The Afflicted Girl

A New Salem Mystery

The Afflicted Girl

— Rory O'Brien

by Rory O'Brien

The Merry Blacksmith Press
2019

The Afflicted Girl

© 2019 Rory O'Brien

All rights reserved.

For information, address:

The Merry Blacksmith Press
70 Lenox Ave.
West Warwick, RI 02893

merryblacksmith.com

Published in the USA by The Merry Blacksmith Press

ISBN—978-1-70059-926-1

For Mike Chandley

From all of us

Acknowledgments

Nobody writes a book on their own. At least I don't. The following were all mission-critical personnel on this project:

My wife, Judith Reilly, who puts up with a lot

Susanne Bohne-Bencivegna, for various kinds of help

Christian Cagigal, for Spanish

Paul diFilippo, an ongoing source of encouragement and inspiration

Tony Gangi, for helping whip this into shape

Rob Proscia just drank, but, you know, whatever

John Teehan, old friend and captain of Merry Blacksmith Press

Elizabeth Wayland-Seal, for proofreading and smart-ass remarks

And to you, for picking up this book

Monday
June 4th

Monday
June 4th

Chapter I

SHE PICKS HER WAY THROUGH SALEM, slowly and carefully. She's been doing this for the last two days. The Salem that she knew is still there somewhere, buried, hidden around corners. Occulted. She walks the almost-familiar streets, feeling her way as she goes.

She returns to the place where her name is carved in stone, memory drawing her back to this place again and again. She traces the carvings with her fingers. The lines are sharp and the stone is cold and rough. Someone has left flowers and pennies, small tokens and remembrances; the flowers weren't here yesterday, but the pennies were. She reaches into the front pocket of her bright, red hoodie for a poppet and places the little figure there, brushing some of the coins out of the way as she does so. The poppet, made of coarse green cloth, with twine around its neck and waist and limbs, has no face; it falls over and she has to stand it back up twice.

Shadows slant across the low granite walls as the sun sets, falling on the stones dedicated to twenty souls, condemned centuries ago. She runs her fingers across her stone again. The stone is still cold.

She's not sure how long she's been there when she hears a voice next to her, and she half-turns, half-gasps, eyes snapping wide. A fat man in a black t-shirt stands a few feet away, sipping iced coffee from a Styrofoam cup. A skinny blonde woman is with him, looking bored, checking her phone.

"*Bridget Bishop,*" the man is standing near and looks past her to read the stone. "*Hanged, June 10, 1692.* Lookit the shit people leave here." He slurps his coffee loudly and adds, "Shit. There's what—ten, eleven cents there?" He looks around at the other stones jutting from the granite walls. "Probably a couple bucks here altogether, then."

"I'm hungry," the blonde woman complains. "My feet hurt."

"Yeah, okay."

"And I hafta pee."

Another deep breath. She flips up her bright red hood and turns away, eyes to the ground, not looking at the two newcomers, the only other people she has seen in this place.

She starts to feel the noose again. The noose that's been haunting her for so long, the noose that tightens and loosens, only to tighten again. Sometimes she forgets it's there, but it never lets her forget for long. Deep breaths, closed eyes.

She glances back to make sure the fat man and the skinny woman aren't following her. The man is moving from stone to stone, picking up the coins.

"Stop it," the woman shrills. "That's probably bad luck or something. They're probably fucking cursed!"

The restaurant looms on her old land, a seafood place called Turner's, the name emblazoned on the broad windows. Her old tavern used to be here, with the apple orchard out back. Her tap room was always loud and smoky as the menfolk drank and laughed and played at shuffle-board. Occasionally, some outraged goodwife would storm in to drag her errant man home. More laughter as he was hauled out the door, as the goodwife gave her a hard look, standing behind the bar in her scandalous red paragon bodice.

It had been crowded last night and she hadn't gone in, but tonight it looks quieter. A couple of guys stand outside on the sidewalk, sleeves rolled up, ties pulled loose, smoking and looking up and down the street. She slips by them, hiding under her red hood, willing them not to see her. They don't seem to notice her pass, but she can never be too sure.

Inside, low lighting: dim but not dark. Tin ceilings and a waiter reciting the specials. Couples at tables, and the velvet murmur of quiet conversation. Glasses and plates clink and soft music plays from somewhere. It's cooler in here than out in the street. She can just faintly smell the apples, the smallest little whiff. She wonders briefly how many others can smell them. Maybe just her.

She crosses the room and shakes her hood back down, lets her dark hair fall around her face. She eases into a tall chair at the end of the nearly-empty bar, runs her fingers along the smooth surface. She scans the menu. There's mac-and-cheese, and she smiles. Comfort food for an uncomfortable time. She orders a bowl, and she orders a Coke. She won't be twenty-one for another few days. Another six days. The bartender sets the glass down and smiles and seems to forget she's even there.

"Well hello there." Suddenly there's a guy standing next to her, beer in his hand and beer on his breath. One of the guys who was outside smoking a few minutes ago. "You from around here? I don't think I remember seeing you before."

She shakes her head and whispers, "No...."

"Well, maybe I can show you around," he says. He puts his hand on the back of her chair, hemming her in, and gestures to her drink on the bar. "That a rum and Coke? You want another?"

She knows *he* can't smell the apples here.

"No."

"Okay, well... what's your name?"

She hesitates for just a second, trying to decide the best thing to do. Then she slides off the bar stool and pushes past him, pushes past the waitress bringing her the steaming bowl of mac-and-cheese. She half-runs for the door. She hears the guy mutter, "Whoa. *Bitch*." as she goes.

Out the door and onto the sidewalk. Deep breaths in the warm night. It's getting dark. It's quiet and she's alone out here.

She has to be careful. She needs to pay attention. She can still feel the noose. She can't let it happen a second time. Can't let them get her again.

She puts a faceless green poppet in the potted plant outside the door. She tucks the little figure deep down into the branches where it won't be seen, but she'll know it's there, outside her old tavern. On her old land.

She crosses the big, flat parking lot, threading her way through the rows of cars, leaving her old tavern behind her. She can't take her eyes from the building looming opposite, the implacably modern building, all brick and beige, drawing her. All she can hear is her own footsteps, her own breath.

It's not the same building, but she remembers what was here before, within sight of her old tavern. It was the old gaol. Long days here, red paragon bodice gray with sweat and dirt; days in the dark, kept awake by the cries of the accused and the abandoned... *I am innocent, God knows.* Telling them what they want to hear. Telling them anything to keep from being dragged out to a rocky hill on the edge of town in a cart.

She shakes the thoughts away. Deep breaths, closed eyes. She takes out another poppet. She only has a few more days to get through.

She slowly approaches the building, mesmerized by its bulk rising in the bright summer night. It's not the old gaol but it's still strangely threatening.

There are people in the parking lot, a couple of shadows in the gloom. She doesn't want them to see her.

She hears a voice. A shocked, angry voice, trying to shout but unable to.

She freezes, stuck. She can't let them see her. Can't let them get her. Not again. But she can't find her legs. All she can do is watch two people struggling: two men, not far away. One falling now, one watching him fall.

But even from here, she can see the blood.

Monday
June 4th

Chapter II

ANDREW LENNOX HAD TWO HEADS sitting on his desk in the back room and now, taking a good look at them both, he couldn't decide which one he liked better.

Most cops had a second source of income. Two of them owned a bar together, another was a silent partner in a pizza place. Some of them just worked as much overtime or picked up as many private details as they could. Shortly after moving to Salem with his family nine years ago, Lennox had decided to open a tourist attraction. The Black Museum was the only true crime museum in town, standing out amongst the haunted houses and witch-kitsch places around downtown. There were dozens of life-sized displays depicting infamous culprits and their crimes, assembled piece-by-piece on nights and weekends, and on days off. The displays had gotten more elaborate and more expensive as time went on, and there was always something to do; there were always repairs and upgrades and little changes.

Like swapping out one of the heads in the front window display for a new one.

The old head had been up for years, glowering at passers-by with a cruel, lopsided expression. He had never quite made up his mind who it was supposed to be; it was just another face in the rogues' gallery of the front window. But the sun had bleached the hair and discolored the cheeks and it was past time for a new one, even if part of him thought the sun damage made the head look even more interesting.

The new head had arrived today: a custom order, 3D-printed by a special effects company in Philadelphia. A long, thin face with hollow cheeks and an unforgiving sneer. The polyester hair was straight and black and swept back over the high, pale forehead; according to the company's website, the hair on the figures was placed one strand at a time.

It was a really nice piece, he thought. Damn well should be, given how much he had spent on it.

Almost too nice. He had found out over the years that the displays had to be good, but not too good. Tourists expected an attraction to be a little cheap, a little dusty and unkempt. If the figures were too high-quality, too polished and perfect, people were somehow strangely disappointed. He could never figure out why it worked that way, but it did.

He tucked the new head under one arm and walked through the main museum space, past Jack the Ripper and Lizzie Borden and Richard Crowninshield.

Outside the month of October, there was usually no need to have a full three-shift rotation in the Criminal Investigation Division at the station, ready to go out on a call. Most crimes could wait until eight o'clock in the morning. But even on a cloudy June night like this, things could happen overnight, and so he was on call until midnight. Three more hours. Enough time to change the heads and then move on to the next thing on his to-do list. And the thing after that. And the thing after *that*.

The Black Museum always seemed quieter to him than anywhere else. There was a stillness he only found here. The only sound was his radio quietly squawking in the lobby. In his first few months on the job, he had slowly learned to tune out whatever chatter there was on the radio that he didn't need to pay attention to, that didn't involve him. But part of him always listened for his name to be called, whatever else he might be doing.

He stepped over the low railing behind the ticket counter, up into the front window. The half-dozen figures arranged here were washed in bright red and green lighting, showing a pair of old-time cops arresting a couple of unsavory characters while concerned citizens looked on. It didn't depict a particular crime. Maybe, he thought, it just represented crime in general. There was one headless figure, in back. He clicked the head into place, squaring it on the padded shoulders. He nudged it a few inches, making sure it was facing the right direction. He'd need to check it from the sidewalk. He carefully swung his legs back over the railing and went outside.

It was warm out, and fairly quiet, but it was only Monday. A young couple walking arm-in-arm dodged around him, laughing as they went. Someone else was walking a dog; another person was arguing on a cell phone. He could hear laughter and music coming from the bar across the street. An easy night. And a quiet night in June was better than a busy night in October.

He stepped back to look at his window. Yes, he could definitely use both heads. He just had to move the older one further back. He knew he had an extra threadbare coat and a dummy form in the back room.

A couple walking slowly by stopped to look at the window and smile. Two women. One was tall and a little heavy with short blonde hair, in jeans and a sweatshirt. The other was short and dark and slight, wearing boots and a denim skirt. The taller woman had her arm around the other's waist.

"Are you open?" the taller woman asked.

"What?"

"Are you open?"

"No. No, we're closed." And he wondered for a moment who the "*we*" was supposed to be.

"We saw you in the window. Didn't know what it was."

"It's a museum."

"Museum?"

"Yeah. True crime museum."

The shorter woman's face brightened and she said, "Ooh! I love true crime stuff!"

"So, wait, like, no witch stuff?" the tall, blonde woman asked.

"Well, there's a section about the witch trials, yeah, but only a little bit." He hadn't wanted to open just another attraction devoted to the witch trials, but that's what people came to Salem for. And nineteen cases of judicial murder, he had reasoned, definitely counted as a crime, so he had set up a triptych of displays: accusation, trial, and execution. "It's really all historic crimes."

"So nothing moves?" He couldn't tell if she was disappointed or not. "Nobody, like, jumps out or anything?"

"No, nothing moves. Nothing animatronic," Lennox said. But the first October he had been open, one of his seasonal help ticket-takers had insisted the displays moved when she wasn't looking. She only lasted a week.

"We went into this one place and somebody jumped out at her and I almost clocked the dude," the tall woman said. "Just a kid in a rubber mask, you know, but still."

"You don't want to go punching people," Lennox said. "Then the police have to get involved and nobody wants that."

"You got Dahmer in there?" the dark-haired woman asked eagerly. "Like, a mannequin of Dahmer? That'd be so cool."

"No, sorry. He's too recent. It's all older cases." He smiled. "Classics."

She smiled and looked up at her girlfriend. The top of her head came to below the other woman's shoulder. She squeezed her arm.

"Can we go in?" she asked, then turned back to Lennox. "Can we come in?"

"Um," he began, "well, we're closed. We open tomorrow at nine."

"Oh." She looked down at the sidewalk.

Why not? he thought. It was just him and it was quiet and there was no harm in letting them in to look around for a few minutes. He still had plenty of time to kill.

"Well," he said, "Okay. Maybe just for a few minutes. But I'm on call, so I might have to kick you out."

"On call? You're a doctor?"

"No, I'm a cop."

He watched for their reaction. They just smiled.

"You're a cop and you run a true crime museum?" the short woman gushed. "That's so cool!"

He returned her smile, and didn't tell her his apartment was in a converted jail.

He led them into the lobby, through the entryway decorated with prop guns and knives and poison bottles, past the figure dressed in wrinkled prison stripes standing just inside the door. The women looked around and smiled. The dim red lighting in the lobby threw shadows across the resin walls painted to resemble blocks of stone. There was a skeleton shackled to the wall behind the ticket counter.

"Who's that guy?"

The short woman smiled and pointed to a figure in the lobby, a tall man in a seventeenth-century ruff, brandishing a blunderbuss.

"That's John Billington. Came over on the Mayflower in 1620, then in 1630 he shot and killed one of his neighbors. So… he's the first murderer we have on record in the New World. They hanged him." He shrugged. "Made sense to have him be the first display you see when you come in."

"Wow," she giggled. "Wow, this is really cool. But you said you don't have Dahmer?"

"No. No Dahmer. Sorry."

"How long did all this take?"

"Took a while."

The shorter woman moved across the lobby, boots clicking on the floor as she went. The other woman looked over to Lennox and smiled.

"Thanks. She loves this kind of shit."

"No problem."

She had stopped to look at the stack of t-shirts when the radio, sitting on the ticket counter next to a cup of coffee that had gone cold half an hour ago, squawked and split the hush in the front lobby.

"Detective Lennox respond."

He grabbed the radio. "Go for Lennox."

"Respond to a body at Church Street parking lot."

The Church Street lot was five minutes away at most. He could walk there as fast as he could drive. And it was around the corner from his apartment building. Literally around the corner.

"Sergeant Ouellette and support personnel already on scene," the dispatcher added.

A body in a parking lot. That sounded like an overdose. Like yet *another* overdose. Opioids had hit Salem just as hard as anywhere else, and sometimes it didn't seem to matter how many doses of Narcan you carried.

"I gotta… take this."

"Oh, shit. Okay, um, yeah." The two women looked at each other awkwardly, not sure what else to say. "Yeah. Yeah, we can go."

"Come back tomorrow," he called as the women went out the door. Then he turned back to the radio.

"On my way. ETA five minutes."

Chapter III

YELLOW POLICE TAPE had already gone up when he arrived a few minutes later, the metes and bounds of the crime scene established. About a dozen personnel were on scene, spreading out and setting up, deciding what needed to be done, what priorities needed to be set. Crime scenes were always strangely quiet; everyone performed their duties in ritual silence, with only nods and gestures. Lennox sometimes wondered if this was out of respect for the dead, or simply because the iron-bound choreography of processing a scene made words unnecessary. The light bars from the cruisers were brighter than the lights at the corners of the lot, and the whole area was washed in a lurid, pulsating blue.

He felt the back of his throat twist. Salem was a quiet city. There were a handful of accidents and overdoses and suicides every year, and every unattended death required investigation, but while Lennox had been forced to deal with only a few dead bodies in his eight-year career with the department, he could never respond to one of these calls without feeling the back of his throat twist.

Detective Sergeant Michelle Ouellette was ranking officer and primary investigator. This was her crime scene. She was a tall, straight-faced woman in a man's silk dress shirt. She pulled her dark hair back into a ponytail, out of her face and out of her way, and her copper cufflinks glinted in the blue light. They had been partnered together for the last seven years, and he knew that the back of her throat never twisted.

"What is it?" he asked quietly.

"Not an accident," she said, turning her head slightly, as if she didn't want the others to hear. "There's a lot of blood."

"Yeah, of course there is."

"ME should be here pretty soon," she added. Police personnel were not allowed to touch a body until a medical examiner arrived, pronounced the victim dead, and conducted a preliminary examination. Until the ME was done, it was look, but don't touch. About twenty feet from where she and Lennox stood, a couple of techs were setting up work lights and taking pictures of a dark shape sprawled on the ground in the middle of the lot. Lennox didn't mind waiting.

The Church Street lot had about two hundred spots, half of them taken tonight. There was never an attendant on duty; customers paid at a blocky, solar-powered kiosk. There was an odd mix of structures clustered around the lot: a square mall with a parking garage, a tall Gothic church, and an apartment building. Standing with hands in pockets, Lennox had his back to a five-story office building that locals still called the Telephone Building, even though the phone company that had built it in the 1950s had long since vacated. Today it was occupied by a mix of small businesses. Lennox had spent a lot of time going in and out of this particular building—the Essex County District Attorney's office took up the entire fourth floor. He glanced over his shoulder at the brick façade, eyes lingering on a plaque by the front door.

"What are you thinking?" Ouellette asked quietly.

"Just that the original jail used to be on this site," he said, nodding up at the Telephone Building. "Where they used to lock up the accused witches. There's a plaque—"

"Not helping," she said. He liked to think they worked well together, but even after seven years, he still couldn't be sure if they were friends.

"Okay. Who found the body?"

She indicated a knot of people off to one side, corralled back behind police tape—a group of blinking, restless faces. One of them was wearing a bright orange Salem t-shirt with the tag still dangling from the sleeve. Another had a shopping bag from a local witch shop. A couple was talking to a young woman in a witch hat, and the three of them turned to look over at Lennox when they noticed him.

"Walking tour," he said quietly.

"Yeah."

"I'll go talk to them," he said. It was their usual division of labor: she supervised official personnel, and he handled the civilians. "Be right back."

"I knew something was going to happen tonight," the guide said, taking off her witch hat and rubbing her forehead. "I just knew it."

She was a short woman, college-age, working a summer job. Her mascara was running. The laminated public guide license tucked into the velvet band of the hat showed her name was Denise, and she worked for Screaming Skull Tours. It was a fairly new company, and Lennox had seen their ads around town, trying to carve out a space among all the other tours in town.

"Why is that?"

"Eleven people," she said, gesturing to the group and shaking her head. "Eleven, plus me, plus Billy. That's thirteen. Thirteen people. Something bad was going to happen."

"I'm only seeing… eight people," Lennox said.

"Shit," she said. "I told everybody to stay. I told them not to leave."

"So five people took off?"

"Must have."

"Okay. Let me come back to that. Just walk me through what happened out here tonight."

"Well, this is where we end, this is the last stop on the tour," she began. She took a deep breath before pointing up to the Telephone Building. "This building sits on the site of the old witch jail—there's a plaque next to the door using the old spelling, g-a-o-l…"

"Yeah, I think I've heard that before somewhere," Lennox smiled. He'd also heard tourists and misinformed guides pronounce the word with a hard G. "So what time did you and your group get here?"

"Ten minutes of nine. We usually get here just about then. Unless it's a big group. Big groups move slow, so it's more like nine. But tonight, ten of. So I'm doing my wrap-up spiel…"

"Where were you when you were doing your spiel?"

"Over there." She pointed to a spot on the sidewalk, about twenty-five feet away from the dark shape.

"Okay. Then what happened?"

"Well, I'm doing my wrap-up and someone says *oh, hey, what's that?* Somebody saw…" She pointed again and took another deep breath. "Over there… I think he thought it was part of the tour at first."

She went into a slow, sickly crouch, wrapping her arms around herself. She was pale as she stared at the ground and tried not to fall over.

Tours in town catered to customers' expectations, giving them blood-and-guts stories of panic and betrayal and innocents being hanged or pressed to death and never given a proper burial. Brutality commodified into a storyline, with pauses for effect and borscht-belt zingers and passing the hat at the end of the night. But no matter how many times a day someone told the story of Giles Corey being crushed or described how the accused were locked up in filthy cells, no one would be prepared to find a dead body lying face-down near where it all actually happened.

Lennox knelt down and put a hand on Denise's shoulder.

"It's okay. Just breathe. None of this is easy. You're doing great."

She nodded.

"You need another minute?"

"No. No, I'm good."

"You want a water or something?" he asked. Then he realized he had no idea where he could find a bottle of water right now.

"I'm okay."

A man in a black t-shirt came to stand over Denise. "You all right?"

"That's Billy," she said. "He's my security."

"Security?"

"Out late, carrying money from tips," Billy shrugged. "They want someone out here with her. I help keep the group together, too."

In Lennox's experience, security usually meant off-duty cop or maybe ex-military. Billy was obviously neither. He was a wiry college student with curly hair. But his shoulders were back and his head thrust forward, trying to look the part anyway.

"So someone noticed the victim," Lennox said. "Who was that?"

"Him." Billy indicated a sweaty man in a t-shirt a size too big. He was on his phone.

"Gotta call you back," he said, when Lennox called him over. He put the phone away.

"So you saw the body?" Lennox asked.

"Yeah. Thought it was part of the show, you know? The big finish. So I pointed him out and was like, *Hey, what's he doing over there?* And I thought he was going to get up or something but then I saw the look on her face and knew this wasn't, like… normal."

"Then what?"

"Then I went to check on him," Billy said. "We've had problems with drunks and whatnot before. But then I saw the blood."

"I hear it's a lot of blood," Lennox nodded.

"There's… enough."

"You didn't touch the body, did you?"

"No. I watch all those shows."

"None of you did?"

Denise and her tourists shook their heads no.

"I told everyone to stay back, don't touch anything. I said to stay here until the cops got here," Billy said. "Till you got here."

"I called 911," Denise added, slowly straightening up, steadying herself.

"But five people took off?"

"Looks like."

"You have their info back at your ticket office, though, right? Names and credit cards and whatever else?"

"I can get that for you in the morning."

"It can wait for now. So you're out here every night about this time. Anything unusual going on tonight?"

"Like what?"

"Like anything. Any suspicious characters, anything that just seemed out of the ordinary. Stuff like that?"

"No."

"So there was nobody else out here at all?"

"Well, Mike was out here with his group."

"Mike?"

"Yeah. He's Gallows Hill History Tours. He stops here, too. All the tours do. He had like fifteen people. They were over by the front door. He was showing them the plaque."

"Anybody else?"

"No."

"Okay. I'm going to have an officer come over and take down everyone's information."

"When can we go?"

"I need you to hang tight for a little bit. We'll try to send you all home soon as we can, but it's going to be a little bit of a wait. Sorry."

He looked back over at the dark shape on the ground.

"You don't know who it is, do you?" he asked. It seemed like a stupid question but it had to be asked.

"Yeah," Denise said. "I recognized him right away."

"You did?"

"Yeah. It's Mr. Halloween."

"Mr. Halloween?" Lennox blinked. "Stuart Pickman?"

"Yeah," she said. "Recognized him right away. It was the sneakers."

Sometimes he really missed the Xanax.

Chapter IV

EVERYONE IN SALEM KNEW who Stuart Pickman was. He made sure of it. He was the executive director of the Salem Spooktacular, the sprawling Hallowe'en festival that took over downtown every October. It was one of the biggest arts and culture festivals in New England, and Pickman oversaw a packed schedule of parades, concerts, fundraisers, contests and other special events that brought tourists from around the world. Pickman bragged he was a self-made man when, in reality, he owed much of his success to tax breaks, corporate sponsorships, and a cozy alliance with the mayor.

But he wasn't always popular with locals. Residents got tired of the noise and the drunks and the traffic and thought Pickman got a lot of money just to throw a month-long party and hold his head up as some kind of civic hero.

Lennox had met him a couple of times. Everybody had. Pickman was a big man with a big voice and the shaggy beard of a Civil War general, always wearing a boxy black suit and a pair of bright orange Chuck Taylor high-tops, the sneakers Denise had noticed. Mr. Hallowe'en had shaken Lennox's hand so hard it hurt.

This was going to be high-profile, Lennox thought now. This was going to be a mess.

"Tentative ID," he told Ouellette. She stood about five feet from the body now. "Stuart Pickman."

It took her a moment to place the name.

"The guy who runs Hallowe'en?"

"That's him. His office is right up there."

He pointed up at the top floor of the Telephone Building.

"That's... not good," she said quietly.

Lennox put his hands in his pockets and watched the squad of evidence technicians continue processing the scene, flashlights sweeping the ground. Occasionally one would set down an evidence marker, and other techs would then photograph and document whatever had been found.

The white apartment building on the opposite side of the lot was called the Essex. Lights were going on over there, and curtains cautiously opened, shadows appearing in the windows.

"See any cameras?" Ouellette asked.

"Not really." The old Telephone Building had cameras mounted at the corners, aimed at the doors, not the parking lot. Too bad, Lennox thought. With the District Attorney on one floor and a Social Security office on another, the security cameras would probably be top-of-the-line.

"No press yet," Ouellette noted.

"Yeah, well, no news happens after five o'clock."

"Just like no crime happens on weekends."

The ME arrived a few minutes later. Minsky was a bald man with a gut starting to work its way over his belt. He had a rolling aluminum case full of equipment that Lennox didn't even want to think about. He smiled, nodded, and looked down at the body, tilting his head.

"Is that who I think it is?" he asked. A hard candy clicked against his teeth.

"Yeah," Lennox said.

"Well, this is something, then," was all Minsky said.

The detectives stepped back to let him work. Lennox could never watch Minsky go over a body anyway. He could practically feel himself getting pale as the man opened his case. They went over to the evidence techs' supervisor.

"Anything?" Ouellette asked quietly.

"Moving outward from the body, we find the usual assorted trash, cigarette butts and candy wrappers and whatnot," the supervisor said. "But there's also this."

He pointed to something next to an evidence marker about twenty feet from the body, and Lennox and Ouellette went over for a closer look.

It was a weird little doll, six inches long, heavy green cloth clumsily stitched with twine. It had no face and the limbs stuck out stiffly. The workmanship seemed almost intentionally rough, as though whoever made it had taken time to make the doll look so careless, so primitive.

"Okay," Lennox said. "Now it's weird."

"What is that?" Ouellette asked.

"It's a poppet. You buy them in occult shops. I bought one for a display over at the museum." Lennox took a picture, but it was blurry and he had to take two more. "You haven't seen them in the windows?"

She shook her head. She had never been to the Black Museum, and didn't pay attention to window displays in touristy witch-kitsch shops downtown.

"Okay. Well, tag it and bag it."

"I'll be right back," Lennox said.

He went over to where Denise was still waiting impatiently with the remains of her group.

"Is this going to take much longer?" she asked.

"Couple more minutes." He held up his phone, showing her the picture. "This look familiar?"

She squinted and shook her head.

"Nope. It's a... poppet?"

"Think so. So it's not one of yours?"

"No."

"You don't give them out on the tour or anything like that?"

"No."

"What about Mike? Gallows Hill History? Does he use them for anything?"

"Don't think so. But…"

"What?"

"Well, like I said, the old witch jail used to be right there." She pointed at the Telephone Building.

"There's a plaque," Lennox said. "Yeah."

"Yeah. They say one of the women used to have poppets and that's one of the things that got her accused. Bridget Bishop."

"Yeah, I know."

"You think that's, like, significant?"

"You never know," Lennox shrugged. "Thanks. Umm, let me see if we can't let you go. I'll check."

"Anything?" Ouellette asked when he got back to her.

"She says it's not hers. So maybe it's the victim's."

"Maybe it's the murderer's," Ouellette said.

"Too early to tell," Lennox replied.

"Done," Minsky announced, raising a hand. Ouellette went over to him; Lennox stayed where he was, a few feet away, no closer than he had to be. "No real surprises. Got it in the neck with a short blade, five inches long, serrated on one edge. Like a little saw."

"You can tell that just from the wound?"

"Still in the side of his neck," the ME laughed proudly. "I'm seeing four neck wounds altogether, so someone was good and angry. A slashed jugular and a nicked carotid will get the job done. Looks like your murder weapon snapped on the fourth try. Defensive wound on the right hand. Would have been unconscious in under a minute, bled out in another minute, maybe two if he was lucky. Or unlucky." He indicated the blade sticking out from the neck. It would stay in place for now, and be removed later in the morgue. "There's your weapon. Obviously."

"No handle?" Ouellette asked.

"Like I said, must've snapped. Must be around here somewhere, right? Could be under him." Minsky shrugged. "Not really my department."

"How long has he been out here?" Lennox asked.

"I'd say over an hour, given the coagulation. Ninety minutes at the outside." Minsky stood up and tossed a couple of probes back into his case. He stretched and rubbed his knees. "Must be getting old or some shit. He's all yours. I have an opening at three-thirty tomorrow, if you want."

"I can be there," Ouellette said.

"Am I still banned?" Lennox called.

"Until further notice," the ME said, not looking up from the forms he was signing. "And don't hold your breath there."

Procedure required at least one detective assigned to a case to attend the victim's autopsy. Lennox had fainted at his first one, and spent the next one vomiting into a trashcan in the far corner. He had been banned from the morgue after that.

"Fine by me."

"Fine by me, too." The ME slammed his case shut.

"Duty calls." Ouellette motioned to Lennox to join her. He felt the back of his throat twist. She ran her flashlight up and down the corpse. Pickman lay face-down, arms and legs splayed awkwardly. The ME had already bagged the hands to preserve whatever DNA or other evidence might be under the nails or elsewhere. One shoulder was oily with blood.

"Let's roll him," Ouellette said quietly.

They turned the body over slowly, an inch at a time, watching carefully as they did. The head rolled vacantly and the beard peeled away from the asphalt where it had been shellacked down by dry blood. The eyes were filmy, drying out, and the face was white. Expressionless. Lennox never understood people who said that the dead looked peaceful, like they were sleeping. To him, the dead only ever looked dead. They only ever looked *gone*.

"No handle," Ouellette shook her head.

She checked the dead man's pockets. A wallet with a driver's license and credit cards and eighty-six dollars in cash. A key ring. An iPhone in a black-and-orange case with a leering jack-o'-lantern on the back. She took the phone and handed Lennox the wallet. She tapped at the screen with a latex fingertip and bit her lip.

"Locked," she murmured.

"Try ten-thirty-one," Lennox suggested.

She entered the code and unlocked the phone.

"Detective," she gave him an eighth-of-an-inch grin. She scrolled through the text messages. "Nothing suspicious, just the usual *love you, be home soon* stuff."

She slid the phone into an evidence envelope. She sealed it and signed it, adding the date, time, and case number.

Pickman's license showed an address in Juniper Point, over in the Willows, a nice neighborhood ten minutes away, overlooking a cove.

"We're doing a notification?" she asked.

"Yeah, I think so." He half-remembered Pickman having a wife or a girlfriend—he couldn't recall which right now.

The ME zipped up the body bag and an assistant helped him load it into a black van with small biohazard labels on the back doors.

Half an hour later, when the techs were finished and the victim's body was on the way to the State Medical Examiner's slab in Boston, Ouellette released the crime scene. Lennox sent Denise and her group home, the police tape was pulled down, the little doll and the broken knife blade were logged as evidence, and the cruisers left to respond to other calls for service. It was 12:47.

"Still have the notification to do," Ouellette said. "You're driving."

As they pulled out of the parking lot, Lennox noticed the lights in the Essex Apartments going off, one by one.

Chapter V

Monday June 4th

THERE WAS NEVER A GOOD TIME to do a death notification, never a good time to give someone the worst news they would ever hear. That they were now "survived by," that they were now the "next-of-kin." Officers and detectives were trained in criminal procedure, interview and interrogation techniques, and were even required to re-qualify with their service weapon every six months. But there was no training for death notifications. No manual, no checklist, not even a guest speaker at the academy. And a death notification set the table for much of the rest of the investigation; bungling it now would only make things harder later on.

Lennox and Ouellette rolled slowly down the narrow lanes of Juniper Point, looking for the right address. A century and more ago, this neighborhood had been a summer retreat for well-off Bostonians, and the wood frame houses were built as getaway cottages. It still felt like a secluded Victorian resort, with the little houses huddled together, all pointed roofs and gingerbread porch rails, wind chimes and patriotic bunting. It might no longer be a summer colony, but it was still for the well-off. The half-moon shimmered off the waters of the cove, silver-yellow, a warm breeze carrying with it the tang of salt.

Pickman's house was a two-story cottage on a one-way street. The porch light was still on. Ouellette pressed the doorbell and stepped back next to Lennox, pointing to the door with her chin. He handled the civilians. He waited a moment, made sure his badge was in full view, and rang the bell a second time.

There was the sound of someone coming down the stairs inside.

"Forget your key?" a muffled voice asked. The door was opened by a young-faced woman with freckles and red hair—bright and metallic red hair that looked expensive. She wore yoga pants and a t-shirt, both a little too small. She blinked and straightened her shoulders at the sight of the badges.

"I'm Detective Lennox, this is my partner, Detective Sergeant Ouellette. Salem Police. Are you Mrs. Pickman?"

"No..." she said slowly. "I mean, we're not married, but... shit. Is Stu in trouble?"

She looked past them, to the cruiser that had followed them. Her eyes showed that she knew two cop cars meant something serious.

"Do you mind if we come in, ma'am?"

"Sure... What's going on?"

"If we could just come in," Ouellette said quietly.

"Okay. Let me get a robe."

She gestured them inside and closed the door. She ran upstairs, leaving them in the front room of the house. A moment later, she was back in a terrycloth robe, wearing glasses now, with her shining hair tied back.

"Okay, what is going on?" she asked, cinching the belt of her robe tighter. Her voice was firmer now, and worry showed at the corners of her eyes.

"I'm afraid I have some bad news," Lennox began. Euphemisms were no good in these situations. Being polite or indirect, leaving her to fill in the blanks herself, was just cruel. But being straightforward didn't feel any less so. "We're here because Stuart died a few hours ago. And it looks like a homicide."

"What are you even talking about right now?" she demanded.

"We're sorry, ma'am," Lennox said.

"But—no. That can't be right." Her voice cracked as she spoke. She hunched forward slightly, squinting at him. "That's not right."

She took her cell phone from the pocket of her robe. Her hands were shaking.

"I'm going to call him," she said weakly. She fumbled with the phone, lifting it to her ear. Lennox knew that, by now, Pickman's phone would be locked up at the station. He imagined it ringing in the evidence room on Margin Street, two miles away.

Her fingers went slack as the call went to voicemail. She half-placed, half-dropped the phone onto a table and steadied herself against the wall.

"Do you want to sit down, ma'am?" Lennox asked.

She moved stiffly over to the couch and sat. She pulled the chain on a little lamp and the room brightened.

"Homicide?" she asked. "He was murdered?"

"Yes."

"Are you sure?" She raised her eyes almost hopefully.

"We're sure. Now ma'am—I'm sorry, I don't even know your name."

"Jessica," she nodded. "Meyers."

"Jessica. What was Stuart doing out there tonight? Was he working late or something?"

"He had a bunch of running around to do," she said. "He always had a lot of running around to do, a lot of little meetings, and things to check on and he didn't really say..." Her voice faltered.

"When did he leave here?"

"Seven-thirty, I think? Jesus Christ," she said, wringing the belt of the robe in her hands. "Jesus God, this can't be happening."

"Was he with anybody when he left?"

"No."

"So you're not exactly sure where he was supposed to be tonight?"

"All over the place, probably." She shook her head.

"Would anybody else know where he was supposed to be tonight?"

"I don't know," she whispered.

"Any enemies that you know of? Anybody who might have wanted to hurt him?"

"Enemies?"

"You don't get to be as successful as him without stepping on a few toes along the way."

"No, no… enemies."

"Any… activities that might get him in trouble with someone?"

"What do you mean?"

"Drugs, gambling, any of that?"

"No. He used to smoke a little pot," she said quietly, "but that was before we even met. And he doesn't gamble. Where did this happen?"

"Right outside the building."

"Mommy—?" a tiny voice came from the stairs. A little girl, six or seven years old, padded into the room, rubbing her eyes. Her pink pajamas had unicorns on them.

"Hey, you," Jessica said soothingly. She came up off the couch, crossing the room in two steps and hoisting the little girl up onto her hip. She brushed her hair back behind an ear with one fingertip. "You shouldn't be up, sweetheart. It's wicked late."

"I woke up," the girl said. She tried to hide behind her mother's shoulder as she whispered, "Who is that?"

"Oh, they're… police," Jessica said. "They just came to… to check on us and make sure we're safe. And we're all safe, so let's get you back to bed…"

She swept upstairs without looking back at the detectives.

"This is awful," Lennox whispered. Ouellette's mouth tightened as she gave a single nod.

Jessica came back downstairs and sat on the bottom steps.

"That's Emma," she said. "That's our daughter."

She folded her arms at her waist and leaned forward, staring at the front door.

"Just tell me what happened," she said.

"We're just getting started," Lennox said. "Anything you can tell us at this stage might be helpful. So he wasn't in any kind of trouble and he didn't have any enemies?"

"Stu throws a big Hallowe'en party every year. He raises money for charity and… and no, he doesn't have enemies."

"We have to ask," Ouellette said.

"And… we also have to ask if you were here all night."

"Of course I was," she said. "I can't leave Emma."

She slowly bent forward, chest to knees. Her shoulders shook for a moment before she straightened up and smeared tears from her eyes.

"I'm sorry," she whispered.

"I'm sorry we have to come and tell you all this," Lennox said. "I'm sorry all this happened. Is there someone we can call? Someone you'd like to have here with you?"

"I have a brother. He's over in Peabody."

"We'll send a car to pick him up," Lennox nodded. "And there's an officer outside who can come in and stay with you until he gets here."

"You don't need to." She wiped her eyes again.

"It's not a problem." He didn't add that it was procedure. "If you want her to wait outside until your brother gets here, that's fine, too."

"I want to see him," she said. "I want to see Stuart. To make sure…"

"Not right now," Lennox shook his head. "Right now he's in Boston… at the Medical Examiner's. They'll follow up with you in a day or two to… make arrangements."

"Arrangements," she whispered. "They're going to… autopsy him?"

"They have to."

"I can't believe any of this is happening."

"We're sorry for your loss. But we'll find out who is responsible for this. We're going to have everyone working on this."

"You should go," she said, lifting her head. "I think I really need you to… get the fuck out of my house. Get away from me…"

"We can come back tomorrow—"

"*Get the fuck out.*"

Outside, Lennox took a deep breath. "That went well."

"Shooting the messenger," Ouellette said.

"You never know how people are going to react."

"That kid is my son's age," Ouellette said.

"Yeah, this is no good. And it only gets worse from here."

They walked over to the cruiser, to tell the officer that she should wait outside until the brother arrived from Peabody. Lennox looked back at the cottage and saw a light go on in an upstairs window. Emma's room, with the pink curtains.

Tuesday
June 5th

Chapter I

Tuesday June 5th

"**How long has it been** since you heard from your daughter, Mr. Conroy?" Detective Sergeant Fred Dworaczyk asked, switching the phone from one ear to the other and grabbing a pen. Shift had started twenty minutes ago and he was sitting at his desk in the CID bullpen at the station. He had a half-empty cup of coffee in front of him and his sleeves were rolled up so the tattoo of St. Michael showed on his forearm.

"Not since the third." Richard Conroy's voice was still fuzzy with sleep, calling from a time zone away. "She got there the day before and called me around noon. She said she was having a good time. But I haven't heard from her since and when I call her it goes right to her voicemail."

"And you know she was calling from Salem?"

"She had a room at the hotel, the big one downtown. She always wanted to see Salem and I got her one of those package deals for her birthday." He sighed. "I pay the balance on her card, and I checked the last few transactions and they're all in Salem. There's a place called Herbologie, some place called Full Moon…"

"Yeah, those are witch shops." Dworaczyk shook his head, glad the father couldn't see. "We have a lot of those downtown, a lot of them are near the Hawthorne—that is the name of the big hotel."

"I filed a missing person report with our local police yesterday here in Milwaukee; they said you'd be able to check that?"

"Yes," Dworaczyk said, tapping his keyboard with one hand.

Richard Conroy had filed the report with the Milwaukee Police Department, District One, yesterday at 7:20 p.m. It was one of eighty-five thousand entries filed under Missing Person in the FBI's National Crime Information Center database. Each entry gave a fairly complete snapshot of the subject: Kelly Conroy was 20 years old, and so still classified as a juvenile. White female, five-foot-five-inches tall, 109 pounds. Medium brown hair, blue eyes (the eye color choices on the form included a box for "maroon"). Size five shoe. No fingerprints on file, and there was a small photo of a sullen young woman with mascaraed eyes, hair close around her face, almost frowning at the camera. Last known destination: Salem, Massachusetts.

"She couldn't just go to Florida like everyone else," her father breathed into the phone. "Had to go to Salem. Had to go see the witches."

"So that is what she is interested in?" Dworaczyk asked.

"It's a phase." He sounded offended. "She'll grow out of it."

"At twenty years old?"

"I haven't heard from her since the day before yesterday. Thirty-six hours. More than that, now, I think."

"Any reason she might not be answering your calls?"

"What do you mean?"

"I mean, how well do you get along with your daughter?"

Silence.

"Mr. Conroy?"

"Yes. I… we get along fine. But…"

"But what?"

"I run a grocery store here in town," Conroy sighed into the phone. "I'm working on opening another one and I need an extra pair of hands in the office. So she was supposed to go on this trip, which I'm paying for, and then come back home and settle down and go to work. So this was kind of her last hurrah before she had to grow up, you know?"

"And how did she feel about that?"

"She wasn't happy, I could tell."

"And how could you tell?"

"We… argued about it just before she left."

"But she still checked in with you when she got here?"

"Yeah. She sounded okay, but… maybe she wasn't. Now I don't know."

"And what about Kelly's mother?"

"I'm… a widower."

"Okay. And who is this Sandy Conroy I see listed in the file? In Chicago? Is that a sister?"

"Yes. I checked, and she hasn't heard from her."

"Tell her to notify us if she does. And you should call everyone—friends, family, whoever—and also tell them to notify us if Kelly gets in touch with them. You have my number."

"Okay. What are you people going to do on that end?"

"I am going to check over at the hotel; I know the head of security. I will see what he knows. I will send out an e-mail notification to a couple hundred detectives—there is a network set up all through eastern Mass and up into New Hampshire. I will have her cell carrier ping her phone and see if they can get a location on her. We will have every cop in town keeping an eye out for her, let me tell you. We will find her. And there is every chance she will come walking through your door in the next five minutes anyway."

Dworaczyk didn't tell the man he was also going to check the hospitals in the area. He also didn't mention he would alert vice detectives, in case a nice young girl from the Midwest had gotten trafficked. It happened.

"If there is one thing I need to know about Kelly, what is it?"

"She's smart but… naïve. Too trusting. No street smarts."

"Salem is not exactly Detroit," Dworaczyk said with a gentle laugh. "Let me just tell you—people come to Salem because they are thinking it will be all witches and magic, like spooky Disney or something. And they get here and it is not what they were expecting and they go home. They go home disappointed, but they go home."

"We argued," Richard Conroy said. "I told her she had to grow up and get to work."

"I am going to check in with you tomorrow," Dworaczyk said. "And remember, call us immediately if anyone hears from her."

"It's her birthday on Saturday."

"Yes, I noticed that in the file. So this was her birthday trip?"

"Yeah... Should I come out there? I should probably come out there."

"Sit tight for now. I will call you tomorrow."

Dworaczyk hung up and turned to his partner, Sergeant Plunkett. Plunkett was one of the elder statesmen in the CID, and went out on as few calls as possible, preferring to count down the days to retirement.

"We have a Missing," Dworaczyk said.

Plunkett licked a finger and turned a page of the newspaper. "Go with God, my son," he murmured without looking up.

Dworaczyk called to Lieutenant Winters across the bullpen. "There is a Missing."

Winters came out of his office, and glanced over the notes Dworaczyk had made while on the phone.

Police departments received missing persons reports regularly. Spouses walked out, kids ran away, and people disappeared—sometimes intentionally, sometimes not. Detectives would make an effort, but until there was a body or a reason to believe there would be a body, the typical missing person case would be eclipsed by a higher-priority case in a day or two. Even in Salem, there were robberies, there were rapes; just last night, Ouellette and Lennox had gone out on a homicide. Serious cases would always knock a missing person investigation down the list. Sometimes far down the list.

"Do what you can with it," he shrugged.

Chapter II

THE SALEM SPOOKTACULAR'S headquarters took up a sunny office suite on the top floor of the old Telephone Building. The main office space was all empty desks right now; it was barely eight-thirty. The walls were hung with framed prints of Depression-era witches and sepia-toned portraits of old Salem, views long gone. Lennox had seen many of the images before, reproduced on postcards and tote bags in shops a few streets away. But of course Mr. Hallowe'en owned the originals.

And there were glass jack-o'-lanterns everywhere: Pickman's famous collection. Every write-up about him mentioned that he had collected over two hundred of them, big and small, arranged on shelves and desks and windowsills. The smallest was the size of a thumbnail and the largest weighed over twenty pounds. They came from all over the world, and Pickman bragged that no two were alike. The sun coming in through the windows threw slices of orange light everywhere.

Lennox was still tired from the late night. He had missed a spot shaving that morning and now ran a finger along the patch of stubble below his right ear. That was going to bug him all day. Ouellette, of course, was sharp and composed as ever.

There was a row of offices partitioned off to one side, and a tall, reedy man with glasses stood in one doorway, very straight. He wore khakis and a polo shirt with the Spooktacular's jack-o'-lantern logo in one corner. He looked at the detectives, noticed the badges, and sighed.

"Jessica called me half an hour ago," he said. "What the hell happened?"

"You're David Nicholson?" Lennox asked. The Spooktacular had a staff directory on its website, with full-color photos and job titles, and he had spent some time that morning going over it. And running each name through the NCIC to check for criminal records. Nicholson had been the assistant director of the festival for five years. "I'm Detective Lennox and this is Sergeant Ouellette."

Nicholson nodded, brought them back into his office, and leaned back against his desk, arms folded tightly, chin tucked. The desk was neat and orderly, and there was nothing on the pale walls. Not even a calendar.

"What happened?" he asked again.

"We're still in the preliminary stages," Lennox went on. "Do you have any idea what he was doing last night?"

"No," Nicholson said.

"When was the last time you saw him?" Ouellette asked.

"Yesterday. We had a meeting with the mayor, then it was back here for a staff meeting, and he left around four, I think?"

"How did he seem?"

"Fine, I guess."

"Anything bothering him? Anything on his mind?"

"Not that I could tell." Nicholson shook his head. "But, he wouldn't say anything to me if there was."

"You're not that close?" Lennox asked.

"More like it just wouldn't have occurred to him to mention it to me," Nicholson shrugged.

"So if it wasn't work-related, did he have any... extracurricular activities that might have gotten him in trouble?" Lennox asked

"No. No, Stu is pretty straight. Really isn't into anything... crazy." Another shrug. "He has a family. A business. Too much to lose."

"Any enemies?"

"Enemies?" Nicholson gave a nervous little smile. "You really do ask that. Ah... no. Who has enemies?"

"Someone didn't like him," Ouellette said.

The main door opened as two staffers came to work. Nicholson pushed himself off the edge of his desk and closed his own office door.

"So you said Jessica called you this morning. Have you ever met her in person?" Lennox asked.

"Yeah. Of course. She used to work here. I hired her."

"She used to work here?"

"Yeah. Events coordinator. But she and Stu hooked up pretty quick, just within a couple of months. Then she got pregnant and went on maternity leave and just… stayed there. I haven't seen her in a little while, though. She used to come by, but not lately."

"Did Pickman ever mention any trouble at home?" Ouellette asked.

"No." Nicholson shook his head.

"Would he have told you if there were?"

"Maybe?"

"Going back for a sec," Lennox said. "You do the hiring and not Stuart?"

"Yeah. I do all the day-to-day around here."

Lennox looked out the glass door of Nicholson's office. A few more employees had arrived for work. One of them, a pale guy in a striped cardigan, was looking back and then turned away so fast that Lennox thought the guy was going to hurt himself.

"Couple other things," he said, taking a photo of the murder weapon out of his worn, leather organizer. "Any idea what this is?"

Nicholson took the photo and looked at it for a long moment, and then tilted his head as Lennox saw the mental click of recognition.

"This… looks like a piece from one of the pumpkin-carving kits. But it's broken." He took a deep, quick breath. "Is this what he was killed with?"

"Pumpkin-carving kits?" Ouellette asked.

"Yeah. Um, we put out these deluxe kits a few years ago. There were little carving knives and sculpting tools and whatnot. They didn't sell real well," he shrugged. "One of Stu's less-brilliant ideas. This looks like one of the saws—there were three of them in the set: small, medium, and large. They were pretty sharp."

"So who has these kits?" Ouellette asked.

"Well, a lot of people, probably, but… I think we gave away more than we sold. They're still around, you can still buy them some places."

"Do you still have any on hand?"

"Yeah, we probably have a couple boxes of them in the merch closet. With the t-shirts and stuff."

"Is there a lock on that closet?"

"No, there's not."

"And if we check, all the kits you're supposed to have are going to be accounted for?"

"I don't even know how many we're supposed to have," David Nicholson ran his hands through his hair, rubbed his temples. "And I think a few ended up in the junk box outside."

"The junk box?" Ouellette asked.

"Yeah, the plastic bin on those shelves by the door. You walked by it when you came in. All the loose crap that doesn't belong anywhere else usually ends up there. I think a couple of those kits got opened and then we had carving knives wandering round the office for a few weeks; then they ended up getting tossed in there."

"Where anybody could have grabbed one?" Ouellette asked.

"You think someone here did this?"

"It's possible."

"No. No way."

"We have to consider everything," Lennox said, taking the photo of the broken saw blade back and exchanging it for one of the green, faceless poppet. "Do you recognize this, by any chance?"

Nicholson looked at the picture and half-scowled. No tilt of the head this time, no little click of recognition.

"No. What is it?"

"Found at the scene. So it's not Stuart's?"

"Don't think so. Never seen it before."

"Okay." Lennox looked out into the main office space: three men and one woman were at their desks, checking emails or messages. "We're going to need to talk to your people before we go."

"They're not going to know anything."

"You didn't email them or text them or anything like that before we got here?" Ouellette asked.

"No. No, I was going to wait until everyone got here and then… break the news. But… I really don't think anyone here has anything to do with this."

"Well, somebody might know something," Lennox shrugged.

"Okay."

"And one other thing," Ouellette said. "Who's in charge now?"

"Well, I am, I guess," Nicholson said slowly. "The board will name an interim director…"

"And would that be you?"

"It could be, but it's really up to them," he shrugged.

"Where were you last night?"

"You're kidding me," Nicholson blinked.

"She's not kidding. We have to ask. It's process of elimination."

"I was home."

"With…?"

"I live alone. I'm… divorced."

"So nobody can verify that?"

"No, but…" he gave a nervous little laugh. "Really? You think I… did this? Seriously?"

"We have to ask."

"And we're going to need to talk to the rest of the staff. Anything we should know there before we do?"

"Like what?"

"Like anything. Anybody in trouble with him lately? Anything like that."

"No... no, nothing."

"Okay, well, we'd like to take a quick look in his office first."

"Yeah," Nicholson said. "Sure."

Pickman's office was the opposite of Nicholson's. Where Nicholson's was sparse and organized, Mr. Hallowe'en's office was a mess. The huge desk was littered with glossy brochures and manila folders and unopened mail. There were a couple of coffee cups—one ceramic, one Styrofoam—wedged in between the teetering piles. The mismatched visitor chairs in front of the desk were almost buried under piles of t-shirts and hoodies—soft mounds of orange and black. There was a table against one wall, piled with more merchandise—mugs and water bottles and fridge magnets. But no pumpkin-carving kits that Lennox could see.

"He didn't really spend much time in here," David Nicholson said, standing in the door as if afraid to enter.

"Why was that?"

"He used to say that his office was all over town. If he had a meeting, he went to see you. Or he met you for lunch or coffee. When he did meet people here, he kept them out in the main area." He gestured behind him.

"There a reason he did that?"

"Showing off the staff? Showing off *for* the staff? Sometimes, he just needed an audience, I guess."

"I don't see a schedule or a planner," Ouellette said, shifting a few things carefully around on the desk. "Did he have one?"

"He keeps most of his schedule on his phone. But I still had to remind him about shit three times a day."

"So did he spend any time in here yesterday?"

"Yeah, but..." Nicholson shrugged.

"Yeah, but what?" Lennox asked.

"Is that... significant?"

"Maybe. We're just trying to find out as much as we can at this point."

"Yeah, he was in here yesterday. A couple of times, but I wasn't really watching him."

"I don't see anything here that indicates what he was doing out there last night," Ouellette said from behind the desk. "So we should probably talk to the staff. Everyone here?"

Nicholson looked over his shoulder.

"Seems it."

"Okay," Lennox said. "Do you want to give them the news, or should we?"

He was relieved when Nicholson said he'd do it himself.

Tuesday June 5th

Chapter III

"**All right everybody, listen up,**" Nicholson announced in the main office area, an open plan space that reminded Lennox of the CID bullpen at the station. "I'm afraid I have some bad news."

The staff turned and glanced from Nicholson to the detectives and back, not sure what was going on.

"I don't know if any of you already know this, but… Stuart died last night."

Lennox watched the reactions, trying to catch everyone at once. There were gasps and murmurs of "Bullshit!" and "What?" and shocked expressions and, as far as he could tell, the staff seemed honestly surprised.

"And right now it's looking like…" Nicholson glanced over at Ouellette. "It's looking like someone may have killed him."

He was taking the kind of soft-sell approach that the police never could. Civilians could never make themselves say the word *murdered*. They used all the qualifiers, all the euphemisms that the police couldn't afford to. And the staff was silent.

"These two are from the police—they have some questions."

"I'm Detective Lennox, this is Sergeant Oucllette. Let me just start off by saying we're very sorry this has happened, and we're still in the early stages of the investigation, so any help you can give us right now would be invaluable."

A thin, blonde, young woman sitting by the window raised her hand like a kid in class. Lennox recognized her from the staff directory: Kara Basilico, special events coordinator. The woman who had Jessica's old job. Kara was somewhere in her twenties, wearing big, round glasses and a denim shirt.

"What happened?" she asked.

"We are treating it as a homicide," Lennox said.

"Homicide?" she said. People usually repeated the word back to him like that. When they could reply at all. She bit her lip and sniffled. She reached for the box of Kleenex on her desk, took two, and blew her nose.

"Sorry. It's this building. I swear to God, this building is making me sick. I don't know if it's something in the vents or if it's the lighting or what, but I always feel sick when I'm here."

"Okay, so looking back over the last few days," Lennox went on, "did any of you notice anything unusual? Was Stuart his normal self or did he say or do anything that kind of sticks out now, in retrospect?"

"Well, it's been getting pretty busy," one man said. He was a square guy, broad shouldered, with spiky hair and a boxy blue and red bowling shirt. He held a big orange ceramic coffee mug in both hands. "Hallowe'en's coming."

"It's... four months away," Ouellette said.

"Summertime is the warm-up," he replied. "Tourists start coming right after Memorial Day. You come over the summer, you still want to go to a haunted house, you still want to see witches. And it just builds and builds."

"What's your name?" she asked.

"Adam Womack."

"What do you do here, Mr. Womack?"

"External relations."

"What's that?" Lennox asked. He had seen the title on the staff directory but had no idea what it meant.

"PR, mostly," Womack shrugged. "Volunteer wrangling. Community liaison."

"What's community liaison?"

"What it sounds like," Womack said. "I work with the locals. We can get people from Florida to come downtown in October but not people from Highland Avenue, you know? Trying to work on that."

"Not really working, though," the lanky guy sitting next to Womack said sullenly. He had gotten a haircut since his staff directory photo had been taken, but Lennox still recognized him: Jason Freitas, ad sales. He wore a skinny blue suit and sat leaning forward in his chair, elbows on knees, looking tired. He had a glass pumpkin on his desk.

"No?" Lennox asked.

Freitas just shrugged.

"Okay," Lennox said. "Who's worked here the longest?"

"That's probably me." A hand went up in the back. The young man in the striped cardigan, the one who had been looking into Nicholson's office. He had lank, dark hair and a long, mournful face with hollow cheeks.

"And you are?" Ouellette asked.

"Zachary Dykstra. I do IT."

"And how long have you worked here?"

"Nine years now, almost ten." He seemed embarrassed.

"Would you say you knew Stuart pretty well?"

"Yeah, I guess." He shrugged.

"So does any of this make any sense?" Lennox asked him. "Can you think of anyone who would want to hurt Stuart?"

"I dunno, man, I think we probably all wanted to at some point," he muttered.

"Jesus, Zachary," Kara said.

"I already told you this," Nicholson said over Ouellette's shoulder. "Whatever happened, it has nothing to do with the festival, nothing to do with anyone here. I wish we could help, but I just don't know what you're expecting here."

Lennox walked over to the junk box, a translucent, 20-gallon Rubbermaid container with no lid. He pulled on a pair of latex gloves as he glanced over the jumble of things in the box.

"Anything in here that could stick me or hurt me?" he asked.

"Probably," Zachary Dykstra said.

He started picking through the contents. Two staplers. A remote that probably didn't go with anything anymore. A tangle of cables that probably didn't go with anything anymore, either. A handful of batteries. An Allen wrench. A few little plastic and metal pieces he couldn't identify. Toward the bottom, he found a few loose pieces from the pumpkin-carving kits: a broad, flat scoop, a couple of narrow scrapers and sculpting loops, and a sawblade that looked like the next size down from the murder weapon. All of them had orange, wooden handles. He took pictures of them with his phone and gently put them back.

"You need something over there?" Zachary asked.

"I'm fine. Don't mind me."

He pulled off the gloves and tucked them back into his pocket. Turning back to the group, he took the photo of the poppet from his organizer.

"Anyone recognize this?"

"What is it?" Kara Basilico asked, squinting.

"Found at the scene last night," Ouellette said. "Any ideas?"

"I think one of the witch shops had those in an ad last year," Jason Freitas said. He nodded over to Kara. "Toni would probably remember."

"And who is Toni?"

"My sister," Kara said. "She does the graphic design and layout for the program."

Every year, the Spooktacular published a fat, glossy guide to the events scheduled around town, with calendars, maps, listings, and even a crossword puzzle and a scavenger hunt. And pages and pages of ads. Lennox bought a pricey quarter-page every year for the Black Museum; he was never sure if it really brought in more visitors but, like most other businesses, he didn't want to skip a year and find out.

"She should be in pretty soon." Kara checked her phone. "We were out kinda late last night and she might have overslept a little... and speak of the Devil."

Antonia Basilico came through the door, paused with her hand still on the doorknob, and blinked as everyone turned to her. With her round face and dark hair and cleft chin, she didn't resemble her sister across the room at all. She smiled with embarrassment and said, "Sorry I'm late," in a small voice.

David Nicholson took a deep breath and said, "Toni, there's some bad news."

"Oh. Okay..."

"Stuart... died last night."

"What? What happened?" She looked around at the others.

"The police," he nodded to Ouellette and Lennox, "say it's homicide."

"Homicide," she breathed. "Murder? But I just saw him yesterday..."

"We all just saw him yesterday," Zachary said from the corner of his mouth.

"Well, yeah, but he seemed... fine." Her dark bangs were a little too long, and she brushed them back out of her eyes. "He was fine."

"Didn't seem like he had anything on his mind?" Ouellette asked. "Nothing was bothering him?"

"No. He was... fine. Someone murdered him?"

"Yes."

Toni's shoulders slumped and she moved over to her desk, between Zachary and her sister. Kara reached over and put a hand on her arm.

"So these were in an ad last year?" Lennox asked, showing her the photo of the poppet. He hated having to question people like this, but it came with the job. Came with a homicide investigation.

"Yeah," she said. "For one of the witch shops."

"Do you remember which one?"

"One of the ones on Essex Street," she said tentatively.

"That doesn't narrow it down much," Lennox smiled.

"The big one that guy owns. Full Moon?"

Lennox nodded. Full Moon was Magnus Moon's shop. Magnus was another one of the local characters, a minor celebrity.

"Okay, detectives, I really think that's enough," Nicholson said. "You can imagine that this is all a serious shock, and we have a lot to figure out." He crossed his arms and continued, "Now, we want to cooperate and we want you to catch whoever did this, but... I think we have to be done with all the questions for right now. If any of us think of anything, we'll let you know."

"You'll probably be hearing from us first," Ouellette said.

Tuesday
June 5th

Chapter IV

THE HAWTHORNE WAS THE GRAND DAME of Salem hotels, five brick stories of Jazz-age elegance. It was the favorite place for proms and weddings, and October reservations were booked at least a year in advance. Dworaczyk had had his own wedding reception there fifteen years ago, upstairs in the Essex Room. He hadn't been able to afford the ballroom—not on a rookie cop's salary.

"So there's a body over on Federal last night and now a missing white girl?" Ed Fuller laughed, shaking Dworaczyk's hand. "Wasn't busy like that back when I was still on the job."

Fuller was a tall black man, a retired cop who was now head of security at the hotel. He wore a sharp navy-blue suit and his hair was beginning to gray. He looked comfortable.

"I have no idea what to tell you, Ed," Dworaczyk said. "Michelle got the homicide and I ended up with the Missing. What room are we going to?"

"Detective Sergeant Michelle Ouellette," Fuller smiled. "And how is *she*?"

"She is not interested. What room are we going to?"

"Four-Twenty-Four. What's the word on that homicide, anyway? Anything to do with your Missing?"

"Doubt it."

Fuller brought him upstairs and knocked on the door of 424. No answer. He opened it with a passkey. The room looked out over the Common, and was pleasantly bland like most hotel rooms.

Housekeeping had already been here—the bed was made, clothing was folded and put away, and the whole room was orderly.

Dworaczyk checked through the folded clothing: there were a few souvenir t-shirts, all red, all with the tags still on. A pile of slick brochures and little stapled booklets from probably every witch shop in town sat on the desk. Dworaczyk checked between the mattresses, under the chair cushions, looking for anything she might have hidden, anything that might hint at where Kelly Conroy had gone.

Dworaczyk got down on hands and knees to check under the bed.

"When are you going to put your papers in and get yourself a nice, cushy, security job?" Fuller asked from the doorway

"Do not get me started," he muttered.

Things always got lost under beds. Lifting the dust ruffle, the beam of his flashlight fell on something the maids had missed. He pulled it out from under the bed and held it up: a small, crudely-sewn doll, no bigger than his palm. The thing was green and had no face. It was creepy.

"The fuck is that?" Fuller asked.

"Might be hers, might be the last person to stay here," Dworaczyk said. "Your maids pretty thorough?"

"Supposed to be."

Dworaczyk took a few pictures of the thing on his phone and put it on the bed.

In the bathroom, he found an amber-colored pill bottle—a prescription drawn on a Milwaukee pharmacy, in Kelly Conroy's name.

"What is Haldol for?" he asked, squinting at the label.

Fuller had his phone out and was tapping with his thumbs.

"Paranoid schizophrenia," he said after a moment of searching. He chuckled.

"The father did not say anything about that when I talked to him," Dworaczyk shook his head. "God damn it. Think maybe that is something you might mention to the police? If your daughter is walking around the city, off her meds, that might be something to tell the nice policeman looking for her."

There was nothing to indicate that Kelly's disappearance was suspicious. Disappearing wasn't a crime. Running away from the father you'd argued with wasn't a crime. The room couldn't be considered a crime scene and, until it was, nothing could be collected as evidence. Dworaczyk took a picture of the pill bottle and put the doll back where he had found it.

"Good luck with this one, sergeant," Fuller laughed.

Chapter V

Tuesday June 5th

SONYA WEAVER WAS A REAL ESTATE LAWYER with an office a few streets away from Spooktacular headquarters, and she had been chair of the board of directors for eight years. She was a stout, round woman in her fifties with big, thick, dark hair only just beginning to gray. She wore rings on every finger. As she gestured to the detectives to sit, Lennox noticed that all the rings on her left hand were silver, and all those on her right were gold.

"David called me an hour ago," she said. "This is just... fucking unbelievable. What happened?"

"We're still working on that."

"And... right out in the parking lot?"

"Afraid so. Do you have any idea what he might have been doing out there last night?"

"He's always running to some event or giving a speech or some damn thing. He says he's always kinda on the clock." She paused. "He *said* he *was* always kinda on the clock." She said the words slowly and carefully, as if trying the past tense on for size.

"Can you think of anyone who would have done this?"

"Stuart? No. He's a charmer. You talk to him for five minutes and he was your new best friend, you know? Everybody liked him."

"Except anybody looking for parking downtown in October," Lennox said.

"Yeah, sure. Some pissed-off tourist came back eight months later for payback," she said dismissively.

"Well, he obviously pissed somebody off."

Sonya just shook her head. Lennox wasn't sure if she was disagreeing, or still couldn't believe Stuart was dead.

"Did you ever meet his wife?"

"Jessica? Yeah. Wait, did they get married?"

"Don't think so," Ouellette said. "Did they seem okay to you?"

"What do you mean, okay?"

"Happy together. Did you ever hear about problems at home?"

"No. Why? Wait, do you think Jessica…?"

"We have to check everything," Lennox said apologetically.

"They always seem fine. I mean, I haven't seen her in a while, but I never heard anything." She shrugged.

"She used to work over there," Lennox said.

"So?"

"Just saying."

"Do you really think she did this?" Sonya lowered her voice to a conspiratorial whisper.

"Like I said, we have to check everything… which brings me to my next question, actually. Where were you last night? After, say, seven o'clock?"

"Me?" she said uncomfortably. "You gotta be kidding."

"No," Ouellette said.

"Oh, fine. I had a meeting starting at seven, went till after nine."

"Where?"

"The Welcome House," she replied. The Welcome House was a trendy, expensive, farm-to-table place on the water over in Marblehead. Lennox had never been there—he didn't think he could or should afford it.

"Who else was there?" Lennox opened his notebook.

"Doug Champlain and Marjorie McQueen."

"They're on the board with you, aren't they?"

He remembered the names from looking over the Spooktacular directory. Champlain was vice-chairman of the board, and Marjorie McQueen was the head of two or three committees. He couldn't remember which ones, right now.

"So this was a business meeting?" Ouellette asked.

"Unofficially," Sonya said.

"Something to do with Stuart?" Lennox asked.

"Yes." She tucked her chin down and looked at her rings. She wasn't going to go any further without being pushed.

"What about him?"

"We were trying to figure out what to do."

"About what?" Ouellette asked.

"About Stuart. About the whole festival, but... that means Stuart."

"Not really following you," Lennox said.

"The festival... isn't doing well," Sonya admitted. "The last three years, we've barely broken even."

"How is that even possible?" Lennox asked. He knew the numbers. Everyone in town did. Another thing Pickman always made sure of. Well over half-a-million people visited Salem in October, pumping over a hundred million dollars into the local economy. October got Salem through the other eleven months.

"People forget where the money really goes. Or they don't realize it to begin with. People come here for Stuart's big Hallowe'en party, sure, but most of their money still gets spent on hotel rooms and meals. Money that doesn't go back to the festival. So October gets bigger every year, but that doesn't mean the festival is getting any richer. And then... we made some bad decisions. Bad financial decisions, I mean. The board is partially to blame there, and by the board, I mean me. He was always coming up with some crazy new idea, and I should have kept Stuart on a tighter leash." She shook her head.

"So pumpkin-carving kits are bankrupting the Spooktacular?"

"Not specifically, but those kinds of decisions, yeah. We let him spend too much and now we're... getting in trouble. A lot of trouble."

"So what was your meeting about?" Lennox asked, but he thought he already knew.

"We were... talking about asking Stuart to step down."

"But isn't it his company?" Ouellette asked. "He started it."

"Sure, but the board has to put the festival first."

"You were planning to get rid of him?" Lennox asked.

"We were planning to save the festival," she said sternly, "and unfortunately asking Stuart to step down is one way to do it. Probably the best way. And it's not like we hadn't given him plenty of warnings before. Every year, the board has this same conversation about what to do with our little problem child."

"So was this an official meeting?"

"No, this was just... friends meeting for dinner."

"So Pickman didn't know about any of this?"

"No. And... this was all very tentative anyway."

"So if you have the same conversation about him every year, was this year any different?"

"This is the first year we actually started talking about... a replacement."

"And do you have someone in mind?" Lennox asked.

"... Yes."

"Who?"

"Wow, really?"

"Yes, really. We're investigating a homicide."

"Well," she said carefully, "we were going to reach out to Phillip Agnew."

Lennox wrote the name down in his notebook. "And who is he?"

"He's currently the director of a theater festival in the Adirondacks. Before that, he was involved in a major music festival, so he seemed like a good fit. He has the right kind of resumé."

"And did Phillip Agnew know anything about this?"

"Oh, God no. Not yet, anyway."

"Did Stuart?"

"We hadn't discussed it, but Stu isn't stupid," Sonya sighed. "Wasn't stupid. He knew we were in trouble and that... all options were on the table."

"You really wanted to replace him?"

"I want the goddamned Spooktacular to survive. Dozens of festivals have folded in the last ten years. Shit, even in the last five years. I don't want us to be another one. If putting someone else in charge is what it takes…" She took a deep breath. "Then that's what it takes."

"Did you like him?" Lennox asked. "Stuart. Personally?"

"Did I like him? Well, yeah, I guess." She gave a dry little laugh. "I mean, the chair of the board and the director are always going to butt heads, but… we were both on the same side. So we had our differences over the years and, sure, he threw some serious tantrums if he didn't get his way. But the next day everything was fine, no hard feelings. He was like that."

"Did he throw any tantrums at anybody lately?"

"Not that I know of. But I haven't seen him in a couple of weeks."

"And the restaurant and your other two board members will all confirm you were there until about nine o'clock last night?"

"Damn well better." Sonya checked the time. "Is that everything? I have a closing in half an hour."

*Tuesday
June 5th*

Chapter VI

THE BIRDS WAKE HER UP, chirping outside. She blinks and it takes her a moment to remember where she is. She sits up in the uncomfortable bed, kicks the musty blankets off. She slept in her clothes. It had taken her a long time to get to sleep last night, even though she had been every kind of exhausted.

She peeks out through the bedcurtains, nervous that she might not be alone. But the house is still empty and she throws the curtains wide. It had been dark when she got here last night, and she had been forced to clumsily feel her way around the room, but now she can see where she is. The windows cast a lattice-work of shadows across the floor, the floor of wide boards that creak under her bare feet as she gets out of bed. The room smells damp. There is some furniture here, all simple and sturdy. There's a table with an open Bible and brass candlesticks and a quill pen. A little, empty, green bottle sits on the narrow windowsill over the table. Across the room there's a flagstone hearth with dull iron cookware, and a couple of chairs over by a second square table under another window.

She yawns and stretches and rubs her eyes. The place is not quite familiar, but it feels right. It's a strange, comforting sensation.

And then she sharply remembers why she is here. She ran here last night, when she had to get away from what she saw in the parking lot, had to find someplace to hide. She remembers now how that blade had flashed white and then red. She screamed and then she froze and then ran once she found her legs again. Ran to this place. And the little village had wrapped its arms around her in the dark and let her know that she couldn't do anything for that man, but she is safe now. She is safe here.

It's a big house. Two rooms downstairs, with more upstairs. It's the only house here that even has an upstairs, from what she can tell. The other room on the first floor is empty, and now she climbs the steep, narrow stairs up to the second floor to see what the rest of the house is like. Two rooms, both empty. Empty and dark, with the shutters still on the little windows. It should be eerie, these blank, dusty rooms in an old house, but it's not.

Back downstairs, she closes the Bible. It's not her book. That stern and vengeful God, with His list of thou-shalt-nots, had never spoken to her—not the way the water and the wind and the Moon always had. She had never prayed unto Him, but had drawn circles on salted floors and lit incense and asked the Universe to grant her wish instead. Now she tucks a poppet into the beams over the door, laying claim to the space.

It had been cold last night. Unseasonable. She wonders if she should light a fire. She wonders if she can even figure out how. But she knows that smoke from the chimney will give her away. And she can't let anyone know she is here. Can't let herself be found out.

She needs a change of clothes, but everything is back at the Hawthorne, and she doesn't want to go back there. She knows it's safe here. But everything is back at the Hawthorne… including her meds. She has to admit the pills help sometimes. The pills tether her to the more mundane world—when she remembers to take them. They help with the practical things and she could probably use a little of that help right now. She wonders if she should go to the police, wonders if she can trust the police, and the pills would help her figure that out. Probably.

But she couldn't rely on anyone to help her last time, when they all turned on her, all cried out on her for sundry acts of witchcraft. Why would it be any different now?

She looks out the window, through the tiny panes. She's still alone. She pulls open the door, a big door of wide planks and iron hinges, dozens of iron nails studding the outside of it. It's a wonder a witch could open an iron-bound door like this, she thinks, smiling at the old myth. It's warmer outside than it is in the house. She feels the sun on her face and listens to the silence for a few moments before deciding it's safe to go exploring.

It's a tiny little village, a cluster of cottages on the harbor. There are crooked pathways, overgrown gardens, and a pond with ducks. She discovered it online, months ago when she was still just planning this trip. It was one of the first places she visited when she arrived. She got a free map from a stand downtown and the village was just off the bottom edge, with an arrow pointing the way. It almost felt like it should have *Here Be Dragons* in curlicue script. It wasn't far from downtown, and when she got here after a twenty-minute walk, she found a dilapidated ticket booth and a padlock on the rusty gate. The village was there, hunkered down behind the fence; she could get little glimpses of it through the trees. She had followed the fence and found a narrow hole on the side that faced the water, but she didn't go in. Too scared. So she had gone back downtown, disappointed. She had other places she wanted to visit. But she remembered it later, when she realized she needed somewhere to hide.

She moves through the village, arms folded tight. She smiles as she goes. She likes it here. It feels right.

It's smaller in the daylight, somehow. Last night, lit only by the stars, it had felt as though it went on forever. She crosses a little bridge over a brook—crossing running water, another old wives' tale. There are a few more tiny houses here, no more than one-room cabins with rough chimneys. A thin wooded area stretches out behind them for some distance, and she thinks there is a neighborhood over that way, over the little hill.

In front of the pair of cottages is a row of benches, arranged to face a set of stocks. The wood is splintered and bleached by the sun and the rain. She runs a finger over the rough wood and laughs. Witchy women who ran taverns ended up punished like this—ended up in the stocks. But not her… no, she had been hanged.

And she feels the noose again for a moment, and she gasps for breath.

She crosses back over the bridge. More little houses here: thatch-roofed cottages, just one room and a loft. No furniture, just a fireplace, and no glass in the window. There's another, larger building opposite—square and stolid. The shutters on the big window are nailed down, but she can peek through the cracks. A forge, an anvil. Hammers and tongs. It's a blacksmith shop. This is where the cookware and the nails at her house come from.

Her house. She smiles as she realizes how quickly she has come to think of it that way, that the house belongs to her. The only house with an upstairs. The only house with a bed, with glass in the windows. Even if she does really belong in one of the ramshackle hovels here, she'll stay where she is. She'll stay in the mansion. Her house.

She goes back to her house and strips out of yesterday's clothes, tossing them behind her. She walks through the village, skyclad, feeling the grass between her toes and the sun on her back, in places it doesn't often touch. She pads over to the hole in the fence and takes a quick look. The tide is in, full-moon high, just ten or a dozen feet away, on the other side of the path running along the fence. There is no one in sight. It's still early. She takes a deep breath, twisting through the opening and sprinting into the water. Up to her knees, then her waist. It's colder than she expected. Goosebumps. Another deep breath and she kneels, skin prickling with the salt water as she dunks her head, digs her fingers into her hair and splashes some water over her back. She rubs her face and her breasts, under her arms and between her legs. The cold water makes her laugh and then cough and then laugh again. She holds her breath and her feet leave the bottom as she floats—she floats because she's a witch. Some kind of witch, anyway. The stinging water wakes her up as much as it relaxes her. Loosens her. Loosens the noose. Lets her forget why she is here. Lets her forget that she saw a man murdered last night. At least for a few minutes.

She splashes back over to the shore, and the air feels warmer as it wraps around her when she leaves the water. She checks to make sure there is still no one around to see her and goes back through the fence, back to her house. Now she's getting cold again. Entering the house, she realizes she doesn't have anything to dry off with, anything to brush the dirt from her feet. She needs a towel. And a change of clothes. And something to eat.

Reluctantly, she pulls the thin tablecloth from the table with the Bible on it and dries herself off with that. She drapes it over the chair to dry when she's done. She pulls on yesterday's jeans and slips her red hoodie over her head. She's still a little damp but it'll be okay. She folds up yesterday's underwear and socks and tucks them under the bed. She definitely needs to pick up some things. She remembers seeing an Army-Navy store downtown. That'll be a good place to start.

She steps back outside, pulling the door shut behind her.

There is a loud, grinding sound, a clash of metal against metal. Her knees buckle and she drops to the dirt, hands on either side of her head.

It's a truck. A heavy truck on the other side of the fence, noisily changing gears and gunning the engine. She can hear it but she can't see it. It's out there somewhere in the park, out beyond her village. She listens to it move away and it takes a couple of minutes for her to catch her breath, to let her heart calm down. She counts to ten, waiting for someone to come walking down the path, but no one does. She's still safe. At least for a little while longer.

She flips her hood up and circles around to the hole in the fence.

Five more days, she tells herself. Five more days and this will all be done.

Tuesday June 5th

Chapter VII

BACK IN THE CID BULLPEN at the station, Lieutenant Winters said, "Update me."

"Victim is Stuart Pickman, executive director of the Salem Spooktacular," Ouellette began. "Age 49. Residence on Bay View Avenue in the Willows."

"Mr. Hallowe'en," Winters nodded. He grabbed a pencil off Lennox's desk and began gnawing on one end.

"Body was found in the Church Street parking lot, across from his work address, with a slashed throat. ME pronounced him at the scene. Murder weapon is a short, serrated blade, recovered at the scene."

"Who found him?"

"Walking tour," Lennox said. "I'm getting the list of names from the office, but I don't expect anything there."

"So who did it, then?"

"Started with the girlfriend, but she seemed genuinely shaken up and people say they were happy together."

"Don't cross her off the list yet. Who else?"

"Board was looking to maybe replace him."

"Replace him with…?"

"Someone named Phillip Agnew, who is in upstate New York."

"Do we know he was in upstate New York last night?"

"Haven't checked into him yet, but he doesn't seem to know he was even in the running."

"And who is in charge now?"

"A David Nicholson, the current assistant director. Helpful, polite. Says nobody at the Spooktacular could possibly be involved."

"What about this knife? Anything there?"

"Identified as part of a carving kit the Spooktacular put out a few years ago," Ouellette said. "They have some in the office."

"So somebody at the organization was involved."

"Can't rule it out," she nodded.

"There are seven different shops downtown that usually carry them, but not this time of year," Lennox added. He had spent forty-five minutes calling around to the various stores when they got back to the station. "But you can get anything on Amazon, any time."

"And the handle was missing," Ouellette said. "Snapped off in the attack."

"Rage killing," Winters nodded.

"But the killer obviously came prepared," Lennox said. "Nobody just walks around with pumpkin-carving knives in June."

"When will you have forensics on the knife?"

"They're backed up right now."

"Of course they are."

"They say maybe Monday. Earliest."

"Anything else at the scene?"

"This." Lennox held up a crime scene photo of the crude little green poppet. "It was near the body, and so far no one has admitted to recognizing it."

"Is that from one of the shops downtown?" Winters sighed. In most other cities, that could have referred to almost any kind of store, but in Salem, "downtown shop" usually meant a witch shop.

"Yeah. It's a poppet."

"Fred," Winters called over to where Dworaczyk sat at his desk, listening. "You found a doll, didn't you?"

"I did." Dworaczyk pulled a photo out of a pile. "This."

He held up a photo of the doll he found under Kelly's bed at the Hawthorne. An identical faceless, green doll.

"God damn. Was my Missing at your scene?"

"And is she a witness or is she a new suspect?" Winters said. "What else did you find in the girl's room?"

"Prescription bottle. Haldol."

"That's for paranoid schizophrenia," Lennox said.

"Funny how you just know that off the top of your head," Dworaczyk said pointedly. "When we spoke this morning, the father did not mention she was on any medication, and now it looks like she may not actually be taking it. And now she is at a crime scene. And missing."

"Better and better," Winters said. "The father didn't mention medication at all?"

"He did not."

"Call him back and see what else he failed to mention. Any other contacts in the file?"

"A sister, lives in Chicago."

"Call her after you talk to the father and see if she has anything to add. No, wait," he turned to Ouellette. "You call the sister. She may be more comfortable talking to a female. Tell her you're working on a related case, but no details."

"Yes, sir."

Winters tossed the mangled pencil onto Lennox's desk as he went back to his office. Lennox nudged it off his desk and into the trash with his old marlinspike as Ouellette made the call.

"Sandy Conroy? This is Detective Sergeant Michelle Ouellette with the Salem Police—"

"Oh my God did you find her?" The sister's words came out in a rush. "Tell me you found Kelly."

"Not yet, but we're working on it," Ouellette said. She heard Sandy sigh with disappointment. "So you obviously haven't heard from her?"

"No, I haven't."

"I'm just calling to go over a couple of things real quick."

"Okay," Sandy said cautiously. "What do you... need?"

Ouellette briefly wished Lennox were the one making this call. For all his awkwardness, all his weird little quirks and digressions, he was usually better at navigating these conversations than she was. He was the one who handled the civilians.

"There was an incident here in town last night, and there's some indication that she may have been present at the scene."

"Did something happen to her?"

"No."

"But she's involved in something?"

"We don't think she was involved, but we do think she may be able to help us. So it's very important for you to let us know right away if she contacts you."

"Okay," cautiously again.

"She's not in any trouble, we just need to speak with her."

"Okay." Sandy was obviously not at all reassured. "So what did you want to go over?"

"Kelly has some psychological issues. Is that correct?"

"Correct." Sandy paused. "Yeah, she has some stuff going on."

"Your father didn't indicate that when he filed the missing-person report." Ouellette glanced across the bullpen. Dworaczyk was on the phone with the father right now, nodding, writing something down. But when he looked up from what he was doing, his eyes locked onto her breasts. He did that shit a lot. She turned away.

"No, he wouldn't," Sandy said, frustration in her voice. "God, I could just kill him sometimes."

"Excuse me?"

"He never should have let her go on this trip," she breathed. "Not alone. I have no idea what he was thinking. He knows she has problems but... just won't acknowledge it. Like, she'll get better and it'll all go away if he just... ignores it all long enough."

"But it's not going away?"

"No, it's not."

"Okay. So she's on medication for paranoid schizophrenia?"

"Yeah. When she remembers to take it."

"How long has she been… sick?" Ouellette couldn't think of a better word for it.

"She was always kind of withdrawn, but… she and Dad got into a car accident when Kell was about thirteen or fourteen. She hurt her neck and it's been giving her trouble ever since. And that's kind of where it started."

"What do you mean?"

"Well, she was always interested in witches and horror movies and that sort of stuff. But after the accident, she started getting all weird and saying she cheated death and why did she cheat death—all stuff like that. And then she did a school project on the Salem witch trials and she got really fixated on one of the witches—Bishop, I think the name was? Bridget Bishop?"

Ouellette wrote it down. She'd heard the name around town before, recognized her as being one of those executed for witchcraft, but that was all. Lennox, of course, could probably give her a detailed biography the minute she got off the phone.

"Why was she… fixating?"

"She… um… she said one night that she thought she was Bridget Bishop in a past life."

"Really?"

"Yeah."

"And why was that?"

"Because she hurt her neck in the accident, and thought that was, like, some kind of memory of getting hung. Dad doesn't acknowledge any of this, by the way, so I'm not surprised he didn't say anything. I guess he figured she'd just grow out of it. I thought so, too, but… here we are." She paused, and Ouellette knew she was trying to figure out how to phrase something. "Now look, she's totally fine ninety-five percent of the time, but every once in a while... I don't know. Things just kind of catch up with her, you know? She gets really, really withdrawn. Really... paranoid. Like the villagers are after her again."

"Does she hear voices?"

"I don't think so."

"Has she ever been violent when... things catch up with her?"

"No. No, she goes inward, not outward, you know? She kind of likes to hide out, go somewhere quiet. If people are after her, she has to get away from them, right?" Sandy Conroy sighed. "I'm sorry, I'm probably not being much help here, am I?"

"Actually, you're being very helpful. Where is your mother in all of this?"

"Mom... Mom was in the car and died a couple days after the accident."

"I'm sorry to hear that."

"Well, it just puts more pressure on Dad and Kell, you know? Survivor guilt, I guess."

"Right. Anything else I need to know?"

"She's... she's just a kid. She's turning twenty-one—Sunday's her birthday. But she's just a kid. I don't know if that helps."

Just a kid. Ouellette's eyes strayed over to the little picture of Roland, her son. Roland was eight. A little older than Pickman's daughter. Just a kid.

But Kelly was a paranoid schizophrenic kid, off her meds, wandering around a strange city, thinking she was the reincarnation of a Salem witch, thinking people were after her.

Merde.

"It does," Ouellette said. "It does. Let us know the minute you hear from her."

"Please find her." Sandy's voice cracked as she said it.

"We'll do our best." She knew never to make promises.

Dworaczyk finished his call to the father just as Ouellette was hanging up with the sister.

"The father does not like my attitude," he said. "He will be here in the morning. And that is all we need right now. What did the sister say?"

"That your Missing thinks she's the reincarnation of Bridget Bishop."

"Really?" Lennox asked. He'd been fiddling with that spike he kept on his desk all during her phone call. He did that when he was bored. Or anxious. Usually anxious.

"Go ahead," Ouellette nodded. "I know you're dying to."

"Well, she's the first woman to hang during the witch trials."

"Great," Dworaczyk said.

"She's supposed to have been this fiery outspoken woman who wore a red paragon bodice—"

"The fuck is paragon?" Dworaczyk asked.

"Some kind of wool."

"Not helping," Ouellette said. Him and his digressions.

"Yes, I am. It explains why she was out in the parking lot. When you're accused of being a witch, they lock you up in the jail that used to be where the Telephone Building is now. So that's going to be an important location for her to visit."

"Okay," she conceded.

"Also explains the poppets. Bridget Bishop's house was where Turner's is now, on the other side of the parking lot from the Telephone Building. According to legend, she kept a tavern there but she didn't—it's just a house with an apple orchard out back. She's probably getting confused with this other woman named Sarah Bishop, who runs a tavern…"

"Okay, and…?"

"And when she's accused of being a witch, there's a laborer who had been doing some work on her house and the guy says he found poppets in the wall—little dolls people used for folk magic. Which is a sure sign back then that she must be a witch. Or so they thought back then."

"So what do we do with this?"

"You might want to check at Turner's to see if she's been in. And have a look to see if she's been over to Gallows Hill, or Proctor's Ledge, or maybe the memorial downtown. All places to keep an eye on, maybe."

"I do not know about that," Dworaczyk said.

"What do you mean?"

"It seems a little far-fetched."

"But you need to take a look anyway."

"Maybe."

"One other thing," Lennox said.

"What?"

"Sunday? That's June tenth. That's the day Bridget Bishop was hanged. It's not a coincidence that she's in town so close to that date," Lennox shook his head. "She's here because Sunday is June the tenth."

"This still seems… pretty out there, if you ask me."

"Just trying to help," Lennox shrugged.

"Ouellette, go to your autopsy," Winters called from his office. "Fred, try to have some progress for the father when he gets here. Lennox, go do whatever it is you do around here."

Tuesday
June 5th

Chapter VIII

LENNOX SPENT ANOTHER HOUR shuffling paperwork on his desk, filling out reports and trying to plan ahead. He finally left at five-thirty. Ouellette probably wouldn't be coming back to the station after the autopsy, so he didn't have to wait around for her. He walked home.

He lived alone in the Old Jail, a stern granite building that had once housed prisoners awaiting trial or serving out their sentences. Decades ago, when it was still an active house of corrections, the inmates had sued over the deplorable conditions and won. Now, the property was all luxury apartments and condos, with granite countertops, professional landscaping, and plenty of parking. He was pretty sure he lived in the smallest, least-luxurious unit, overlooking the graveyard out back. He'd lived here since the divorce, and once he'd settled in and gotten past the irony of a cop living in a former jail, he realized the place suited him in some way he couldn't quite describe. He'd decided to stay, even though he'd gotten a letter from the office last week, saying that the rent was going up.

He put his badge and radio on the table and locked his service weapon in its gun box and put it on the bookcase. He wondered if he wanted coffee. There was still some cinnamon-hazelnut left. He didn't like it—it gave him heartburn and would probably keep him awake till after midnight. But it was AJ's favorite.

AJ. Amy Johnson. The evidence technician he had been… seeing? Dating? Involved with? She had turned forty-one a month ago and said that she didn't like "the g-word" anymore. She had her own drawer in the bedroom, her own collection of shampoos and soaps in the blue-tiled bathroom (where she had recently proven the shower was big enough for two), and her own go-bag of evidence collection equipment in the closet. And her own b-word who still wasn't quite used to having anyone around.

He lay down on his Ikea couch, jammed a pillow behind his shoulders, and found his page in *The Devil In Massachusetts*. Comfort reading. He had lost track of how many times he'd re-read it, how many times he'd taped the cover back on. There were a few pages on Bridget Bishop, and he started searching for them when there was a knock at the door.

He crossed the room to squint through the peephole, and saw Mrs. Chevoya from down the hall, smiling and bulbous in the fisheye lens. She lived with her husband and a couple of teenagers and he had the vague idea she was a retired teacher. He only knew her well enough to say hello by the mailboxes. He didn't know any of his neighbors particularly well, though.

"I hope I'm not bothering you," she said, when he opened the door.

"Um, no?"

"Do you mind if I come in for a minute?" She lowered her voice and glanced down the hall.

"Sure..."

"You're not busy?"

"I have to go out later, but not for a little bit. C'mon in."

She took a few steps into his apartment and looked out the window.

"You can see the graveyard," she said. "I don't know if I'd want to see a graveyard. That'd be... weird. You can't from our unit."

"Right."

She turned from the window and startled.

"What is—that?"

She pointed unhappily at a four-foot-tall figure in the corner, a mannequin dressed like a Dickensian schoolboy, which had glass eyes and a grim mouth.

"That's Jesse Pomeroy. Youngest serial killer in American history."

Jesse Pomeroy had started his criminal career at an early age, beating and torturing a handful of other children but leaving them alive. In 1874, at the tender age of 14, the Boston Boy Fiend had been convicted of killing two other teenagers, dumping one body in a marsh and hastily burying the other in the cellar of his own mother's dress shop. Sentenced to hang, his sentence had later been commuted to life in prison, and he spent his days writing poetry and an autobiography. Lennox had tracked down a copy of Jesse's autobiography via a rare book dealer in New Orleans, and the thin, worn little book had arrived last week. On the same day as the letter saying that rent was going up.

"It's for my museum," he added. "Down on Derby?"

"You have a museum on Derby Street?" Mrs. Chevoya blinked. "Is it a museum of serial killers or something?"

"Kind of. Can I help you with something?"

"Yes," she said slowly, trying not to look at the pint-sized killer staring at her from the corner. "You know we all feel safe having a cop in the building. We all feel… safe."

"Okay," he nodded. "Great. Thanks."

"And I was just wondering… have you seen the guy in 110?"

"Not really." Although he had. A tall man with shy body language who didn't make eye contact when Lennox saw him by the mailboxes.

"So you don't know anything about him?" she asked.

"Can't say that I do."

"Because some of us were wondering… he doesn't seem to… fit, you know?"

"No, I don't."

"He just seems like a weirdo."

"A weirdo?"

"Yeah. And I don't know if you can, like… check up on him or something? I just think there's something going on with him. And, you know, a lot of us have kids in this building."

"What do you think is going on with him?"

"I don't know. But there's just... something."

"Has he done anything? Has he bothered you or the kids?"

"Well, no, but..."

"But what?"

"There's just something about him we don't like," she said firmly.

"We?"

"My husband and I. And a couple of other people we were talking to. We just thought maybe you could... look him up? See if he has a record or something? We just don't know what's going on with him."

"Well, if you see anything suspicious, let me know," he shrugged.

"You can't just go talk to him?"

"About what?"

She took a deep breath and straightened her shoulders. She glanced out the window at the headstones, and then over to Jesse Pomeroy in his corner.

"Forget it," she snapped. "Never mind. Forget I even came. But when something happens, don't say I didn't try to warn you."

She slammed the door behind her as she left.

"Neighbors, huh?" he asked Jesse, as he sat back down on the couch and tried to find his page again.

He read for another hour, skimming, looking for information on Bridget Bishop. He put the book aside a few minutes after eight o'clock and got ready to go back out to the Church Street Lot, just around the corner.

He told Jesse, "Don't wait up."

Tuesday
June 5th

Chapter IX

REVISITING A CRIME SCENE twenty-four hours later was standard procedure: people kept schedules that put them at the same place at the same time every day. The parking lot would have regulars. Someone who always parked in the same spot when going to work, or someone who always took the same shortcut home. It could even be someone who always chose a particular doorway to get high or drunk in. People kept schedules and any one of them might have seen something.

The Church Street lot had been a little neighborhood once, bulldozed decades ago in the name of urban renewal. He had seen black and white photos of old houses with clapboard sides and gambrel roofs and old cars parked out front. All of them were gone now. But St. Peter's Episcopal, the church that gave Church Street its name, still stood, with a stolid, Gothic Revival tower and stained-glass windows and a group of ancient headstones clustered around the front door. The building was from the 1830s and the congregation was a century older. The land had once belonged to Phillip English, a wealthy merchant who had been arrested for witchcraft but escaped. English was legendary for having exhumed the body of Sheriff George Corwin after the witch trials were over and holding it for ransom, until the family returned the property the sheriff had confiscated. Lennox had always assumed that included the parcel upon which St. Peter's now stood.

Half the parishioners were Spanish and called it San Pedro's now. A parking lot with a church at one end seemed like some kind of weird, modern village green. Changing times.

There were a few people standing around a buzzing floodlight, about twenty feet from where Stuart Pickman's body had lain the night before. As he approached them, no gun on his belt, badge in his pocket, he saw the flowers and candles and plastic pumpkins of a makeshift shrine, piled up at the foot of the lamp post. There were lilies and some roses: some real and others made of silk or plastic or paper. Most of the candles were flickering LEDs but a few were wax, including a pale beeswax pillar that made Lennox glance over his shoulder. There were photos of the victim, most of them copies of the one from the Spooktacular staff directory: Stuart Pickman, Mr. Hallowe'en, arms folded, head tilted to one side, smiling. It looked more like an actor's headshot than anything else. There were coins and pentacles and some little folded notes tucked among the flowers and the candles. Lennox knew he was going to have to check all the notes, but he'd have to wait until no one else was around. He might have to come back after midnight.

"I moved here because I love Hallowe'en," a young woman was saying as he approached— a plump goth with black hair down to her waist. She tugged absently at her studded collar as she spoke, not looking up from the little shrine. "Hallowe'en is so exciting here, but now... now I'm really worried."

"About what?" someone asked.

"That it's going to change," she said, trying to wipe a tear without smearing her makeup. "That, you know, the city will decide it's too dangerous now and they'll shut it down. Or like the cops, maybe. Public safety or something."

"Maybe I'll be able to find a place to park downtown in October if they do," an older man said out of the corner of his mouth. He had a paunch and unruly white hair stuck out from under his Sox cap. He sipped from a Dunkin' travel mug and added, "I mean, I don't wanna see anyone get killed, I'm not saying that, poor bastard. But look at what happens to this town every October. It's a fricking zoo, and these people are the ones responsible. Last year, some fricking drunk drove her car right up the walkway outside my building—and that's a pedestrian walkway I'm talking about, by the way. She gets to the end of the walkway and she *keeps going*. Damn near took the corner offa the building. Had to call a tow truck to get her outta there."

Lennox smiled to himself. He remembered that story from last year. The responding officer had written every citation she could think of.

"That's not their fault," the goth woman's boyfriend said. He wore an identical studded collar and laid a protective hand on her shoulder. "Can't blame this guy for something like that, dude."

"The hell I can't. I've lived here all my life and we never had shit like this until these idiots come along and now the city's a carnival every October. All those frickin' tourists." He swigged from his mug and shook his head.

"But the tourists bring in money," someone else said—a slim guy in his thirties, in chinos and loafers. "He saw an opportunity and capitalized on it. Smart businessman. Have to admire that."

"And look where it got him."

"There was nothing here twenty, thirty years ago." The guy in the chinos and loafers nodded toward the flowers and candles. "Pickman saw the potential. He put this place back on the map. He understood."

"Understood what?"

"How to make us a destination. Understood people are looking for an experience. And Hallowe'en in Salem is one hell of an experience."

The townie in the Sox cap finished his coffee and shook his head again.

"Look, all I'm saying is that without this festival, without this organization, Salem would just be another West Springfield," loafers and chinos said.

"Wait," the girl said. "What's in West Springfield?"

"My point exactly." He looked over to where Lennox stood a few feet away from the group. "What do you think?"

Lennox took a deep breath. The guy was probably right. Twenty years ago, Salem was just another burned-out New England mill town; like everywhere else, shipping vanished in the nineteenth century, factories disappeared in the twentieth. For a long time, Salem didn't seem to be anywhere in particular. Hallowe'en and witchcraft weren't really part of Salem history the way the spice trade or Nathaniel Hawthorne were. Witch City and the Hallowe'en Capitol were just masks that Salem wore from time to time, as needed.

"So… did any of you know him?"

"So what are you, a cop?" the townie asked.

"Um… yeah, actually." Lennox took his badge out of his pocket, holding it up with a tight unhappy grin. It glinted in the light from the little LEDs. "This is my case. So did any of you know him?"

Four people shaking heads.

"Were any of you out here last night?"

Four more nopes.

"So what are you people doing with this?"

"We're… investigating. Following up on some very promising leads."

"You had any solid leads, you wouldn't be out here talking to us." The townie lifted the mug again, scowling when he realized it was empty.

"Just dotting my T's and crossing my I's." Lennox said. "No turn unstoned."

"Oh, and he's funny, too."

They were interrupted by a skinny young man with dark, lank hair and hollow cheeks. Zachary Dykstra. The Spooktacular's IT guy. Head bowed and shoulders hunched, he slipped past the goths and stared at the makeshift little memorial to Mr. Hallowe'en. He wiped at his nose and didn't seem to notice anyone else.

"You gonna ask him if he knew the guy?"

"I'm all set," Lennox said.

Zachary glanced over at Lennox, startled, and whispered, "Fuck."

His hand went to a pocket and Lennox tensed the way cops always did when someone reached into a pocket. He removed a folded slip of paper and hesitated for just a moment before kneeling down and thrusting it in amongst the flowers, near one of the photos in a plastic frame. He straightened up, bit his lip, and left without looking back.

"The hell was that?" the townie asked.

"It's getting late," the goth's boyfriend said. He gave a "let's go" toss of his head and they left, hand in hand.

"Yeah, it's late," the townie said, giving Lennox a shrug. "Good luck with this, huh?"

The man in the loafers and chinos simply said good night before he left.

Lennox was about to reach for Zachary's note when someone else walked up. A reporter from the Salem *Argus*, the young woman had a camera around her neck and a notebook under one arm. She smiled.

"Well, well, well, fancy meeting you here," she said.

"Where's the other guy?" Lennox asked. When a reporter from the *Argus* showed up, the reporter from the *Advertiser*, the competing paper, usually wasn't far behind.

She ignored him and studied the haphazard pile of flowers and candles and photos. She took a step or two in one direction, and then another few steps back, looking for the best angle. She snapped a couple of pictures and reconsidered. She reached down and nudged a candle closer to one of the framed photos, took a few flowers and laid them down in front, then nodded at her own arrangement and took a few more pictures. She adjusted the lens a few times, took a few more photos, and then looked over at Lennox.

"Okay, let's get one with you in there."

"Nope."

"C'mon. Salem's Finest, on the case. Paying your respects. Here…" She picked up a silk lily and held it out to him. "Just let me get a couple of shots of you laying this down all reverently and we'll have you on the front page. Above the fold."

"Yeah, did the front page thing before once," Lennox shook his head. "Not really my thing."

"Don't know what you're missing," she said, tossing the fake lily down and then firing off another flurry of shots. "Can I at least get a statement? Like a really cute quote?"

"Can we maybe go with 'no comment'?"

"Adorable," she said, putting the camera away. "You had your chance."

They both turned as the short, heavy reporter from the *Advertiser* approached. He stopped and went from a scowl to a smile.

"Well, now," he said. "Greetings, citizens."

"Beat you to it," the woman from the *Argus* said. "And don't even bother with him, he's not talking."

"Oh, I already got my quote," the guy smiled.

"Who?" she tilted her head.

"Ken Cromartie, the old partner."

"Bullshit. How'd you even find him?"

"Google is your friend," he smirked. "Cromartie's up in Maine."

"So what's the quote?"

The guy from the *Advertiser* unfolded a piece of paper and cleared his throat.

"This is devastating news. Stuart was a brilliant, generous man who loved Salem very much and I knew from the beginning of our friendship that he was destined for great things. The Spooktacular was his yearly love letter to the city and I was always very proud to have helped him bring his vision to life. This is a great loss to everyone."

"That's it?" the woman from the *Argus* laughed. "That sucks. Why'd you even bother?"

"Shut up." The man folded the paper back up and shoved it into his pocket.

Lennox smiled and waited for the guy to take his pictures, making sure to stay out of the frame. After a few minutes, he put away his camera and the two reporters left, walking off side by side. Lennox waved and looked around, making sure he was alone before diving for the note Zachary had left, rooting around through the flowers and the coins and other offerings. It took him a couple of minutes to find it. Just a small slip of white paper, folded once. He got out his phone to take a picture.

Two words, in angular, precise handwriting:

I'm sorry.

Wednesday
June 6th

Wednesday June 6th

Chapter I

"**Where is she?**" Lieutenant Winters asked.

Lennox looked over at the empty chair behind Ouellette's desk in the CID bullpen.

"No idea," he said.

It was eight-fifteen; Ouellette was never late. Dworaczyk was out checking on something and the second unit detectives had the day off. Lennox was alone, sitting at his desk, flipping back through the pages of his notebook, and wondering what to make of Zachary Dykstra and his note.

"She was supposed to have the autopsy results," Winters said.

"She cc'ed me on that last night. No real surprises there," Lennox said, pulling it up on his screen. She had sent him a copy of the preliminary results last night; the final results would follow much later. He took a deep breath and continued: "Stabbed in the neck, bled out within minutes. Which is what he said at the scene."

"Any word on forensics?"

"No. They're still behind."

"What about your girlfriend?"

"What... about her?" Lennox asked uncomfortably, shifting in his chair. He and AJ had kept things mostly quiet. They weren't a secret, but it didn't seem like something he wanted to announce. He wondered how Winters knew.

"Can she move things along a little?"

"It's... not her scene. And even if it was, asking for favors doesn't look great, does it?" It was bad enough, he thought, that a detective was dating an evidence tech, even if they weren't working the same case.

"Fine. Give it another day or two, but then, we should start pulling some strings. Need to get this thing figured out. Fast."

"Sorry I'm late," Ouellette said, coming around the corner,

"Nice of you to join us," Winters muttered.

"Traffic," she said.

Traffic hadn't seemed too busy on Lennox's own way over to the station, but he didn't bring it up.

"Lennox said the autopsy was pretty much what you expected?" the lieutenant said.

"Yeah," she nodded. "Nothing unexpected, nothing helpful."

"And apparently we are still waiting on forensics." Winters gave Lennox a look.

"Monday earliest is what they told me," she said.

"TV makes it look so easy."

"So no updates here?"

"Maybe?" Lennox said. "There's a little shrine out in the parking lot, and Zachary Dykstra left a note there." He pulled up the photo on his phone.

"Maybe," Winters said. "Keep it in mind, but... keep looking."

"What about Dworaczyk's missing girl?" Ouellette asked.

"I don't think he has anything yet, either," Winters said. "So this is all going really well so far."

"Still early, sir."

"Lieutenant?" A uniform stopped just outside the half-wall that formed the bullpen. Officers rarely entered the space. It was some kind of unspoken rule, part of the departmental caste system. The officer had a civilian standing behind her: a rumpled, middle-aged man with a travel bag slung over one shoulder.

"Asked to see you," the uniform said.

"You must be Mr. Conroy," Winters said.

"Rick," he nodded. He looked like he had been up all night. He probably had.

"You must have just gotten in."

"Red-eye," he replied. "Have you found her?"

"Not yet, but we are checking on a few things."

"You're checking on a few things? That's it?" Anger mixed with the exhaustion in his face now. "What things? What are you checking?"

"We are just in the preliminary stages right now, Mr. Conroy."

"Rick."

"Okay."

"We have an idea, though," Lennox blurted, staring at the deck prism he used as a paperweight. A souvenir from his time in the Coast Guard, like the marlinspike in his desk drawer. "A theory, anyway."

"What theory?"

"Well, we understand that Kelly is interested in the witch trials, and this Sunday is the anniversary of the first hanging, a woman named Bridget Bishop."

"But it's only a theory," Winters warned them both equally.

"So what does that mean?" Conroy asked.

"Well, if she's here close to that date, then it makes sense that she's here because of that date… so it makes sense to think she might be out at the site on Sunday."

"The site?"

"Where the… executions took place."

"But we're going to find her before Sunday." Winters held up a hand.

"Are you the one I talked to yesterday?" Conroy asked Lennox.

"No," Winters answered for him. "Sergeant Dworaczyk spoke with you. He's out right now."

"And why aren't these two out with him? And somebody called my other daughter and told her that Kelly might have something to do with another case? You had a murder here a couple nights ago? Did I read that right? You think Kelly's mixed up in a murder?"

"Mr. Conroy," Winters raised his voice without actually yelling. Yet. But there was an edge. He could be yelling in another second. He had been a cop for over thirty years, ten of them in uniform in Southie, and still had the old beat cop's way of squaring his shoulders and making everything sound like a command. Lennox had been on the business end of such commands a few times. "We can talk in my office."

Conroy shifted his bag to his other shoulder as he followed Winters.

"I do not envy that guy," Lennox said as the door closed.

"Dworaczyk is not going to like you telling the father about your theory, you know," Ouellette said.

"He doesn't like me to begin with."

"Not sure the father is real impressed with you, either."

Something was bothering her, he thought. Maybe. She was hard to read, but she was rarely late, and traffic hadn't been that bad. Whatever it was, he knew better than to ask her, and she probably wouldn't tell him anyway.

Winters closed the door of his office and said, "Have a seat, please. You must have had a long trip. Can I get you coffee? Water?"

"No. No, thanks." Rick Conroy half-fell into a chair.

"All right. I have my people working on finding your daughter. Sergeant Dworaczyk, who you spoke to, is one of my best men. But missing person investigations are not easy, especially when the missing person does not want to be found, which may be what we have here."

"Why would she not want to be found?"

"That's a question we're working on right now. We have reason to believe that Kelly may be connected to another investigation being handled by Sergeant Ouellette—that's her out there. She's a very capable detective. She could be sitting in this chair in another couple of years if she wants it. And her partner is a hell of a lot smarter than he looks, trust me. They're a good team and they'll be working very closely with Sergeant Dworaczyk."

"So everyone's very good," Conroy sighed. "Everybody's your best, sure."

"Actually, yeah, they are," Winters said sternly. "Because if they are not very good, if they are not the best, they don't get to stay here."

"So what's this other case?" He bit his lip. "Do you think she had something to do with this… murder I was reading about?"

"It is that case, but we don't think she's actively involved. We just need to talk to her and find out if maybe she saw anything. So obviously, the sooner we find her, the better for everyone." He let Conroy sit for a minute before asking, "Where are you staying?"

"I don't know. I just got here. Kelly's staying at… I don't know. The Longfellow?"

"The Hawthorne. There's another place. It's closer, it's on the water. I'll have an officer bring you over." He knew that letting the man stay in the same hotel his daughter vanished from would only make him crazy. "We'll talk more once you get settled."

Winters steered Rick Conroy back out into the bullpen and handed him over to a uniform. As the officer led him down the hallway, Winters turned to Lennox and Ouellette.

"Don't you two have somewhere to be?"

Wednesday June 6th

Chapter II

THE PINK CURTAINS IN THE UPSTAIRS window were still fluttering in a warm, salty breeze when they arrived back in the Willows. The man who answered the door was a slightly younger version of Jessica. The same chin, the same eyes. The brother from Peabody.

"I'm sorry," he said. "Jessica isn't really seeing anyone today…"

Ouellette held up her badge, flashing it quickly and sliding it back into a pocket.

"Right," he blinked and bit his lip. He stepped back and murmured, "Okay, then."

"And you are…?"

"Trevor. I'm her brother. She's in here…"

Jessica Meyers was sitting tightly on the couch, holding an empty coffee cup and talking to a gray-haired man in a black suit. It wasn't until the man turned and stood that Lennox saw the collar. A priest.

"Father," Ouellette nodded.

"This is Father Dutra," Jessica said in a dry voice. She cleared her throat and added, "He just came by to… check on me. Did you find out anything?"

There was a look in her eyes, hoping they had found out something but also not wanting to know.

"We're still working on a few things," Ouellette said. "Nothing definite yet. Sorry."

"I can go," Father Dutra offered.

"We won't be long," Lennox said. "We stopped by to check in, too. Just wanted to see how you are holding up." Part of any investigation was making sure the survivors or other bystanders didn't feel forgotten.

"How well did you know him, Father?" Ouellette asked.

"I tend to see more of Jessica than Stuart," the priest said with a soft smile. "But he would occasionally come along."

"He liked to sleep in," Jessica said.

"A lot of people do these days." Another soft smile.

"The… medical examiner called. They asked me about… making arrangements. We never talked about that." She shook her head. "I don't really know what Stu would have wanted."

"We were just talking about it before you came in," Dutra told the detectives. "The service will be on Saturday. It'll be at Harmony Grove."

Harmony Grove was a rambling garden cemetery not far from downtown. Lennox had always liked it there. There was a lot of history to the place.

"I think he'd like it there," Jessica said quietly.

"Where's your daughter?" Ouellette asked.

"My wife has her today," Jessica's brother said. "Took her to Boston. Going to a museum, I think, or a gallery, something like that. Just trying to keep her occupied."

"Does she know?" Lennox asked.

"She's *six*," Jessica said. "She thinks Daddy went on a trip. I don't know what to tell her."

"We'll work on that." Father Dutra laid a hand on her shoulder. "Like I said, we can tell her together."

"Maybe. I don't know yet. This is… oh, fuck. This is so fucked up." She wiped at her nose and her eyes, and mumbled, "Sorry, Father."

"*Ego te absolvo,*" he said. "I've heard worse. Said worse a few times. In my younger days, of course."

Her little laugh was closer to a sob.

"So," she turned back to Lennox and Ouellette. "Nothing? Really? Nothing?"

"I wish we had better news," Ouellette said. "But it's still early yet."

"Do you need anything from us?" Trevor asked from over her shoulder.

"Not right now. You should all just sit tight until you hear from us."

"So, Saturday?" Lennox asked.

"Eleven o'clock," Father Dutra nodded. "We decided to keep it private, but you're welcome to attend."

"We can be there."

"Good."

Trevor followed them to the door, stepping outside with them.

"She's really not handling it well," he whispered.

"You can't expect her to," Lennox replied.

"I guess not." He looked back at the little house, up to the pink-curtained window on the second floor. "I don't know what she's going to tell Emma."

"It's not going to be easy," Ouellette said. "Never is."

"How well did you know Stuart?" Lennox asked.

Trevor leaned against the door frame and tilted his head thoughtfully. He was a few years younger than his sister, but had the same tired look around his eyes.

"He was great to my sister. I mean, he never married her," he shrugged. "But other than that, he was always good. Took great care of Emma. My wife and I have kids and Uncle Stuart always got them tickets to stuff around town at Hallowe'en." Another shrug. "He was generous."

"So you two got along?"

"Yeah, sure. I guess. I just... I don't know what's gong to happen now."

"What do you mean?"

"I mean... he never fucking married her," he said, lowering his voice and glancing back over his shoulder. "They had Emma together, but… I don't know how screwed Jess is going to be here, you know? I think… I think it's his house, and she might not be on the deed or anything… I just don't know." He shook his head and was silent.

"So, I have to ask… where were you that night?"

"Me?" he laughed. "I was home."

"And what did you do between six and nine?"

"Ah… got home from work a little before six. Had supper, stayed in and watched TV. We have kids—little kids. We don't go out a lot no more, my wife and me."

"Okay."

The three of them stood there awkwardly, none of them sure what to say. Trevor eventually shook his head and went back into the house.

Lennox's phone rang as they were getting back into the car.

"Sergeant Lennox—?"

"Detective Lennox," he said, not placing the voice right away. "Who's this?"

"Adam Womack. From the Spooktacular." Now he recognized the voice. "Can you—can we meet?"

"What's up?"

"Well, some of us were talking last night," Womack said. It sounded like he had one hand cupped around the phone. "And there's something you should know."

Wednesday
June 6th

Chapter III

Kelly wasn't in the shelter downtown. She wasn't at the campground out at Winter Island. None of the kids or homeless along Essex Street, tourist central, had seen her, or would at least admit they had. Nobody liked to talk to the cops. Dworaczyk had spent the morning checking with Salem's handful of registered sex offenders and now wanted a very long shower. He had gotten a call from the lieutenant, saying the father had arrived, and it might be nice to have an update for him. But Kelly was still missing. And probably still off her meds. And she may have witnessed a murder.

Dworaczyk was following up on a list of credit card charges, and now he entered Magnus Moon's shop on Essex Street. The cluster of bells on the door jingled when it closed.

He wasn't sure if he had ever been in this shop or not; they all looked the same to him, all smelled the same. Crystals and herbs and candles and little velvet bags. The same merchandise being sold to the same people.

There was a basket of poppets just inside the door, over-full. A few of the grotesque little dolls had fallen to the floor. Nine dollars each—buy twelve, get one free. The witches' dozen, according to the hand-lettered sign.

"Can I help you?" the woman behind the counter asked. She was probably about Kelly's own age, looking strangely out of place in a neat cardigan and white blouse buttoned to the throat, hair held to one side with a prim barrette.

"Sergeant Dworaczyk, Salem PD," he told her, sliding a photo of Kelly and a printout of credit card charges across the counter. "This girl was in here on Saturday; she spent over seventy-five dollars. I would like to know if she has been in again, and, if you could tell me what she bought, that could be very helpful."

"Yeah, she was here. I remember." The young woman nodded. "Give me one sec…" She slid off her stool, pulled a beaded curtain aside, and called, "Dad? There's a cop here?"

Magnus Moon swept out of the back room. He was a big man, tall and broad, with bushy hair and a devil's beard, both deep black, both very obviously dyed. He wore a velvet shirt, mostly unbuttoned, with a jumble of amulets and talismans and charms around his neck. Brooding pictures of him, almost always gazing meaningfully at a skull or a crystal ball, decorated the walls of the shop; signed headshots were available at the counter for ten dollars. Dworaczyk had seen the guy around town but never had to deal with him. Lennox had once said he had a soft spot for Magnus, but Lennox was the department weirdo, so he would.

"Constable!" his voice boomed. "Hail and well met! Welcome to Salem's première emporium of witchery!"

"I am looking for a missing girl." Dworaczyk held up Kelly's photo. "She was in here Saturday?"

"Yes," Magnus said. "Saturn's Day. We remember. We remember her very well."

"Why is that?"

"She wanted to meet us." Magnus straightened his shoulders, ready for his close-up.

"She did?" Dworaczyk smirked. "Why?"

"We are not unknown throughout the witching community, constable," Magnus said. "We are, in fact, famous."

"She cashed out about one o'clock," Dworaczyk checked the charge slip. "How long did she stay?"

"I rang her up around one, but she came in probably half an hour before, maybe forty-five minutes even," the young woman said. "Lots of browsing. She seemed really excited to be here. Then she asked if Dad was here. She was real shy about it."

"What is your name?" Dworaczyk asked, opening his notebook.

"Hel," the young woman said. "One L."

He hesitated, and decided to let questions about the spelling go.

"And was she with anyone?" he asked.

"No."

"And did she seem okay? I mean, she was not hurt or anything?"

"Nope."

"And did she seem at all disoriented? Maybe under the influence?"

"No, nothing like that."

"What did she want to talk to you about?" he turned back to Magnus.

"As we have already told you, we are somewhat famous—not to say infamous!" He gave his best devilish grin.

"Did she ask you about anything in particular?"

"She asked if we had anything on Bridget Bishop. And we do." He pointed to the rack of booklets on the counter. "We have been busying ourselves in writing brief biographical treatises on all the martyrs of 1692. The booklet on Goodwife Bishop has done very well."

Dworaczyk took one and thumbed through it. The same booklet he had seen back at the Hawthorne, along with the other things Kelly had collected from around town. It looked like it had been printed at the copy shop a few streets away. He put it back on the rack.

"She bought one," Hel said.

"Yeah, I know. What else did she do while she was here?" Dworaczyk asked. He held up the copy of the credit card charges. "She seems to have bought a lot of stuff."

"Poppets. We're running a special. And a book on reincarnation."

"Anything else?"

Hel looked over the copy of the charges. "Maybe a couple of candles or a smudge stick. But no real big-ticket items."

"Big-ticket items?"

"Like a cloak or an athame or a besom."

"Besom?"

"You would call it a broom, inspector," Magnus chuckled.

Dworaczyk saw tourists walking around town with brooms from time to time, the straw wrapped in tissue paper, price tags fluttering in the breeze. A few years ago there had been an assault case involving two drunk girls, each wielding a broomstick. One of them had swung a lot harder than the other.

"And the other thing?"

"An athame. A ceremonial blade."

"But you say she did not buy those things, right?"

"No," Hel said. "I'd remember, and the charges don't add up to enough anyway. I remember her buying a lot of little stuff."

"How did she seem? How would you describe her overall demeanor?"

"Shy but enthusiastic," Magnus said. "Very happy to be here. She said she is from Milwaukee and there is nothing like our shop there."

"A fangirl," Hel said. "Kid in a candy shop."

"When did the poor child go missing, inspector?"

"Night before last."

Magnus thought about it for a moment and asked, "Was that the night Mr. Hallowe'en was killed?"

"Yes. Same night. And there may be some overlap, so it is important that we find her as soon as possible."

"Overlap? Is she somehow... involved?"

"I cannot really comment, but we do have to check into everything."

"Is there any reason to believe that she may be in danger?"

Dworaczyk flipped his notebook closed. This clown was getting on his nerves. Maybe he should have let Lennox come talk to him.

"Thank you, you have been very helpful."

"We employ a number of gifted psychics and clairvoyants, all licensed, of course. If one of our professionals can be of service to you, you need but ask…"

"The Salem Police Department does not rely on outside help."

Magnus's body language shifted, softening slightly but noticeably. Less of a pose. He looked over at Hel for a moment—his daughter, about the same age as Kelly.

"Let me know if there's anything I can do," he said quietly.

Wednesday June 6th

Chapter IV

WOMACK WAS NERVOUSLY WAITING just inside the door of the Cauldron, a narrow coffee shop a few streets away from Spooktacular headquarters. The Cauldron was a new place with no chairs, just tall tables and counterspace. Lennox had tried it a couple of times, but the coffee was bitter and made him jittery. The place smelled delicious, though.

"Thanks for coming," Womack said, looking past the detectives and out into the street, like he was making sure of something. He led them over to the corner of the counter where Freitas stood, looking just as nervous and picking at nonexistent lint on his skinny tie.

"So like I said," Womack continued, "some of us were talking last night."

"Who was talking?" Ouellette asked.

"Well, mostly just the two of us," he gestured over to Freitas, who nodded slowly.

"Mostly?"

"Okay, just us, then."

"What were you talking about?"

Womack took a deep breath and said, "Zachary."

"What about him?"

"We were talking about it, and… and we think it's him."

"What do you mean?"

"We think maybe—"

"We think definitely," Freitas said quietly.

"We think Zachary killed Stu." Womack seemed like he was trying not to move his lips as he spoke.

"And why do you think that?"

"Well, you met him yesterday. He sits over in his corner and barely talks to anybody. The guy's weird."

"If weird bothers you, then you might be living in the wrong town," Lennox said.

"Tell him about the fight," Freitas said.

"Right. So, last Friday, Stu calls Zachary into his office. Zachary was working on a new app, it's going to be a guide to the festival—like the program book, but an app."

"Okay."

"And it was supposed to be rolled out like a month ago. And it's not ready. And it's never going to be ready for October if he doesn't get his shit together. And Stu wants to know what the hell was going on. Zachary says it was *still in development*. Like that. *Still in development.*"

Lennox nodded. That must be the IT version of *following up on some very promising leads,* he thought.

"And then Stu just rips into him," Womack shook his head. "I've never seen him like that before. He was… furious."

"Yup," Freitas nodded.

"Stu said if Zachary can't handle it, he'll get someone who could."

"That's harsh," Lennox said.

"Yeah, no shit. That's not like Stu at all. This is…"

"Outta character," Freitas said.

"Exactly."

"So how long did he get yelled at?"

"It went on for like five minutes."

"That's some pretty serious yelling," Lennox said.

"No shit."

"Both of them yelling?"

"Oh, yeah. Zachary took it at first and then just started yelling right back at him."

"So then what happened?"

"Zachary came out of the office and he was white as a fucking sheet. Thought he was going to cry."

"Looked like it," Freitas said. "Tell him about the pumpkin."

"Yeah. Well, you've been to the office, you've seen the jack-o'-lanterns all over the place."

"Pickman's collection," Lennox nodded.

"Well, Zachary grabbed the nearest one and just… throws it."

"Chucks it," Freitas nodded.

"Right against the wall. And the pieces went everywhere, man."

"Shattered."

"Who else saw this?"

"Everybody saw this. Everybody saw the whole thing."

"Then what happened?"

"Then he left," Womack shrugged.

"Coulda grabbed a saw out of the junk box as he went," Freitas said into his coffee cup.

"Did you see him do that?" Ouellette asked.

"No, but we were all trying not to watch him, you know?"

"All right. What happened after he left?"

"Toni swept up the pieces. David was out at a meeting or something but when he got back, he and Stu locked themselves in Stu's office for like, twenty minutes, but neither of them said anything about it after. I left early."

"Me, too."

"And what about Monday?"

"Wasn't in Monday. He called out sick. The day it happened."

"He wasn't in?"

"Nope. We thought maybe he quit, but then he showed up yesterday."

"Weird," Freitas muttered.

"Why didn't anybody mention this yesterday?"

Womack looked down into his coffee cup and shrugged.

"Didn't want to say shit with him sitting right there, you know?"

"Why would Nicholson not have told us about this?" Ouellette asked.

"Wasn't even there when it happened," Womack said. "So, what are you going to do?"

"We appreciate you getting in touch," Ouellette said after a pause.

"That's it?" Womack said from the side of his mouth.

"What do you mean?" Lennox asked.

"Well, aren't you going to… do something?"

"We have a lot going on with this investigation right now," Ouellette said, "but thanks for letting us know about this."

"That's it? That's just it?"

"This is very helpful," Lennox said.

"Helpful? Yeah, it's helpful and you appreciate it. We just gave you a solid… what do you call it?"

"A lead," Freitas offered.

"We just gave you a solid fucking lead and that's it? Go arrest him."

"Doesn't work like that," Ouellette said.

"We pay your salary," Freitas said, quietly but pointedly.

"Do your job," Womack added. He drained the last of his coffee and put the cup down without looking up. He shouldered past the detectives and out the door, with Womack a step behind.

"That went well," Lennox said.

"I hate it when they pull the I-pay-your-salary shit."

"Me, too. So, go have a talk with Zachary Dykstra?"

"You're driving."

Wednesday June 6th

Chapter V

LENNOX AND OUELLETTE ARRIVED at the Spooktacular office before Womack and Freitas got back. The two Basilico sisters fell into a guilty silence when the detectives got there; Zachary Dykstra, in his corner, didn't even look up.

"Is he in?" Ouellette pointed at Nicholson's closed door.

"Yeah, but he's in a… meeting," Kara said.

"That's okay," Lennox said. "We don't mind."

Ouellette knocked on the door and opened it without waiting for a response. Nicholson stood, leaning back against the edge of his neat desk, just as he had the day before. There was a tall man standing in the office with him. Nicholson looked up from the papers he was holding as Lennox and Ouellette entered.

"I'm sorry, I really do not have the time for this right now," he began. "We have a shit-ton of stuff to get straightened out right now."

"You didn't tell us everything yesterday," Ouellette said.

"Excuse me, what's this about?" the other man asked. He was heavyset, in a suit and tie, and held a pair of eyeglasses in one hand.

"And who are you?"

"Nicholas Bedrossian. I'm the festival's legal advisor." He took a business card from a pocket and handed it to Ouellette with a flick of the wrist. "What's this about?"

"We understand that Pickman had a blowout with Zachary Dykstra last week?"

"On Friday," Lennox said quietly.

"Yes," Nicholson said.

"What was it about?"

"I wasn't here for it," Nicholson said. "I had a meeting."

"Which means he really has nothing to say on whatever allegedly happened," Bedrossian said.

"We hear that Zachary is behind on an important project, some kind of app for the festival? And Stuart wasn't happy about it," Ouellette said.

"Irrelevant," Bedrossian said.

"Was there usually a lot of tension between them?" Lennox asked.

"No." Nicholson folded his arms.

"We understand things haven't been going so well lately."

"Is there a question, detective?" Bedrossian asked.

Nicholson stiffened and said, "Don't know what you mean."

"We also hear that the Spooktacular might be in some financial trouble."

"We have some… challenges ahead, sure."

"And maybe Stu has been feeling the pressure lately?"

"Maybe a little, yeah."

"And he took it out on your IT guy?" Lennox asked.

"Your IT guy, who smashed one of Pickman's pumpkins and then called out the day of the murder," Ouellette said. "Why didn't you tell us this yesterday?"

"I already told you, I wasn't even here when it happened."

"Do you think that Zachary is capable of something like this?" Lennox asked. "Capable of murdering Stuart?"

"You don't need to answer that," Bedrossian said quietly.

"All right," Ouellette said. "We're going to have to talk to him."

"Can they do that?" Nicholson looked at Bedrossian.

"Yes."

"Right now," Ouellette said.

Lennox told Zachary they just had a few quick questions, and it would be better if they talked outside. Bedrossian warned him that he didn't need to go, but Zachary sighed and shut down his computer, and they rode the elevator down to the first floor in silence.

He was pale under the stubble, and he squinted in the sunlight as they exited the building, shading his eyes with one hand. He looked over at the little shrine in the parking lot. Lennox thought it had probably grown since last night. More flowers, more candles.

"We can talk in the car. More comfortable."

"Um, yeah. Okay. Whatever."

They put him in the passenger seat, with Lennox in the driver's seat and Ouellette in the back, right behind Zachary. It wasn't an interrogation room at the station, but it was good enough: taking Zachary out of his environment and putting him in theirs. Lennox considered starting up the car and driving somewhere else, anywhere else, moving him further away from his comfort zone, but decided not to. No need to get that serious just yet. And they could see the shrine from where they were parked; it was warm in the car and Zachary was staring out the window at it.

"So how long have you worked here?" Lennox rolled down a window and balanced his notebook on one knee.

"Nine years now."

"Is this really the kind of job you stay in?" Lennox asked. "I mean, this looks like a stepping-stone to something else? Something bigger?"

"Like what?"

"I don't know the IT field. But maybe a bigger company or something? Something corporate."

"I'm happy here. Happy enough, anyway."

"You've been here the longest? Didn't you say that the other day?"

"Yeah. Ken hired me," he nodded.

Ken Cromartie, the old partner.

"Must get pretty crazy around Hallowe'en though, right?"

"Yeah, it can. But it's not so bad. I don't have to deal with the public much. Not face-to-face anyway. So that's nice."

"So what's it like working for Mr. Hallowe'en?"

"He could be… tough."

"You didn't sound real happy with him yesterday." Lennox turned back a few pages in his notebook. He hadn't written Zachary's words down, but wanted him to think he had. "You said everyone probably wanted to hurt him at some point or other. What did you mean by that?"

"He wasn't always the easiest to work for, you know?"

"Did you get along better with Ken?" Lennox asked.

"Yeah, sometimes, I guess. Maybe…"

"Maybe what?"

"I dunno. Sometimes I think maybe Ken should have been in charge from the beginning, you know?"

"We heard that you and Pickman had a blowout last week," Ouellette said, leaning in from the back seat. "You smashed a pumpkin."

"There it is. I was starting to wonder." He twisted around to look at her. "So he's the good cop and you're the bad cop? That it?"

She tilted her head slightly and gave Zachary her Look. Lennox had seen her do this with suspects before. Michelle Ouellette had a kind of forceful poker face: not angry, not accusing, but serious. A look that said she was not fucking around. A look that said she expected something, and expected it now.

"Just tell us what happened," she said patiently.

"All right," he breathed. "So this year's big project is an app, a guide to the festival. Like the program book. But… it's just being a bitch and a half. The functionality is all pretty standard, but Stu didn't want standard, he wanted cutting-edge. He kept saying that: cutting-edge. So it's going slow, but it's getting there. And then… Stu did some interview a couple weeks ago talking about all the great shit we're doing for this year and he says we'll have this cutting-edge app out in another two weeks." He shook his head. "I never said two weeks. It can't go live in two weeks. No way. But he shoots his mouth off and now it's two weeks. And… I had to tell him it wasn't going to happen."

"And he gave you hell for it."

"Yeah. He did."

"And then you called in sick Monday," Lennox said.

"Yeah, I was sick to my stomach. Because of all this shit. I swear, this place is going to give me an ulcer or something."

"You were upset."

"Yeah, I was upset."

"You were angry."

"Yeah… okay, I see where you're going with this. You think I killed him. Jesus, you think I killed him over an app? No."

"It's not just about an app, though—he really went to town on you and everybody knew it," Ouellette said. "That must have been embarrassing. And you thought he was a piece of work to begin with."

"And you had all weekend to stew about it."

"Did you grab that little saw out of the junk box when you left Friday? Or did you have one kicking around at home already?"

"Where are you even getting this?" Zachary shook his head.

"Look, Zach—"

"Zachary," he said sharply.

"You were over there last night," Lennox gestured toward the shrine. He took out his phone and pulled up the photo of the note. *I'm sorry.* He held it out, but Zachary didn't look up. "What were you sorry about?"

Another deep breath. Zachary let his head fall back against the headrest.

"You looked at that?"

"My job."

"You look at all the notes, or just mine?"

"I'm a cop, Zachary. This is a homicide investigation. I look at everything. So…?"

"So… the last time I saw Stu, we argued. Because I let him down. And now he's fucking dead. And I'm sorry about that. Okay?"

"Where were you that night?"

"I went home early. Fell asleep and woke up around... six? Six-thirty?"

"And were you home all night?"

"No," he said reluctantly. "I went back out."

"Where and when?" Lennox asked.

"I... I went over to BitBar... the place with all the video games."

Lennox nodded and wrote it down. BitBar was a bar-restaurant with dozens of old arcade games lined up along the brick walls—Space Invaders, Ms. Pac Man, Centipede. He knew the place because it was downstairs from him in the old jail. He'd been in a couple of times but hadn't stayed long. He'd never played a lot of video games when he was a teenager, and now the beeping and flashing just made him nervous and gave him a headache.

Zachary had just placed himself around the corner from the crime scene.

"How'd you get there?"

"I walked. It's like a twenty minute walk."

"So what time did you get there?"

"Like seven-thirty, maybe."

"And?"

"And... I had a couple of drinks."

"Drowning your sorrows?" Lennox asked.

"Yeah, something like that. I had a shitty day, okay?"

"Is the bartender going to remember you?" Ouellette asked.

"It was... crowded. Like, really busy for some reason."

"So the bartender isn't going to remember you, is what you're saying."

"Maybe? But... I met a girl. She was playing Star Castle and I loved that game when I was a kid. So... we got talking and I bought her a drink, and... I bought her a couple more drinks. And... we went back to my place." He took a quick, nervous gulp of air. "I don't usually do that kind of thing."

"She said she didn't either, right?" Ouellette asked. "Did you walk back to your place?"

"No. She called an Uber."

"She called, not you?"
"Yeah. Her."
"So you don't have a receipt for the ride?"
"No."
"What time did you two leave?"
"Nine... thirty?"
Lennox always wondered how civilians could be so careless about knowing the time.
"And what time did she go home?"
"She... stayed over."
"She was with you all night?"
"Yeah."
"Well, we're going to have to check all this with her," Lennox said. "How do we get in touch with her?"
Zachary blinked. "No idea."
"You don't have a phone number or anything?"
"Um, no. No, it was... we really didn't plan on seeing each other again."
"Okay. What was her name?"
"Stacey," he said hesitantly.
"Stacey what?"
"Just... Stacey."
"And what did Just Stacey look like?"
"Short. Kinda dirty blonde hair, down to her shoulders. A little chunky but cute." He shrugged, adding uncertainly, "Kinda big tits."
"Tattoos or anything like that?"
"Yeah, a little bunch of stars." He pointed behind his left ear. "And... a little heart."
"That behind her ear, too?"
"No, um..." He pointed downward, below his belt buckle.
"That's great," Lennox said. "What did she say about herself? Anything about where she lives, what she does for work?"
"She said she was a medical transcriptionist," he said, obviously proud he could remember. "Works from home."

"Did she say where home is?" Ouellette asked.

"No. She said she was from somewhere in Pennsylvania originally. Prussia, maybe? Something like that?"

"King of Prussia," Lennox said absently. "So... Stacey the medical transcriptionist originally from Pennsylvania who likes to play Star Castle and has dirty blonde hair and one... visible... tattoo."

"And kinda big tits," Ouellette added. "But only kinda."

"And you have no idea how to find her again?"

"Nope."

"You argued with the victim a couple of days before the murder," Lennox said. "Smashed one of his jack-o'-lanterns. And you just told us that you were near the scene at about the right time. Now if I were you, Zachary, I would figure out how to find Stacey real quick."

"If we check your apartment, are we going to find anything to indicate she was there?" Ouellette asked. "Maybe she dropped an earring or something?"

"That's if I let you in to check out my apartment," he said, straightening up in the seat. "Don't you need a warrant for that or something?"

"Not if you give us permission," Lennox said. He knew they could never get a warrant for this, anyway.

"Well, I'm... not giving you permission."

"You're really not helping yourself here, Zachary," Ouellette said.

"What do you want?" He rubbed his eyes. "Am I under arrest?"

"No."

"Then fuck it, I'm going back to work. Got an app to finish."

He turned around and shoved the door open angrily, slamming it behind him as he went.

"That went well," Lennox breathed, watching Zachary stomp back into the Telephone Building. "Does he really seem like he could charm a girl into going home with him?"

"Someone out there for everyone," Ouellette said. "I think he's in first place for this. You?"

"I think we need to see if we can find Just Stacey first."

"Bet you we can't."

"Let's go," she said. BitBar was just around the corner.

Chapter VI

Wednesday June 6th

"Bridget Bishop, thou art a witch!"

She cringes. She's been so careful. She keeps her hands in her pockets, head down, hood up. No eye contact. No polite hellos to people in the street. And now a man cries out on her. Has she been betrayed? Again? She half-turns to find her accuser, looking sideways, trying to be careful. It's a young man, no older than she is, in a tall, floppy hat and buckle shoes. A young man in a Puritan costume. She shivers in the June heat.

But the man isn't addressing her. He angrily points to a short woman who now turns to face him, scarlet skirts swirling. She wears a red paragon bodice, cut lower than anything she would have worn in her day. The woman's blonde hair is tucked up into a mob cap. She heaves in and out of the red bodice as she shouts back.

"I am innocent of a witch!" the woman in the red bodice shouts. "I am clear!"

"Bridget Bishop, thou art a witch!" the man repeats, louder, turning to sweep his finger at the tourists who have stopped to watch. "Thou art a witch and all gathered here know it!"

"If I were any such person you should know it," the woman says. The little crowd laughs, but Kelly trembles, hearing the words coming from someone else's mouth now.

"Witch!" another woman in antique garb calls. She motions to the crowd to join her, and in a moment she has them all chanting with her: "Witch! Witch! Witch!"

The tourists laugh and chant and take pictures.

"Bridget Bishop, I arrest thee on the charge of practicing the detestable arts of *witchcraft!*" the man cries, grabbing the woman roughly by the shoulder. "All of you good citizens of Salem are invited to come and witness the trial of Bridget Bishop! This way, good people! This way!"

He half-drags the woman after him. The tourists look at one another, some laugh and some shrug, but most of them follow along.

"I am no witch! I know not what a witch is!" the woman protests.

"Then how do you know that you are not one?" the man asks.

Kelly gets push-pulled along by the crowd. It's a group of thirty or forty people now—tourists out for a nice day—following close behind the man dragging the woman in the red bodice. After a hundred yards, the woman drops to the ground, kneeling on the bricks, refusing to move. The crowd circles around her.

"Witch! Witch! Witch!"

Kelly realizes she's the only one not chanting, not laughing.

The man hauls the woman back onto her feet and shoves her forward. The crowd surges again toward a stern brick building that frowns down a side street. The man in the buckle shoes drags the woman in red through the door and into the building. Another man in a bright orange witch-on-a-broom t-shirt stands by the door.

"The witch trial of Bridget Bishop is about to begin! Tickets are sixteen dollars and ninety-two cents. We accept cash and all major credit cards. No personal checks!"

A few in the crowd turn and walk away, but most stay and take out their wallets. Kelly wants to leave but she can't. She looks up at the pitiless old building. It's terrifying, the way it looms, the way it won't let her leave. Not warm and welcoming and safe like her little hidden village. She doesn't want to enter, but she knows she must.

She hands the guy a crumpled twenty-dollar bill and feels the noose tighten. She doesn't wait for her change.

The windows are tall and broad, washing the floor and walls in bright sunlight. The walls are pale and the floor is old, blond wood. More people in costume, directing people to their seats. Kelly sits in the back, making sure she can still see the woman in the low red bodice, still see Bridget Bishop.

"Goodwife Bishop, you stand accused of practicing witchcraft," a black-robed magistrate intones. He looks about twenty years old, and is wearing sneakers under the robe. "How dost thou plead?"

"I am innocent!"

"Thou art a witch!" another woman in an apron and mob cap cries out. "Thou art too outspoken and last week thou afflicted my cow and now her milk is sour!"

"Aye, and she doth afflict my husband as well," another goodwife calls luridly. The audience laughs as Goodwife Bishop tugs her bodice up a little higher.

"Yeah!" a guy off to Kelly's left yells. "Yeah, and last week, she didst give me a hummah!"

"Now goodman, you have spent too much time in the tavern, methinks," the man in the hat says, giving the guy a smile that isn't friendly. "Do any others have evidence to offer here?"

"I saw her at a witches' sabbat," another tourist calls.

"And what was thou doing at a witches' sabbat, goodman?" the magistrate demands.

"I... um... got lost in the woods," the tourist laughs.

"Say you that you saw Goodwife Bishop with her sister witches?" the magistrate asks, stepping toward the tourist. "With the Black Man?"

"Yeah, sure."

"Thou art a liar! Never have I met with the Black Man in all my life! I am no witch—I scorn it!"

"Goodwife Bishop, is that not a witch-mark upon thy throat?" the magistrate asks triumphantly.

The woman in red raises her hand to cover a small wen on the side of her neck.

"'Tis nothing," she says. "It hath been there since I was but a child, and it means nothing."

"It means thou art a witch!" the woman in the mob cap cries. "Dost thou deny that this is a witch's mark?"

"I do."

"And dost thou deny that thou hast been to a witches' sabbat in the woods?"

"I do!"

"And do you deny that you have afflicted this goodwife's cow? And that goodwife's husband?"

"I do. Upon my life, I do deny it all!"

"Good citizens of Salem," the magistrate turns to the crowd. "What say you? Is Bridget Bishop guilty of witchcraft, or is she innocent? Thou hast all heard the evidence against her: what say you?"

And then outside, a cloud moves across the sun and the hall darkens suddenly and that's when it happens. She's wondered since her first night in town, wondered if she'd find others like her—others called back to Salem through time and space, others from the old days. But she hasn't seen anyone else. Not until now.

Now she half-recognizes, half-remembers some of them in the crowd. She can't quite put names to the faces, but she knows them just the same. The man sitting a couple of seats over—the one in the khakis and sandals—he had been at her trial, wearing breeches and a long vest.

The woman standing trial? The woman in the red bodice, pretending to be Bridget Bishop? An old neighbor from a few muddy streets over. She can't remember what the goodwife's name had been, she just remembers that she had been at the trial, had been at the hanging, wearing the same stern expression now that she had then. Only too happy to see Goodwife Bishop hang.

The cloud passes and the room brightens and the flicker of recognition is gone.

The crowd murmurs. People turn to one another and whisper, "I dunno—what do you think?"

Someone to her left murmurs, "Hang the bitch."

A moment ago, she remembered that man in a tall hat and a short cape, but the recognition is gone now.

The woman sitting with him slaps his knee and said, "Innocent, asshole."

"What? I paid like seventeen dollars—I wanna see her hang," he protests.

"By a show of hands, how many of you say that Goodwife Bishop be innocent?" the magistrate asks sternly.

Only a few hands go up. More laughter.

"And how many say she is guilty?"

More hands. Many more hands.

"Goodwife in the back—I did not see thee vote?"

He's pointing right at her. She's in the back, trying to be invisible, like she used to try to do in school, but the teachers always called on her like the magistrate is doing now. She feels the noose tighten.

"What say you?"

"A witch," Kelly whispers. The whisper echoes in the room. "A witch... but not guilty."

"A witch but not guilty!" the magistrate repeats, and the crowd laughs.

"Now, ladies and gentlemen," the other man says, taking off his hat and smoothing his hair, "we are Certain Detestable Arts, and we are a local theater troupe here in town. We offer these performances to help remind you how easy it can be for well-meaning people such as yourselves to get caught up in paranoia and finger-pointing. Here in the twenty-first century, we are every bit as susceptible to those things as they were in the seventeenth! Most of you were ready to send Jenny to the gallows!"

"Yeah, hey, thanks for that, everybody!" Jenny smiles brightly, giving them a thumbs-up.

"Our troupe likes to use the past to look at the present and you can learn more about what we do on Facebook and Twitter and Instagram, hashtag Bridget Bishop..."

But Kelly gets up and makes her way to the door, slouching along the aisles, head down, hands in pockets. Fleeing. She's sick to her stomach. She gets outside where she can breathe. She goes around the corner, trying to get away from the witch trial, the witch trial which is too close to the way she remembers it. She's trying to ignore the noose, but she can't. She never can.

Wednesday June 6th

Chapter VII

"**We're actually closed,**" the bartender called as Lennox and Ouellette opened the door to BitBar.

"We're on duty." Ouellette held up her badge.

BitBar was a tall space, but not a big one, with warm brick walls and narrow windows, like the rest of the old jail. There were iron bars and some old cell doors mounted here and there, too-obvious décor choices.

The bartender sighed. She was a sinewy woman in a neon tank top, her left arm tattooed from shoulder to wrist with flowers and vines, her lopsided hair dyed at least four different colors. She stopped wiping down the aluminum-top bar and said, "We don't allow minors after eight o'clock and I card everybody, so I *know* you're not here about anything like that."

"No," Ouellette said. "We're checking on something."

Lennox took out his phone and showed her Zachary's photo from the Spooktacular staff directory.

"Have you seen him recently?" he asked.

The bartender pushed some disobedient hair out of her eyes and looked at the screen.

"Maybe," she said. "Yeah, I think."

"You think?"

"I think he's been in here a couple times, yeah."

"When?"

"A couple times," she shrugged.

"When was the last time he was here?" Ouellette asked.

"Tuesday? Or… maybe last Tuesday? Maybe Monday."

"You're kidding me," Lennox said. "We need to know where he was Monday night. Was he here?"

"Maybe," she shrugged. "It's been real busy lately and nights start to blur together after a while. He might have been in, but I can't swear to it." Another shrug. "Sorry."

She came out from behind the bar and moved down a bank of dark, silent arcade games along the wall. Lennox had never even heard of half of them—his older brother had been the video game champ when they were teenagers. Malcolm had regularly bragged about setting high scores in the little arcade on whatever Army base their parents were stationed on. The bartender reached behind each machine, throwing a switch on each garish plywood cabinet, and the screens began to flicker as tinny music started beeping. Each game had a little shelf next to it for the player's drink. When she finished with the row of video games, they followed her into the back room where she started up the pinballs.

"Wish I could help," she said over her shoulder. "What did he do, anyway?"

"We're also looking for a young woman who was with our guy," Ouellette continued, ignoring her question. "Named Stacey. Dirty blonde hair, tattoo of stars behind her left ear. Likes to play Star Castle. Ring any bells?"

The bartender turned, the annoyed look on her face sharpened by the flashing yellow lights on the nearest pinball.

"You're kidding me, right?"

"Thought she might be a regular," Ouellette said.

"We get a lot of regulars. And we get a lot of people who come in once." Yet another shrug. "I don't know what you want from me here."

"We're in the middle of a homicide investigation," Ouellette said.

"Oh, shit," the bartender said. She folded her arms and the vines and flowers flexed as she did. "Is it the girl you're talking about? Stacey? Did the guy… hurt her?"

"No, it's not her. You must have heard about the body around the corner?"

"Mr. Hallowe'en?"

"Yeah. That's our case. That's this case. We're just trying to work out who was where, and when."

"Let me see him again."

Lennox handed her his phone. She stared at the photo, really trying to recognize him, but still couldn't. She shook her head.

"Sorry."

"All right, well, if a young woman comes in, dirty blonde hair, stars behind her left ear, answers to Stacey, you call me." Lennox gave her his card.

"Okay, but that sounds like a lot of girls."

"Plays Star Castle," Lennox said.

"Kinda big tits," Ouellette added.

"Not a lot of help."

"Okay. Which one is Star Castle?" Lennox asked.

"Back out there." She pointed. "Fourth one down. The one that says… Star Castle on the front."

He went back out to the empty barroom and found the machine. The screen was a little blurry, a little out of focus, and he had to wait a minute or two for the display screens to cycle around to the list of high scores. Malcolm had always gotten to enter his initials when he claimed anther high score back when they were kids, and one machine after another had MDL taking up the top slots. None of the high scores on Star Castle started with an S. Or a Z.

Ouellette nodded to the bartender and pushed the door open. They stood outside in the shadow of the old jail.

"I live right upstairs," Lennox said. "I can come down tonight and camp out at the bar and see if anyone matches the description."

"Just Stacey won't be back anytime soon."

"Why's that?"

"It's a one-night stand. No intention of seeing the guy again. If she wanted to see him again, he'd have a number. He'd have a last name. She's not going to show up here for a good while because she doesn't want to run into him."

"Probably right," Lennox said.

And then her phone rang.

"Ouellette. Yes, sir. Yes, we might have a new lead that's looking pretty good, actually. Yeah, we can be there in fifteen minutes. We can be there in less than five. Okay."

She ended the call and put the phone back into her pocket.

"That was the lieutenant. The mayor wants to see us. *Merde.*"

Wednesday
June 6th   **Chapter VIII**

"So how are you settling in?" Dworaczyk asked, looking around Richard Conroy's hotel room, all beige and bland.

"How do you think?'

Dworaczyk nodded and said, "Okay, well, I have some good news for you. I spoke with someone earlier today who saw your daughter on Saturday, and he said she was fine."

"Who?"

"One of the local… merchants. Kelly was in his shop. And she was fine."

"But that's Saturday."

"And there is no reason to think that she is not still fine right now. Like I told you, Salem is not a dangerous city."

"But you had a murder here a couple nights ago."

"That is not my case, but I know the detectives working that investigation and you have nothing to worry about there."

"Nothing to worry about." Richard Conroy shook his head. "I never should have let her come here."

"But she is here now, and we will find her," Dworaczyk said.

"I talked to one of the other detectives when I got here," Conroy said. "And he had a theory?"

"Did he?"

"Yes. He said that Kelly might be out where they used to hang the witches. This Sunday. He said it was the day of the first hanging, so maybe she'd be out there to… I don't know. Mark the occasion or something."

Goddamn Lennox, Dworaczyk thought. The department weirdo couldn't keep his mouth shut. Had to be the smartest kid in class and tell the father of a missing girl his crazy theory. But Lennox wasn't stupid. He was probably even halfway smart, but he didn't really look it, sitting at his desk, staring off into space, tapping that damn spike he kept in a drawer. Dworaczyk never thought Lennox was really cop material. He wondered how he'd gotten this far. Wondered how much longer he would last before it was all too much and he quit and ran away to read books all day.

"Does that sound like something Kelly might do? Visit that location?" Dworaczyk asked. "Does it sound like something she would definitely *not* do?"

"I guess it makes sense. I mean, none of this makes any goddamn sense, though." He rubbed his temples. "Do you think this other guy knows what he's talking about?"

"I think it… could be something to keep in mind," Dworaczyk admitted.

"I think he's probably right. It's the kind of thing that Kelly will know. She'll know where to be and when." Richard Conroy nodded. "Yeah, it seems like he's probably right."

Dworaczyk hated it when Lennox was actually right.

"But that's still four days away," Richard said.

"We might get lucky and find her before then."

"All right." Richard leaned back in the chair upholstered in pale, flowery fabric. "What should I do in the meantime? I already ran off a bunch of posters."

He pointed over to a cardboard box filled with bright yellow flyers: *Missing. Have You Seen Kelly???* There were two photos of her: the moody one Dworaczyk had already seen, and another, brighter one, like a family portrait, no less carefully posed. She seemed more relaxed in the moody one, he thought.

"I put my number and the police station number on them. I wasn't sure if that was okay."

"It would have been better if it was just our number." Dworaczyk rubbed the back of his neck. "But this should be okay. I just do not want you to get a bunch of crank calls, or crazy people thinking they saw her."

"But what if they really have?"

"Then you let me follow up on it. You do not respond to anything on your own. And you do not agree to meet anybody who calls or anything like that, okay?"

"All right," Richard said weakly. "Should I go to the newspapers or something? A friend of mine back home said I should get the media involved."

"No. That would actually be a very bad idea. I think that, for right now, it would be best to keep this under control, if you see what I mean. Going to the newspapers can open up a whole other can of worms. You should definitely hold off on doing that."

"My friend also said maybe hire a private detective."

"Not a great idea," Dworaczyk shook his head. He didn't like private investigators. Most cops didn't. They were usually just amateurs trying to draft off the official investigation, or worse—weird double agents trying to get dirt on the department. "No, a P.I. is not going to know Salem the way I do. A P.I. is just one person and I can tell you right now that every cop in town is looking for your daughter. One more out-of-towner is not going to help, especially when all he is going to do is walk around from nine to five and then bill you for it."

"I just... have to do something." His shoulders slumped. "My goddamn kid..."

"Put up your posters," Dworaczyk said. It wasn't a great idea, but much better than going to the newspapers or hiring a P.I. It probably had the least chance of backfiring. And he needed something to do, somewhere to put his energy. Dworaczyk couldn't just leave him sitting here in a beige hotel room, waiting for the cops to call. That would just be cruel. "But you call me if anyone gets in touch with you, okay? Immediately."

"Okay," Richard nodded. He straightened up, now that he had something to do. "I guess I'll go do that. Do you... do you have kids?"

"Yeah. We have two."

"How old?"

"Fifteen and twelve. One of each."

"So you can imagine what this is like, then."

"No," Dworaczyk said. "No, I am not sure that I can, Mr. Conroy."

"Rick."

"Rick, then."

Wednesday June 6th

Chapter IX

JOSIAH PYNCHEON WAS IN HIS FOURTH TERM as mayor and showed no signs of going anywhere. He was a charming egomaniac with a fondness for Italian suits, foreign cars, and much younger wives. Everyone in town had met the mayor at least once, in the same way that everyone had met Stuart Pickman once. Both men made sure of it.

The assistant was silent and made no eye contact as she showed the detectives in to the mayor's office and shut the door.

Tall and broad-shouldered, in a wide pinstripe suit and an almost-loud tie, Pyncheon sat at a polished desk, his back to a heavy-curtained window overlooking Washington Street below. He was signing his way through a stack of papers with a fountain pen, not looking up, making them wait for him. Pyncheon posed himself as carefully as Pickman always had; they were both almost too aware of their public personae, too aware that so much of their job was theater.

His office was also laid out for effect. One wall was hung with framed honors and certificates, another with pictures of Pyncheon smiling and shaking hands with various celebrities. There were trophies and gleaming awards arranged on a table, along with a row of leatherbound books on display, and Lennox was pretty sure Pyncheon had never read them.

After a long minute, the mayor put the pen aside, leaned back in his chair, and said, "What can you tell me?"

"That we're working on it," Ouellette said.

"What's it been? Thirty-six hours? You should have someone by now."

"We would love to have someone by now, but this is getting complicated. There may be some overlap with another case under investigation."

"Do you have a suspect or not?"

"We might, but you know I can't go into that with you."

"With anybody," Lennox added.

"I'm not anybody. I'm the fucking mayor."

Anyone else would have stood up and leaned across the desk. But Pyncheon knew he didn't have to.

"Sir," Ouellette said. "You know we can't discuss an active case."

"Especially when you're personally acquainted with the victim," Lennox said.

"How long have you two been on the job?"

"Eight years now," Lennox said.

Ouellette said, "Nine."

"You weren't here when I got elected." More than an observation, but not quite an accusation. "Hallowe'en was bad that year. There were a lot of… problems. A lot of vandalism, a lot of drunks, and a lot of lawsuits afterward. And of course people blamed the previous administration for that." Pyncheon smiled. He was just the type who would never mention an opponent's name, not even years later.

That Hallowe'en night fifteen years ago was still being talked about at the station. Lennox had heard all the stories—the broken windows, a couple of overturned cars, even a few fires. There had been a record number of injuries and assaults—records that still stood to this day. It was the year that Salem finally realized it had a Hallowe'en problem, the year that what to do about Hallowe'en became a talking point in the campaign for office.

And Pyncheon had quickly positioned himself as the candidate who would get Hallowe'en under control. If the incumbent won another term, he warned, October would only get worse and worse. He would make Salem safe again, but without sacrificing tourist dollars. And a week after Hallowe'en, Josiah Pyncheon rode that message to victory and was sworn in as mayor. But there had been some whispers at the time that Pyncheon himself may have quietly orchestrated some of the mayhem in order to swing the election to him. And those whispers had never quite died down.

"Stu was just getting started back then," Pyncheon went on. "He had a lot of big ideas but didn't know how exactly to implement them. We had a meeting a month after I took office. He sat in that chair right there. Ken was still with him. I more or less put Stu in charge of Hallowe'en. Getting it organized. Getting it under control. Told him I could… expedite a few things for him if he needed. Got him set up in his first office space. I was a good friend to him over the years," he nodded. "And every time I came up for reelection, I knew I could rely on him. I took care of you people, too," the mayor went on. "Made sure you got extra funds, extra officers, made sure you got all those crowd-control toys you like to roll out every year."

Pyncheon never let anyone forget what he had done—especially what he had done for them.

"He was here the night it happened, you know." Pyncheon leaned back in his chair.

"He was?"

"Yes."

"Just here at City Hall, or here with you specifically?"

"There was a committee meeting I had to go to that night, and we spoke for a little while afterwards."

"Can I ask about what?" Ouellette was cautious.

"He had some concerns. His board of directors wasn't happy with him—not for the first time, I might add. He wanted to make sure that I would be on his side if anything happened."

Pyncheon was an ex-officio member of the Spooktacular board. Of course he was.

"What time was that?"

"Eight-thirty. Give or take. Now, you said you have a suspect?"

"We have someone we need to look at, yeah," Ouellette nodded.

"When are you making an arrest?"

"We're still pretty far away from that. There's a lot to do first."

"Stuart Pickman was a personal friend, and an important asset to this city. And I would like you to make an arrest. Tomorrow."

"It's not that easy—"

"This is not some fucking junkie who got stabbed over in the Point. This is Mr. Hallowe'en. People know who he is, and they know what he has done for the city. You need to arrest someone for this."

"We're going to work on it."

"Good. Go get to work."

He picked up his pen again. They were dismissed.

As they left the office, Lennox heard the assistant quietly tell the mayor, "Phillip Agnew is on line one for you."

Phillip Agnew. Sonia Weaver's choice to replace Pickman.

"Not wasting any time," Lennox said.

Wednesday June 6th

Chapter X

"**What did you tell the mayor?**" Winters wanted to know.

"That we might have something," Ouellette replied. "An employee who is behind on a project and had a blowout with the victim the week before, and then did not show up day-of."

"And where was he night-of?"

"Says he met a woman at a bar and took her home, but can't confirm it. No information on the woman, and the bartender probably won't remember him or her."

"So what do you think?"

"His story could just be a story. It's the kind of thing that sounds more specific than it is, you know?"

"And you've checked with the bartender?"

"She doesn't remember him. Or the girl he allegedly picked up."

"But he does admit to being in the area at approximately the right time. Do you think it's him?"

"Looks like our best bet right now."

"What's next?" Winters asked.

"Start looking for his one-night stand, talk to his neighbors."

"He told us that she called an Uber to go back to his place," Lennox said. "I'm trying to check with them about that. They're going to have a record of the trip. But… they want you to create an account and submit a request, which they'll have to verify is legit before getting back to me."

"Did you tell them you were the law?"
"That's the procedure when you're the law."
Winters shook his head.
"You two have your work cut out for you."

Lennox spent a few minutes searching for Ken Cromartie online. The old partner. The old partner who Zachary thought should have been in charge of the Spooktacular. Maybe Zachary was more serious about that than he seemed at first. Maybe with Pickman out of the way, Cromartie might return. At least in Zachary's mind.

Mr. Hallowe'en's old partner was now the head of an events management company headquartered in Augusta, Maine. The website showed him in a jacket and tie—a headshot similar to Pickman's—welcoming visitors to KC Events, Inc. Lennox called the number under the photo, pressed "1" when prompted, and was surprised when Cromartie himself answered.

"This is Detective Lennox from the Salem Police," he began.

"Oh, God. You must be calling about Stu. Yeah, I heard. What the hell happened?"

"We're working on that. When was the last time you spoke to him?"

"I haven't actually heard from him in a couple of years now, to be honest," Cromartie laughed slightly. "I'm still on the mailing list, so I get the program every year and every once in a while they send me a new t-shirt or whatever else with a little note, but that's about it, really."

"So you two weren't close anymore?"

"Well, I guess not—no. But, I mean, there were no hard feelings when I left."

"Why did you leave?"

"Well, the chamber of commerce used to put on Hallowe'en events every year, and Stuart and I helped them out a lot back then; when it all got to be more than the chamber could handle,

Stuart and I kind of took it all over. Stuart was a great ideas man, but he wasn't good at organizing, you know? That's what I did. He was kind of messy—Mister Improvisation, Mister Loose Ends, you know? And I'm not. He needs someone to do the day-to-day stuff for him."

Lennox had heard the stories. Everyone in town had: Pickman told and retold the tale in every interview, burnishing the legend with each telling. The Salem Spooktacular had started out as two guys living in a crappy third-floor apartment, noticing more and more tourists arrive in town every October. Pickman the visionary, Cromartie the programmer. They launched a website, an online guide to Hallowe'en. The next year, they started calling it the Ultimate Online Guide to Hallowe'en, and started selling ads. The third year, Pickman always said, when we started getting calls for interviews, we realized we were really onto something big—something spectacular.

"But I started to get a little uncomfortable with it all, you know?" he went on. "I mean, c'mon—twenty people got killed and now we're throwing a party all month long? I'm a logistics guy, I love organizing, I love putting things together… but it all started to kind of rub me the wrong way, you know? It was getting to be like Mardi Gras and… it just started to seem kind of gross after a while. And my wife had just gotten pregnant and so it seemed like a good time to cash out and spend more time with her."

"Did you… ever think of coming back to the Spooktacular?"

"No, I'm pretty well settled up here. I work on a lot of fairs and festivals up here, plus some colleges. If you need a hypnotist or a folk singer, you let me know." He paused, and then his tone lowered as he asked, "Do you know anything about a funeral?"

"Yeah, it's Saturday. Eleven o'clock. Over at Harmony Grove."

"I talked to a reporter a couple days ago and he didn't know. I'm going to try to be there," Cromartie said. "I have a few things to wrap up here first, but I can probably make it down there."

"So you said you weren't in touch with Stuart—how about anybody else?"

"At the Spooktacular? No. I don't think there's even anyone left over there that I knew."

"I was talking to Zachary Dykstra yesterday," Lennox said carefully. "He remembers you."

"Zachary? Really? Yeah, Zachary. How's he taking it?"

"Everyone over there is pretty upset right now. You and Zachary got along pretty well when you were still there, right?"

"Yeah, we did. He's kind of an odd duck, but I always liked him, I guess."

"Odd duck how?"

"Wasn't always real good with people, but he was a computer guy, so… par for the course, huh?"

"He seems like a smart guy."

"Yeah, and he knows it, too. He always kind of thought of himself as the smartest guy in the room, you know? And that kind of shit doesn't make you real popular."

"No," Lennox said. "No, it doesn't."

"Well, I'm just about to go into a meeting here. I'll look for you when I get down there Saturday?"

"Yeah. I'll be there."

Wednesday June 6th

Chapter XI

WEDNESDAY WAS DATE NIGHT, and it was a quiet summer evening in the Witch City.

Andrew Lennox checked his watch as he headed to the restaurant. Almost seven o'clock. He was going to be late. Late for a late dinner with AJ. Their schedules hadn't always aligned over the past eight months, and even when they were both supposed to be off-duty on the same night, it hadn't always worked. Neither of them had predictable hours, and date night plans could always be disrupted by one of them being suddenly ordered to a crime scene. That had happened last date night, when she had been called out to help process an accident scene, leaving him alone, re-reading *The Devil In Massachusetts*.

She was waiting at Rockefellas, at their usual table—one of the big ones looking out onto Essex Street. He still wasn't quite used to seeing her in civilian clothes, somehow; he still always seemed to picture her in the crime scene coveralls and baseball cap she'd worn when they'd first met. He wondered if that was normal, or if it was some weird hangup, some strange kink.

She smiled and gave him a quick kiss as he sat down.

"Sorry I'm late," he said.

"Pretty used to it by now," she said with a happy little smirk that dimpled her cheeks.

"Busy day?"

"Yeah. I was at a scene just a couple hours ago, so, you know…" She shrugged. "You?"

"The usual."

And that was as far as that conversation went. Eight months ago, on their first date at this very same table, AJ had insisted that shop talk needed to be forbidden. Lennox had agreed it was a good rule. She didn't want to hear about him checking alibis or questioning suspects and he didn't want to hear about hair and fiber evidence or spraying for bloodstains. Talking about work was just too easy. And he wanted to make sure they had other things to talk about.

The place was crowded tonight. The waiters and bartenders recognized AJ, greeting her with nods and smiles and not paying much attention to Lennox, seeming to regard him simply as her quiet date. She was vegetarian and ordered a towering mushroom and goat cheese salad; Lennox wasn't vegetarian but ordered the same thing. He thought eating meat on date night was rude.

"So have you given it any more thought?" she asked quietly, not looking up from her plate.

He sighed. He knew this was going to come up. She had first raised the question of moving in together a month ago, and he knew he could only stall for so long—only tell her that he was in the middle of a huge case and couldn't make decisions like that right now, that he needed time to think about it, a finite number of times. He wasn't sure what the exact number was, but he was pretty sure he was getting close to it.

Divorced and on his own for over a year now, he wasn't sure he was ready to share a space with someone again. And he couldn't believe that anyone would want to share space with him.

"My lease is up in two months," she said. She had a small apartment in Beverly, with shelves and shelves of snow globes. But she liked Salem better, she said, and his apartment in the old jail was big enough for them both. And her snow globes. Her snow globes and his books, old true crime and witch trials volumes in no real order on the built-in shelves. "So I kind of need to figure out what I'm doing."

"Yeah, um… I—"

"Need more time to think about it?"

"Well, yeah, it's a big... thing."

"Way to make a girl feel wanted." She stabbed at her salad.

"It's not that."

"Once bitten, twice shy," she said. "I get it."

She wrinkled her nose at him. A nose that was nothing at all like his ex-wife's.

"I need to figure out what I'm doing and... I think maybe we need to figure out what we're doing, Andrew, you know?" She reached across the table to give his hand a reassuring little squeeze. Her hand was soft and warm and fitted his so perfectly.

"Oh, God. Drew—?" came a voice. The voice was both disappointed and accusatory.

Ellen.

Ellen, his ex-wife. Ellen, looking great, dressed for a night out.

"Oh, hi," he said, standing up so fast he knocked his chair over. He stood there, awkwardly wondering how to greet her in front of his new... g-word. Was he supposed to just nod? Shake her hand? He shoved his hands into his pockets and said "Hi" again.

Rockafellas wasn't really Ellen's kind of place. She was someone who made elaborate meals at home; she'd always said she hated eating out when she knew she could make something just as good, or better, herself.

Over her shoulder was Martin Frazier, another professor at Salem State—the colleague she'd left him for after eighteen years of marriage. They both taught in the history department, and he offered courses titled *Firebrands of Hell: Witchtrial as Culturewar*, and *The Bad Goodwife: Misogyny and the Salem Witch Trials.* He nodded to Lennox, looking like he was handling this better.

"It's date night," Ellen explained, "And, you know, I've walked by this place a thousand times and never been in, so... why not, right? Have you heard from Allison?"

Allison, their daughter, heading into her sophomore year at Salem State.

"Yesterday," he nodded. "You?"

"Not all week," she said. Even if it was summer vacation, he wondered how she could not have heard from her own daughter, and he was secretly pleased that he'd heard from Allison more recently than she had.

"And I'm AJ."

"Right. Amy—Amy Johnson," Lennox stammered. "AJ."

"I'm Allison's mother," Ellen smiled, looking at AJ appraisingly. "What is it you do, Angie?"

"AJ. I'm a crime scene tech. I collect evidence."

Martin Frazier turned green.

"That must be very interesting," Ellen said.

"It is. I help catch bad guys." She gave up and picked at her salad some more.

"Well, I guess we should let you get back to your dinner," Ellen said.

"Right—right. We shouldn't keep you."

"Bye, Drew," she whispered, so low than only Lennox heard her. And there was a tiny flash of the woman he'd fallen in love with so long ago, a little hint that this might be as awkward for her as it was for him.

"So," the waiter said, "coffee and dessert here?"

AJ said, "Nope."

They walked down Essex Street a few minutes later, arm-in-arm.

"So you're really not ready for me to move in, are you?"

"No. I guess I'm just really obviously not," he sighed. "I'm sorry."

She gave his hand another reassuring little squeeze.

"Yeah. It's okay," she said. "But just so you know, though... I am."

Thursday
June 7th

Thursday June 7th

Chapter I

"**The father went to the newspapers,**" Winters announced, holding up copies of the *Argus* and the *Advertiser*. Both papers had the same sad-eyed photo of Kelly Conroy, and very similar pictures of her concerned father. Seeing them side-by-side, Lennox noticed the resemblance now: the same oval faces, the same broad chins and narrow mouths. The *Argus* headline was *Where's Kelly?* while the *Advertiser* went with *Missing Girl In Salem*.

Officially a media case now, Lennox thought. But it was always going to be.

"Yeah, I spoke to the father yesterday," Dworaczyk said. "I told him not to go to the papers. He asked about it and I told him no."

"Damn well hope so," Winters muttered.

"He told me he was going to put up posters downtown, and I said that would probably be fine. He asked if I thought he should hire a private detective and I said no. We have enough going on without a P.I. getting in the way. And you," he looked at Lennox accusingly. "You talked to him about your theory."

"I was just trying to help," Lennox said. "I wasn't trying to step on your toes or anything. I just thought that the guy's daughter is missing, he should know where we are."

"What do you even have at this point?" Winters stepped in.

"I have one confirmed sighting here in town. At that weirdo's shop, the friend of yours," Dworaczyk nodded over to Lennox. "She was in his shop on Saturday. She was alone, and not acting suspicious. And now, this morning, five messages, all because of the newspapers. All saying that they have seen her somewhere. One of the calls came from..." He turned pages on the pad on his desk. "Outside of Albany."

"Albany?"

"No story stays local. People love a missing white girl story. Thank you so very much, Twitter."

"Do any of them seem credible?'

"Two of them, maybe. One says she was at a coffee place on Essex and another has her out on Highland. I do not know what she would be doing out there."

"But you're going to follow up."

"But I am going to follow up."

"Follow up those two yourself and send uniforms out to check on the less-likely ones."

"What about Albany?"

"Forget Albany for now. We have enough here to keep us busy. The father's in town, the newspapers have the story, and the mayor is watching. So you tell me what you need, Fred. You need extra bodies, overtime, expert help—tell me."

"I will put together a list."

"Just find her and keep the father away from the goddamn newspapers. Which brings me to you two." He turned to Ouellette. "Yesterday you had a suspect. Do you still have a suspect today?"

"Following up on him today," Ouellette said.

"Following up on what, exactly?"

"Checking up on his one-night stand."

"And you're still thinking that Fred's Missing is your witness?"

"We are."

"All right, well, let's just try to stay off the front page today, okay?"

Winters went back into his office and closed the door. Dworaczyk got up from his desk, straightened his tie, tried to ogle Ouellette without her noticing, and left the bullpen, going to check on those reported sightings.

Thursday
June 7th

Chapter II

ZACHARY DYKSTRA LIVED in a three-family house over in the Bridge Street Neck. The area was older than it looked—it had been part of the original Puritan settlement, back when Salem was still called Naumkeag, but it had been built up and built over so many times that it didn't look historic anymore, it just looked old. It was a dense neighborhood with narrow streets named for privateers and merchants and old square-riggers.

Records showed that the house had been built in the 1920s and gone condo nine years ago. The first floor was occupied by a Carla Sanchez, who had no criminal record. A John Rushlow lived on the third floor; a quick check revealed he had collected over thirty unpaid parking tickets in the last seven years. Lennox wasn't looking forward to talking to him.

He clipped his badge to his pocket and rang the bell for the first floor—a little electric buzzer next to the original painted-over doorbell that probably hadn't worked in years. Ouellette stood behind him, slightly to one side, on the top step of the front porch.

Carla Sanchez was a slim, middle-aged woman; she had very dark hair with traces of gray at the temples. She was short, well below Lennox's shoulder, and she blinked up at him.

"Yes?" she asked uncertainly.

"Ma'am, we're from the police and we just have a couple of quick questions, if you have a minute?"

"Yeah," she said. "Okay."

Somewhere behind her, an older woman's voice called, "*Qué quieren esos?*" in a gravelly voice.

His Spanish was rusty and not even very fluent to begin with. It mostly consisted of a handful of useful phrases and the Miranda warning. But the woman's tone carried her suspicions clearly enough.

"It's just the police," Carla said over her shoulder. "Sorry, my mom's visiting. What do you need?"

"We're here about your upstairs neighbor."

"Oh, that guy." Carla rolled her eyes.

"You don't get along?"

"Not really. He's kind of a jerk. He's… really a jerk. Never takes his shoes off."

"Yeah, I had a neighbor like that once," Lennox said. "It was a couple, actually, and we had hardwood floors in that building." He shook his head. "I know how it is."

The story wasn't true, but it did the trick. Carla smiled and nodded.

"So did you maybe hear him stomping around on Monday?"

"Monday? I dunno. Maybe? Not sure. Why? He in trouble?"

"We're just trying to figure out if he was home that night or not."

"Maybe he had a guest?" Ouellette said. "Maybe you… heard something from upstairs?"

"A guest?" Carla asked.

"An… overnight guest," Lennox said.

"A young woman," Ouellette added.

"Oh. Yeah, well. He doesn't seem like the type, you know?"

"Cause he's kind of a jerk?"

"Yeah."

"So you're not sure if he was home?"

"I'm really not sure. I kind of try to ignore him."

"*Qué quieren?*" her mother asked.

"Nothing," Carla replied.

"Was your mom visiting on Monday?"

"No."

"Diles que hay fantasmas."

"Ma, stop."

"Something is... fantastic?" Lennox asked.

"No. No, my mom thinks the house is haunted. She says there's a ghost. Every time she visits, she says there's a ghost and I gotta get rid of it. I gotta get someone to get rid of it." She shrugged.

A silver-haired woman peeked around a corner over Carla's shoulder. She looked at Lennox, then at her daughter.

"Él puede," she whispered.

"Is she okay?" Ouellette asked. "It's just a ghost that's bothering her? That's all?"

"Yeah."

"You're sure?" Lennox asked. He never knew what was going to be on the other side of a door, never knew what he might be walking into. Anything from a gun to a ghost. And his Spanish wasn't good enough to know what Carla's mom was saying.

"Yeah, she's just being weird."

"Pregúntale."

"Ma, *para*," Carla said.

"Pregúntale!"

"She wants you to chase the ghost out," Carla sighed, giving in. "She thinks you can do it."

"That's... a little above our pay grade," Ouellette said.

"Por favor."

"Para!"

"Um... I'll do it," Lennox said.

Carla and Ouellette both stared at him.

"Protecting and serving," he shrugged.

"We have work to do," Ouellette said. Then she added, "Five minutes."

Lennox looked at the old woman and nodded. She stepped forward and grabbed his arm, pulling him into the hall and through to the parlor. It was a bright room with big windows and a flatscreen and the same Ikea couch he had in his apartment in the old jail. She started pointing.

"*Abre la ventana.*"

"Open the... windows?"

"Yeah," Carla said patiently. He wasn't sure if she was trying to be patient with her mother, or with him. He opened the three front windows in the bay that looked out over the street, pulled the curtains back. He nodded to the old woman.

"That it?"

She shook her head.

"*Asustarlo afuera*"

"*Mama, por favor!*"

"There's more?"

"*Que use la medalla.*"

"What did she say?"

"She says you need to use your medal to scare it away."

"My medal?"

"Your badge," Ouellette said, before the daughter could answer. She was standing in the doorway, arms folded, with an eighth-of-an-inch smile on her face.

"This?" He unclipped his badge from his front pocket.

"*Si.*"

"Okay." He glanced around the room, not sure what to do next. Then he held his badge out in front of him. Brandishing it. "Go!" he said quietly. And then, a little more forcefully, "Go! You are not welcome here! Leave! *Vamanos!*"

The old woman was nodding and clapping her hands now. He took a couple of dramatic steps, squaring his shoulders and taking a deep breath, readying himself for the final push, the final banishment of the ghost.

"The... the power of Christ compels you!" he said. He was trying not to smile now.

And his knee bumped a flimsy little table. He froze, and could do nothing but watch it teeter forever until it sent the vase of flowers on top of it crashing to the floor.

Where it exploded.

"Shit."

The pieces went everywhere, spinning and skittering across the floor, vanishing under things and behind things. Everywhere.

Carla's mother didn't seem to care. She rushed to the windows, slamming them closed, one after the other.

"Ay perfecto!" she cried. *"Gracias!"*

"I'm... so sorry." He pointed to the shards of the vase at his feet. He bent to pick up some of the bigger pieces.

"Don't worry about it," Carla said. "My mother-in-law gave us that vase. It's the kind of cheap shit she likes. I don't even know why I keep it around."

"Gracias," her mother said again. She reached to take the broken pieces from him. *"Puede venir la próxima semana, si encaso que regrese?"*

"Ma!"

"What?" Lennox asked.

"She wants to know if you can come back next week. In case the ghost comes back."

"Well... my schedule is pretty tight right now," he began.

"He can be here," Ouellette said. "I'll remind him."

"Sure. Yeah, I can be here."

They stepped back out onto the front porch, Carla's mother smiling, hands over her heart. "All right, so just to be clear: you aren't sure if Zachary Dykstra was home on Monday night?"

"No," Carla shook her head. "Sorry. I mean, he might have been, but I can't swear to it."

"Okay, well, thanks for your time."

"Thanks for putting up with my mother's craziness."

"No problem. She seems really nice. I'm really sorry about that vase. I'll pay for it. Please don't sue the department or anything."

"Don't worry about it. And you don't really have to come back next week."

"I can if you want. Gets me out of the office."

"I'll remind him," Ouellette said. "We're going to check with the third floor. Have a nice day."

When Carla closed the door, Ouellette turned to Lennox and said, "So that was fun."

"We've had weirder," he said, ringing John Rushlow's doorbell.

"Hi…" John Rushlow said cautiously, his eyes going from Lennox to Ouellette. Then he saw the badges. "Oh, shit. Really? You're kidding me, right? They send cops out now for parking tickets?"

"We'll get to that in a sec," Lennox said. "Need to ask you about your downstairs neighbor."

"The Sanchezes?"

"No. Zachary Dykstra."

"Okay," Rushlow said, relaxing slightly. He was a reedy man with tiny glasses and blond stubble. "What about him?"

"Was he home Monday night?" Ouellette asked.

"How am I supposed to know?"

"He lives right downstairs."

"And I'm supposed to be paying attention to him?"

"Look, we're just following up on something and we'd like to know if he was home Monday night."

Rushlow crossed his arms and leaned against the doorframe thoughtfully.

"Well, do you need him to be here or not?" he asked.

"Excuse me?" Ouellette asked.

"I'm asking… where do you want him to be?"

"We just need to find out if he was here on Monday," Lennox rubbed his eyes. "It's a yes-no question."

"And I'm saying I can help with that," Rushlow nodded. "Do you want him to be here or not? And, you know, maybe you can help me out with those stupid parking tickets—none of them should've ever been written, by the way—"

"Doesn't work like that," Lennox said, trying not to smile.

"If you say so, boss." Rushlow scratched his ear idly.

"We are not fucking around here," Ouellette said. "This is serious. We need to find out where he was that night. Now do you remember him being here or not?"

"I... don't?"

"As in, you remember him not being here, or you don't remember him being here?"

Rushlow took a deep breath and let it out slowly.

"I don't remember if he was here or not," he said. "He might've been. Might not. I can't be sure. I kind of steer clear of him anyway."

"Why's that?"

"Cause he's an asshole," he shrugged. "Don't put out the trash, don't shovel the walk. Wakes me up all the damn time, stomping around his apartment."

"But you live upstairs from him," Lennox said.

"Yes, I do."

"Okay, so he's loud."

"And he's an asshole. This one time, over the winter, he had to have a plumber come in to do some work. We all have problems with frozen pipes sometimes. Plumber parked behind me, kinda blocked me in. So I asked him if he could have the guy move and he was really, really pissy about it. He actually yelled at me and slammed the door. I mean, Jesus." He shook his head. "Kinda haven't really talked to him after that, you know?"

"So he's got a temper?"

"Yeah." He gave an exaggerated nod. "You can say that again."

"Fine," Ouellette said. "So you're honestly not sure if he was here on Monday or not?"

"Yeah. I mean, no... I'm honestly not sure."

"Does he ever have visitors?"

"Visitors?"

"Yeah. Like overnight visitors?" Lennox asked.

"Women," Ouellette added.

"Not that I ever noticed."

"All right, well, thanks for your time. If you think of anything, let me know."

Lennox handed over his card.

"So that's it?"

"Yeah, that's it."

"What about the parking tickets?" Rushlow called as the detectives stepped off the porch.

"You're going to want to pay them," Lennox said without looking back.

His phone rang as they walked toward the car. He glanced at the number. A 978 area code. Probably local, but he didn't recognize the number.

"Lennox," he said.

"Detective?" a small voice said on the other end. "It's Toni Basilico, over at the Spooktacular?" Her voice went up at the end, making it a question.

"What can I do for you?"

"I'm really worried about Zachary. Can you... can I come talk to you?"

"Sure. What's going on?"

"I just need to talk to you."

"Okay. Where are you?"

"At work."

"We'll be right over."

"Okay," she breathed, sounding nervous now. "Sure. I'll be out front."

"What was that?" Ouellette asked as he ended the call.

"Toni Basilico wants to see us. She's really worried about our suspect."

*Thursday
June 7th*

Chapter III

RICK CONROY SAT IN A COFFEE SHOP on Essex Street, thinking Salem was nothing like what he had expected.

He wasn't exactly sure what he'd expected, but it wasn't this. Kelly had once said that witches ran the city, but it looked like any other tourist town, just with weirder souvenir shops than usual. It was old here, though. There was a house a few streets away, painted black, with a steep roof and tiny windows—the Judge Somebody House. One of the judges from the witch trials lived there, or something. He'd heard someone call it the Witch House. It was twice as old as anything back home. It was the kind of thing Kelly would have loved.

My daughter, the witch.

This witch thing of hers was getting out of hand. But he'd watched her, made sure she was taking her meds, made sure she got outside and didn't stay locked up in her room with the shades drawn. She hadn't been moody. Not too moody, anyway. He thought she was getting better. He thought she was growing out of it.

He hadn't wanted her to come here, and told her so. What if she went away and then, being in the middle of all this, some switch got flipped in her head? He hadn't said that, but he hadn't needed to—she must have known what he was thinking. He considered going with her, but what twenty-year-old wanted her father coming with her on vacation, as she turned twenty-one? He couldn't stop her from going, and they hadn't spoken for a day and a half before she left.

I'm a shitty father, he thought. I never should have let her come on her own. And Sandy had barely spoken to him the last couple of days. He'd called to give her updates but she didn't have anything to say to him.

He'd spent the day making the same desperate circuit over and over, not sure what else to do. Up and down Essex Street, up and down Washington Street, down Derby and New Derby, and back along Hawthorne Boulevard. He put up Kelly's poster with tape or thumbtacks all along the route, and now she stared back at him every damn time he turned around.

Two days, he thought. Two goddamned days and I have no idea where she is. Two days of posters, checking with the police, who never had anything new to tell him. Two days of asking people if they had seen his daughter, and none of them had. Two days of nothing but the fear that she might never be found.

His breath shook in his chest as he sipped his coffee, trying not to cry.

He forced himself up, forced himself back out into the street. He was exhausted. He hadn't shaved and he was still wearing yesterday's shirt—at least he thought it was yesterday's. He probably looked like a bleary-eyed crazy person.

He was almost out of flyers, but he would stay out here until they were all gone before going back to the hotel for a rest. The street was busy with day-tripping tourists in t-shirts they had probably just bought, with "Hanging Around in the Witch City" in Old English script. There were little groups of teenagers, blackly overdressed for the sunny June weather. Other people walked firmly by, not stopping to look in shop windows or up at the buildings, people clearly on their way somewhere. Some of them took a flyer as they went, glancing at it but seeming to dismiss it once they realized it wasn't for a free tarot reading or a discount walking tour. Some twisted away from him when he held one out, refusing to take it. Only a very few of them mumbled an apology, and some of them said they couldn't help—they were only here for the day and didn't know the city. But he knew these were just excuses, people not wanting to get pulled into his own personal disaster.

And now he was standing here on an unfamiliar street in a strange city—a very strange city—handing out flyers with his daughter's face on them. The face with his eyes, and his wife's nose.

There was a bar up on the corner. And then on the next corner. And the next street over. He had been noticing them as he made his rounds. He hadn't had a drink since the accident. Because of the accident. But now… it was tempting, he had to admit.

Someone walked by and he robotically thrust out a flyer. He didn't even look at people's faces anymore, just at Kelly's.

"Have you seen my daughter?" he asked for the millionth time.

The man stopped and took the flyer, studying it for a moment.

"I saw this in the paper," he said. "You're her father."

"Yes, I am. Have you seen her?"

"No, I'm sorry. I can't imagine what you must be going through."

"It's been awful," Rick said. "Just… awful."

"Have the police been able to help?"

"Not really, no."

"Sorry to hear that. The Salem police aren't very good," the man shook his head and looked cautiously around, like he didn't want to be overheard.

"No?"

"No. This city doesn't exactly attract the best and brightest—I mean, would you take a job here if you had anywhere else to go?" He laughed a little bitterly. "Do they at least have an idea?"

"My daughter is… interested in the witch trials." He didn't want to use the word "obsessed" with a stranger. Didn't want it to sound like his daughter was crazy. "That's why she wanted to come here. They think she might go out to the site where the witches were… executed." His breath shook again, and he only got the word out with effort. "I don't even know where that's supposed to be, but they think she'll be out there Sunday. That's when they hanged one of the women back then."

"Do you think they're right? Think she'll be out there?"

Rick shrugged. "God, I hope so. I mean… I think?"

"What else have the police told you?"

"That they're working on another case—a murder. And they think Kelly might have seen something, so they want to find her for that."

"What did they say about the murder?" The man took a step forward.

"They're not telling me anything about that. I think they don't want to scare me, or they don't trust me or something. But the officer who is handling it, he's the one who thought Kelly might be out where they used to hang the witches. Lennon, I think?"

"Oh… I was worried you were going to say that."

"Why?"

"Well… like I said, the Salem police aren't very good. And Lennox there is one of the real bad ones. I wouldn't trust him to find my daughter, I can tell you that."

"Why not?"

The man hesitated. Rick could see his own reflection in the man's mirrorshades, looking desperate.

"He's not a very good detective and, last year…" the man's voice dropped to a whisper. "Last year he *shot* someone."

"What? Why?"

"There are a lot of rumors," the man shrugged. "People in town know that Lennox is dirty, and my guess is that the guy knew something, or knew too much, so… he had to be dealt with."

"Oh, my God."

A dirty cop is looking for my daughter. A dirty cop who shoots people. Rick ground the heels of his hands into his eyes. He felt faint.

The man gave a weird little smirk.

"Can I keep this?" He held up the poster.

"Yeah, of course."

"This is your phone number here?"

"I'm the 414 number; the cops are the 978."

"Yeah, I won't be calling them." Another smirk. "I'll definitely be keeping an eye out for your daughter, though."

"Thank you," Rick breathed. "Thank you so much. Please, call me if you think you see her. Call any time." He held out a hand. "My name's Rick; I didn't catch yours."

But the man was already walking away.

Thursday
June 7th

Chapter IV

SHE'S WALKING DOWNTOWN, walking the streets she has gotten to know these last few days. It's nice out: warm, stopping just short of hot. The skies are clear blue and the sunlight feels beautiful on her face and the summer breeze runs its fingers lovingly through her hair. It takes a little bit, but she is able to forget about the noose, to put it off to one side and try not to feel it. Walking and breathing and feeling the sun and the wind and not the noose.

Walking here is different from walking around in Milwaukee. She doesn't quite know how, but it just is. It's not the faint tingle of salt from the ocean when the wind changes direction. It's not the locals who smile and nod as she passes. Or the cars that stop to let her cross. But there is something, something nice, that lets her take a little break from why she is here, lets her just enjoy being in Salem on a summer afternoon, if only for a couple of hours.

Yes, she thinks. Just a couple of hours. Just play tourist and ignore what she hasn't been able to ignore since she got here.

She wants ice cream. Ice cream is perfect on a perfect day in June. The perfect way to take a little time away from why she is here. There's a shop on the next corner, across the street from her old tavern. A knot of people stand outside, all laughing, all balancing two or three scoops on cones: chocolate and vanilla and strawberry.

Once she's inside, the guy ahead of her in line looks back over his shoulder, glancing at her once, then twice, giving her a quick up-and-down appraisal. He probably thinks she doesn't notice, probably thinks he's sly. He gets his cone and gives her another look as he leaves. She half-watches him, but only to make sure he is really gone before she steps up to the counter.

She looks up at the menu board. So many choices! All the usual flavors, plus… green tea? And what is maple walnut? Three different kinds of sherbet. No, four. And all kinds of toppings to go with it. Her eyes dart from one flavor to another before she settles on black raspberry. Two scoops. A guy her own age hands the cone over with a smile. She pulls a crumpled five from the front pocket of her hoodie, where her wallet sits next to a small poppet. She puts the change into the tip jar and steps back outside into the sun.

The ice cream is wonderful. Smooth and freezing on her tongue. Almost immediately, it's running down her chin and dribbling down her knuckles and it's going to be a sticky mess in another few minutes. The breeze sends some of her hair waving right into the ice cream. She laughs and pulls it free. It's all so completely worth it to just walk and breathe and have ice cream on a warm June afternoon in a tourist town.

The next corner up from the shop, she stops in the middle of the sidewalk and screws her eyes shut as the brain freeze hits her. Hits her hard. She can't see as her forehead and temples frost over and she tries to step out of the way of people she knows must be trying to pass her. It feels like it will go on forever. It feels like it will never stop. But then it does. Her head slowly thaws out and she laughs and keeps walking.

She walks down the street, her own reflection flashing in the shop windows at the edge of her vision as she goes. Maybe she needs another change of clothes. Maybe another hoodie. But there is a dress in a window that she stops to admire. A burgundy sundress, flimsy and short but cute. Not the kind of thing she usually likes to wear but… she looks down at her jeans and her sneakers, a little dull from the last couple of days. The dress is nice, and it might be good to wear if she doesn't get ice cream all down the front of it.

But it's for a different occasion, a different set of circumstances. It doesn't fit into what she needs to do here. Which is too bad, because she can actually imagine herself in this dress on a different day.

Down the street, wandering, turning onto Essex, busy with tourists. Busy with *other* tourists, she thinks. For an hour, for a couple of hours, she wants to be just another tourist. Please.

She finishes her ice cream cone, carefully avoiding more brain freeze and tossing the purple-stained napkins into a garbage can. She takes a moment to lick the dried raspberry off her fingers. She giggles and breathes as she trips down the street, carelessly weaving along behind the other tourists.

And then she sees him. A dozen feet away. Maybe closer.

He's wearing sunglasses and a baseball cap now, but she knows him instantly: the slope of his shoulders, the cruel slant of his mouth. She only saw him once, a few nights ago, out in the parking lot by the old gaol, harshly lit by the buzzing streetlights, but it's him. She'd know him anywhere. She'd seen him kill that big man with the bushy beard, watched him cut the other man's throat with a little knife that flashed white and then red.

And they hadn't noticed her; neither of them had, not until she screamed as the big man went down, collapsing to the ground, coughing and gurgling. She'd screamed and the cruel man with the knife had turned and looked her right in the eye. And she screamed and ran—ran for the brightly lit door of the mall on the other side of the parking lot. She ran track in high school and she was fast. She's still fast. He chased her only a few yards and then stopped. She ran into the mall, looking back over her shoulder to see if he was still following her, but he wasn't. She ran through the building, past the shop windows, dodging around the last few shoppers, and out a door on the other side and didn't stop running until she was streets and streets away and the man wasn't after her. But she kept running, knowing where she wanted to be but not really knowing where she was going yet. And then she realized she had dropped the poppet back in the parking lot.

And now that man is here. A dozen feet away.

And talking to *Dad*.

What's Dad even doing here? Looking for her, of course. How long has he been here? He looks exhausted. Stooped and rumpled and old.

And why is he talking to that man? The man who had the knife? The man who...

She feels like she's going to throw up. Yes. She's going to throw up the ice cream and there will be sick purple vomit everywhere and everyone will see her and she'll be caught.

The man pulls back from Dad, done talking to him, walking quickly away as Dad half-turns and gestures.

She spins now. She couldn't move a second ago and now... now it's all she can do. Move. Trying not to move so fast that she gets noticed, so fast that she slams into anyone. She flips up her hood and her fingers are still sticky. She lowers her head, shakes some hair into her face, bunches her shoulders, trying not to look like herself. Knowing she doesn't look like anyone else. She's heading for the corner. She knows, somehow, that if she can just get around that corner she'll be safe, she'll be okay.

And then she starts seeing the posters—the posters she probably saw before but willed herself not to. Her own face, staring out from under the desperately red word *Missing*. It's an old photo, taken last year or maybe the year before, back home, out with friends. She'd never really liked the picture but her father always did, or said he did.

It has her name, her description, right down to her shoe size. Pleas to contact her father or the Salem PD if seen. Various numbers with Salem's 978 area code, and one with Milwaukee's 414. Dad's cell.

She pulls one down, half folding and half crumpling it, shoving it into her pocket. She crosses the street, hooded head down, hands in pockets. There are more posters—on streetlights, on telephone poles and mailboxes. She walks past them, trying not to cry, feeling her own eyes follow her as she goes. And now she feels it, feels the noose chafing under her chin.

Thursday June 7th

Chapter V

ANTONIA WAS WAITING OUTSIDE the Telephone Building when they got there, standing by the square Witch Gaol plaque, eyes fixed on the wilting flowers and lumpy candles of the memorial. She glanced over nervously as the detectives approached.

"That was fast," she murmured. "Thanks for coming."

"Sure," Lennox replied. "You sounded worried."

"Yeah, I am. I—" She stopped to blow her nose and clear her throat. "Sorry."

"Looks like you have Kara's cold," he smiled.

"It's not a cold, it's this building." She looked up at the brick and concrete façade. "I don't know if it's the lights or bad air in the vents or what, but… we've both been feeling really sick ever since we started working here. It's a sick building. It's good to be outside." She took a slow, deep breath: in through her nose, out through her mouth.

"So you're worried about Zachary?" Ouellette said.

"Yeah. I am."

This wasn't going to be the same as talking to Womack and Freitas. Those two had been eager to make their accusations, but Toni was obviously scared of whatever it was she had to say. Lennox could see it in her eyes. She already regretted placing the call.

"You questioned Zachary," she began.

"We talked to him, sure."

"He said you questioned him. Like a suspect."

"We talked to him," Lennox said gently. "We have to talk to everybody in a case like this. And he was helpful."

"He says you think he did it." She squinted in the sunlight and suddenly looked very, very young. "That he… killed Stu. Do you?"

Lennox looked over to Ouellette and her expression said that this interview was up to him.

"I can't really go into that with you."

"Oh, God. You do."

"Like I said…"

Toni swallowed hard and looked ill.

"Is there something particular on your mind here?"

"He didn't have anything to do with what happened. He couldn't have."

"Okay. What makes you say that?"

"He just couldn't have. He likes Stu too much. I mean, he liked Stu too much. And he loves working here." Her words came out in a rush now. "He was kind of pissed when Stu wanted the app ready but he kind of saw it as a challenge, you know? Like he wanted to see if he could do it."

"They had a blowout a few days ago," Lennox said. "You swept up the pieces of that jack-o'-lantern that Zachary broke."

The front door banged open and Toni jumped as a few people exited the building, laughing at something and looking over in their direction for just a second. People who didn't know this was part of a murder investigation, just a few feet away. Unconcerned people who were probably just wondering where to get lunch.

"So you and Zachary are pretty close, then?"

"We're just… friends."

Lennox had heard it a hundred times. The little pause, the slight hesitation when someone said they were just… friends. It always meant there was more to it.

"He wouldn't do this," she said finally.

"Okay. Good to know. Who do you think did?

"I… don't know."

"Okay," Lennox said. He wasn't sure what else he could say to her. "Well, thanks for letting us know."

She nodded slowly without looking at him.

"Was there... anything else?"

"He was with me that night," she blurted.

"Wait—what?"

"He was with me Monday night." She glanced at the shrine and then at Lennox. Took a deep breath. She straightened her shoulders. No going back now. "Yeah."

"What did you do that night?" Ouellette asked pointedly.

"We were at his place..."

"Over in Castle Hill?" Lennox asked. "Across from the convenience store?"

"Yeah. He made coffee." She gave a little smile. "He had to go get milk at that place across the street. We watched a movie—one of those anime ones he likes."

"But he doesn't live in Castle Hill, Toni," Lennox said as gently as he could. "And there's no convenience store across the street."

"Oh." She bit her lip and went red in the cheeks and along her forehead. "Why can't you just leave him alone?"

She pushed herself off the building, slipping between them and heading for the door. She yanked it open and didn't look back.

"That went well," Lennox said. "Sick building, huh?"

"You could say that."

"Why do people lie to the police?"

"Because people just lie," Ouellette replied.

"So she's into him, and even she's worried he did it."

"And willing to lie about it."

"And she probably couldn't even tell you why." He looked up at the top corner of the building, to the Spooktacular's windows. "Think she's involved?"

"I think she's... just confused and scared."

"Poor kid." Lennox rubbed his eyes. "I think I hate this case."

"Not helping."

"So what do you think?"

"I think Zachary still looks good for it. We can't rule him out just yet."

"So where do you want to go with this next, Sergeant?"

He watched Ouellette think for a minute.

Finally, she said: "I'm going to polygraph him."

"Wow. Really?"

"Yeah. Really." She shook her head. "Too much lying going on."

Lennox had a polygraph display at the Black Museum: a stern interrogator looming over a terrified suspect hooked up to a black metal box, with a roll of paper spilling onto the floor, showing a jagged record of attempted deceit. There was a card explaining that lie-detector machines were unreliable, and the results were questionable. More trouble than they were worth. They didn't even have a polygraph back at the station. He had never actually seen one, and had built the display prop after looking at pictures online. They were used far more in the private sector and, if they wanted to use one, they were going to have to call one of the companies in Boston that offered such tests and schedule an appointment.

"It's not ideal, but it might give us something to work with," she said. "You can set it up when we get back to the station."

"Yes, ma'am."

Thursday
June 7th

Chapter VI

DWORACZYK SPENT HIS AFTERNOON following up on the supposed Kelly sightings. Wasting his afternoon, he thought, as he got back to the station. None of the calls had panned out, but he hadn't expected them to anyway. Appeals to the public were a last resort, and usually just made more work. Too much more work. And they brought out the kooks and publicity hounds. But he'd been lucky so far; Salem had its own brand of kooks and publicity hounds, and he hadn't gotten any calls from local mystics today. Maybe tomorrow.

He was eight to four, and it was after five now. He could always use the overtime. They were putting in new kitchen counters at home.

He had just finished writing up the various dead ends he'd spent the day working on when his phone rang.

"CID, Dworaczyk."

"Hi, um, I'm over at the farmers' market," a woman's voice said. It wasn't a good connection. "I think I just saw that girl in the paper? The one you're looking for?"

"What happened?" He grabbed a pen. He wanted to make sure this really was something before he went out on it.

"She might have just stopped at my table. Young girl in a red hoodie. Light brown hair. Bought a bag of apples."

"She pay with a card?"

"No. Cash."

"Still there?"

"Yeah, I'm still here."

"No, is she still there?"

"Oh. I think. Let me check."

He listened to the woman breathing into the phone for a few moments. He could hear the crowd, hear music. He heard the woman make little frustrated sounds.

"Yeah, she's still here. She's… over at a table looking at homemade soaps."

"All right. I will be right over. Keep an eye on her."

Kitchen counters weren't cheap.

The farmers' market set up once a week in Derby Square, a small brick plaza in front of Old Town Hall. Dworaczyk had only gone once, sometime last summer. It was a few dozen tables and tents, with everything from tomatoes to wine, soap to cheese and honey. There was someone playing a guitar and mourning her way through a song he half-recognized from the radio. People milled around on a summer afternoon, and he scanned the crowd as he got out of the car, looking for a girl in a red hoodie. There were probably a hundred people slowly wandering through the square. Not enough to be considered crowded, but more than enough to make finding a particular person require some effort.

There were four different vendors selling apples, of course. He found the one he wanted on the third try. He held up his badge.

"You called me a few minutes ago," he said. "Which way did she go?"

"That way," the vendor pointed. She was a skinny, hippie-grandmother type with little wire-framed glasses. "But that was a few minutes ago now."

He was already moving, shouldering his way through the little crowd. Someone held out a free sample—something on a stick—and he shook his head, ignoring it. There was a flash of red glimpsed between the moving bodies… but it was just a guy in a t-shirt. He nearly tripped over a row of children, sitting on the ground, listening to the singer. Everybody else was moving so slowly, so aimlessly. Everybody was in his damn way.

He found the guy selling soaps. He held up his badge and said, "Girl in a red hoodie come by in the last ten minutes?"

"Red? Yeah. She came by a couple times. Didn't buy anything."

"She with anyone?"

"Nah."

"Which way did she go?"

"I think that way." He gestured. "Or... not." He looked in the opposite direction and shook his head. "Sorry."

Dworaczyk left, shaking his head. Why didn't civilians ever notice or remember anything, dammit? He went up and down the rows of vendors. Derby Square wasn't big, and it only took a few minutes to complete the course through the stalls. It took even less time to do it a second time. There were a lot of people in red, but none of them were Kelly. None of them were even close.

There were three flights of stairs on the front side of Old Town Hall, each leading up to its own green door. Dworaczyk bounded up the granite steps, two at a time, and turned to look out over the square. The tents and the canopies and the fluttering signs actually made it harder to see anything from up here.

The square was right on Front Street. She could have left that way. Or she could have gone down one of the brick walkways or alleys that led away from the square. She was probably gone.

Goddammit, he thought. This looked good a few minutes ago. Well, it looked like a possibility. It looked better than any of those other leads he wasted his afternoon chasing down.

There was a coffee shop down a walkway to his left, and he saw a young woman step outside. She wore a lightweight hoodie; it was probably closer to pink but it was red enough. She had sandy brown hair down to her shoulders and carried a little paper bag of apples in one hand, and a cardboard cup in the other. The tag from a teabag fluttered in the breeze.

He bounded down the stairs, trying not to trip as he went after her. She turned and started walking away, not seeming to notice him.

Twenty feet away from her. He wanted to shove some of these people out of his way as he closed the distance. Ten feet.

"Kelly," he called, trying to sound happy and friendly. Trying not to sound like a cop. "Kelly?"

She kept walking.

He was behind her in another few steps. He reached out to tap her shoulder.

"Kelly—"

She turned and looked at him, more puzzled than alarmed.

"What? No," she said.

He couldn't be sure right away. He only had those two photographs to go on. Two very different pictures, neither of them recent, from what the father had said. This girl… looked familiar. She was a little tall, elbows sticking out, standing awkwardly, weirdly familiar posture, squinting at him. Her hair blew into her face and it looked like she needed a haircut.

"Kelly Conroy," he said slowly.

She shook her head *no*.

"Salem Police." He opened his jacket so she could see the badge on his belt. "What is your name?"

"What's *yours*?"

"Detective Sergeant Dworaczyk."

"Okay, then you know my dad," she said.

"And who is that?"

"Detective Andrew Lennox."

"You have got to be kidding me," Dworaczyk sighed.

She shook her head slowly as she sipped her tea, watching him over the rim. Yeah, this was Lennox's kid. He could see it in the shape of her face now. That's why she looked familiar.

"All right, well, show me some ID anyway."

She set the bag of apples down and got her wallet out of her purse. She flipped it open so her license showed in a plastic window.

Allison Lennox. The department weirdo's kid.

"All set?" she asked.

"Yeah, yeah. You are fine. I will say hi to your dad for you when I see him."

Chapter VII

Thursday June 7th

STRINGS OF PARTY LIGHTS LED the way to the door of BitBar. Lennox walked slowly by the patio scattered with tables around a bar on wheels. Eighties music was playing from a speaker mounted on the corner of the building—a song that sounded familiar but he couldn't quite remember. He paused to scan the people eating and drinking out here: little, loud, college-age groups of three or four, none of them with a blondish-haired woman with stars behind one ear. He headed for the door, not wanting to linger out on the patio looking like a creepy middle-aged guy checking out the younger women.

It was warm out, getting humid, and a rush of air conditioning and noise hit him as he opened the door. The beeps and bells of the games mixed with a couple dozen conversations echoing off the brick walls.

"How many?" the perky hostess asked.

"I'm just going to sit at the bar."

"Kay. Cool."

"Hey, you card everyone, don't you?" he asked.

"Well, yeah, but I think you're old enough." She gave him a smile.

"No, not me," he said. He slid his badge out of his front pocket, and held it out in a cupped hand. "Do you remember carding a young woman in here Monday night—dirty blonde hair, star tattoos behind her ear?"

She looked at the badge, and then at him, wrinkling her nose.

"What'd she do?" she asked hesitantly.

"Just need to talk to her."

"I card a lot of people. She might've been in here but..." She shrugged.

"Okay, well, thanks anyway."

He took a seat at the far end of the bar, away from the door but still where he could see it, and looked around. The indoor crowd skewed older than the groups at the outdoor tables—outside they were twenty-something, indoors they were all over thirty. More men than women, he noted. A very white crowd. Mostly men standing at the various games, leaning in, some lost in concentration and others laughing and glancing over at whoever was standing near. Every little shelf seemed to have a half-empty glass on it.

No one matching Stacey's description, at least initially.

"What can I getcha?" the bartender asked, putting a square blue napkin down in front of him and leaning in close to be heard over the noise. It was the same bartender he and Ouellette had spoken to yesterday. She tilted her head and blinked, surprised.

"You came back," she said.

"I live upstairs," Lennox shrugged.

"Don't remember seeing you in here before," she said. "Before yesterday."

"Yeah, I don't get out a lot."

"You just missed him," she said. "The guy you were asking about."

"He was here?"

"Yeah. Left about fifteen minutes ago."

"Well, damn. How did he seem?'

"Seem? I dunno—a little cautious, maybe? Ordered a beer and just... kinda looked at me funny. Like he knew something was up."

"What did you say to him?"

"I didn't say anything," she replied, defensive. "I just gave him his beer."

Lennox nodded. She had given him a beer and a funny look to go with it. And Zachary had probably been getting funny looks since yesterday. Probably a lot longer than that.

"Was he alone?"

"Yeah."

"Seem to be waiting for anyone?"

"Not that I could tell," she shook her head.

"Talk to anybody?"

"Nope. Sat at the bar, finished his beer, and left."

"And that's it?"

"That's it. You actually going to order anything?"

"Yeah. I'll have a ginger ale." He was technically off-duty, but if Stacey showed up he'd be back on-duty, and couldn't be drinking.

"Living it up," the bartender said as she shook her head. "This on an expense account or something?"

"I don't get one of those..."

She filled a glass from the soda gun, put it down, and seemed to forget about him.

He looked back over the crowd. Still no one fitting Stacey's description. He wondered how long he should give it. Being a cop meant that half the time you were walking around trying to find out what had happened, and half the time you were sitting and waiting for something to happen. And the other half of the time was paperwork. Maybe he wanted a cheeseburger while he watched the bar. He was probably going to be here for a while. It was rude to eat meat in front of AJ... but she wasn't here right now.

He wondered if she really would like it here, if she would really like living here in the old jail with him. She had said one morning that it was strange to wake up to the graveyard view out the bedroom window, but she could get used to it. There was some part of him that thought she was just being polite, just glossing over another one of the weird quirks her middle-aged b-word had: his books and his museum and his graveyard out back.

He ordered a cheeseburger and scraped the pickles off it when it arrived.

He remembered the first time he met Stuart Pickman. He had seen him around town before, of course—Mr. Hallowe'en always made sure he was always highly visible—but had not actually met him face-to-face. He finally did when the Black Museum first opened. He and Ellen had still been married back then, and she suggested they have a ribbon-cutting to drum up some publicity. Mayor Pyncheon's office had said the mayor's schedule was full that day, and every other day that Lennox suggested, and he just assumed that Pyncheon wouldn't bother appearing at the grand opening of some tourist attraction that would probably be gone by the time it started snowing. But Pickman's office called back quickly and the community liaison—Lennox couldn't remember who it was back then, but it hadn't been Adam Womack —said that Pickman would be there. Always happy to help out one of Salem's finest.

The next morning, a small handful of reporters and bloggers and curious locals showed up and waited. Lennox smiled nervously, told them that Pickman would be joining them soon—any minute now—and checked the time again. He was twenty minutes late. A few people in the little crowd wandered away, bored.

Pickman finally arrived, trailed by some kind of assistant, and nodded to Lennox without an apology.

"Ready?" was all he asked. "Scissors?"

The scissors. He had been so busy trying to get people to show up, so busy getting a ribbon to cut. He had ordered a roll of crime scene tape from a party store on Amazon; he thought it would be more fun to use police tape rather than the usual red ribbon, and the lieutenant wouldn't allow him to use real department-issue tape. He had completely forgotten to buy a pair of giant, ceremonial scissors.

And when he had told Pickman that, he saw the anger flicker across Mr. Hallowe'en's face. Not just anger—rage, kept just under control. His face flashed red, his lip curled upward from his teeth as he quietly hissed, "Fucking idiot. I came down here and you don't… have… scissors."

This wasn't about cutting a ribbon on a new attraction. This wasn't about helping out Salem's Finest. This was about Stuart Pickman. Everything always was, Lennox realized then.

Lennox scrambled, hoping he had a pair somewhere, maybe in the back room, while the little group gathered on the sidewalk looked impatient. The new ticket-taker, the one who would quit a week later because she said the displays kept moving and freaking her out, helped him look. After a few harried minutes, they found a pair he couldn't even remember buying, couldn't remember even owning: a small pair with rounded, childish ends. He handed them over to Mr. Hallowe'en without looking him in the eye.

Pickman turned to the little crowd and smiled, telling them how happy he was to be here. How happy he was that they could all be here, too. That it was always a pleasure to welcome a new business opening in Salem, always a joy to see a new addition to the community. He wished the Dark Museum the best of luck for the future. The crowd applauded and Pickman cut the yellow tape and never stopped smiling. He waved, posed for a picture shaking Lennox's hand, and was gone.

Lennox didn't see him again for weeks. When he did, at some Spooktacular-related event at the Hawthorne, Pickman clearly didn't remember him—just shook his hand and smiled and moved on. Lennox didn't say anything about getting the museum's name wrong, didn't ask for the scissors that Mr. Hallowe'en had pocketed that day.

He scanned the barroom once again now, almost automatically. The crowd was slowly changing over, getting younger and louder but still very white. The music transitioned from eighties to grunge. Halfway through his cheeseburger, he started to wonder if he should try a video game. He hadn't played one since he was about fifteen. Back then, they had seemed so sleek and high-tech, they seemed like the future. Now, they just seemed hopelessly retro, old TVs in plywood cabinets.

Maybe he should spend the rest of the night playing Star Castle and waiting for Stacey to show up and challenge him to a game. But he didn't want to have to say he had been playing video games when he found the suspect's alibi witness. He could already imagine the headlines, calling him the Space Invaders Cop. Winters would not be happy.

When they had gotten back to the station that afternoon, he had started calling polygraph companies to see if any of them could set something up for tomorrow morning. Polygraphs might be inadmissible and unreliable, but he still found four companies in Boston alone offering their services. One firm claimed that its team of highly-trained specialists used proprietary artificial intelligence software to track the microscopic eye movements and voice stress analysis that betrayed liars every time. He wasn't sure the department would sign off on cutting-edge artificial intelligence, and went with Peterson Risk Management, one of the more traditional companies.

He wasn't sure how he felt about it. Polygraphs were based on the Victorian idea that lying made the subject nervous, and the sensors would detect and record the heightened anxiety that indicated deception. But he knew from hard experience that liars could be perfectly calm, and honest people could be nervous wrecks. He probably wouldn't be able to pass a polygraph test himself, he thought, taking a final bite of his cheeseburger. And failing a polygraph was no more an indication of guilt than a pimple or a mole was a sign of being in league with the Devil.

But the police still occasionally used them. Suspects sometimes confessed outright when threatened with a lie detector, when they were convinced the machine was infallible and their lies would be documented. Reliable or not, it was another tool. As Ouellette had said, at least it was something to work with.

He stayed until last call, when he ordered one more ginger ale and then went back upstairs to his apartment, hoping to dodge both Mrs. Chevoya and the guy from 110. He pulled off his shoes and stretched out on the bed, where he could see headstones, stark and crooked in the moonlight, right outside the window.

Friday
June 8th

Friday June 8th

Chapter I

THE POLYGRAPH OPERATOR ARRIVED at nine-thirty and asked Ouellette where she would like him to set up. She and Lennox led him down to Interrogation One, off the lobby. He was a thin man with a beaky nose and a skinny tie, and he said the traffic from Boston hadn't been too bad.

"I guess I was expecting something bigger," Lennox said as the man opened up a laptop. "Bulkier?"

"Like in the movies? The big black box and the roll of paper and the needles? Nah. Haven't used that stuff in years. I've actually never even used one of those old-school machines. All computerized now. Still works the same, though," he shrugged and smirked. "Lying's lying."

"How accurate are they though, really?"

"Over eighty percent accurate in the hands of a skilled operator," the skinny guy said patiently.

"And you're a skilled operator?"

"Wouldn't still be working for the company if I wasn't. Going on eight years now."

"Still not admissible in court, though," Lennox said casually.

"And do you always agree with what the courts say, detective?"

"Do you need anything from us?" Ouellette asked, giving Lennox a look he interpreted as *behave*.

"Nope. Couple of forms for you to fill out before we get started, but nothing else aside from that. When the subject arrives, I'd like to administer the test alone, just the two of us."

"No," Ouellette shook her head. "Can't leave civilians unattended in the station."

"You leave lawyers alone with their clients, don't you?"

"Are you a lawyer?"

"No."

"And he's not your client, we are. I'll be here while you test him."

"Me, too," said Lennox. "Eighty percent, huh?"

"Why don't you go get Dykstra," Ouellette suggested. "I'll stay here. Take a uniform with you."

"He doesn't have to go, though, does he?" the uniform asked on the way over to Spooktacular headquarters.

"No, he doesn't," Lennox said. "But he's cocky and probably cocky enough to think he can beat it."

"But even if he fails…"

"It's still leverage."

The staffers tried very, very hard to ignore them when they came through the door and crossed the open studio space to speak quietly with Zachary Dykstra.

"Need you to come down to the station."

"What now?"

"Just need to go over a couple of things."

"What's going on?" David Nicholson stood in the doorway to his office, arms folded.

"Need to borrow Zachary for a little bit."

"How long?"

"Shouldn't be long. An hour. Maybe two?"

"I have a lotta shit to do," Zachary said, glancing over at Nicholson for help. "I have this *app*…."

"We'll have you back quick as we can."

Zachary looked at the officer, eyes going from badge to gun.

"Maybe you should just go," Nicholson suggested. "We said we'd cooperate."

"Such bullshit," Zachary Dykstra muttered, slamming his laptop closed and standing to go.

"We haven't been able to find Stacey," Lennox said as they drove back to the station.

"Not my problem." Zachary stared out the window.

"Going to be a big damn problem for you if we can't confirm your alibi."

"I think this is the part where I'm supposed to say *You Got Nothing*. Right?"

"Got more than you think," Lennox lied. "Is there anything you want to tell me before we get to the station?"

"Like what?" Zachary laughed.

"Like anything." The station was in view now. "Kind of trying to help you here, Zach."

"Zachary. Yeah, right—you're supposed to be the good cop."

And the bad cop, Lennox knew, was the machine waiting for them in Interrogation One.

He turned and drove past a *Police Personnel Only* sign and parked.

"Seriously, though, if you have anything to say, now's the time."

"Now's the time? What kind of B-movie shit is this?" Zachary looked up at the stern and square brick façade of the police station. "Am I under arrest?"

"No." Lennox shook his head and waited for a moment.

"All right, well—whatever it is, let's get it over with."

"Okay. The sergeant is inside."

Zachary stiffened when Lennox opened the door and he saw the polygraph machine on the table. Ouellette and the skinny, birdlike operator looked up from the screen.

"What the hell is this?"

"It's a polygraph."

"You're kidding me," Zachary blinked. "You are absolutely fucking kidding me."

The operator slowly shook his head.

"I've read about these things. They're bullshit. They don't even work."

"The new ones are a lot more accurate," the operator said, quietly adding, "… and this is one of the new ones."

"I don't have to do this," Zachary shook his head.

"No, you don't," Lennox said.

"But here's the thing," Ouellette said. "Our lieutenant wants a result on this case. If you refuse, he's going to take that as a sign of guilt and then…" She shook her head.

"Then what?"

"Then it gets real serious."

"And if you take it and pass," Lennox said, "Then he'll tell us to cross you off the list and look for somebody else."

Zachary stood under the harsh fluorescent lights, shifting his weight from foot to foot.

"Yeah," he said finally. "Yeah, screw it. Let's get this over with. What do I do?"

The operator nudged a clipboard across the table, and Zachary spent a couple of minutes signing and initialing forms. That clipboard was whisked away into a case and replaced with another, several pages of yes-no questions for Zachary to answer.

Zachary shook his head, and for the next ten minutes, the only sound in the room was the scratch of his pen checking boxes, the rustling of the pages, and his sighs of frustration as he finished each sheet.

"What's next?" he asked, as he finished.

The operator hooked him up to the machine. A blood pressure cuff went around one arm, rubber tubing around his chest and stomach, and sensors were clipped to his fingertips.

"Now just relax. I'm going to ask you a few test questions to get us started with a baseline reading."

"Fire away."

"Just answer yes or no."

Zachary struggled to keep a straight face.

"This shit's unbelievable," he muttered.

"Just relax. Answer yes or no, and just tell the truth. Ready?"

"Yeah."

The operator went to the first page of questions that Zachary had just answered and started reading them off.

"Is today Tuesday?"

"No."

"Is today Friday?"

"Yes."

"Good. Is your name Zachary Dykstra?"

"Yes."

What evil spirit have you familiarity with?
None.

Have you made no contract with the devil?

Lennox's uncertainty about the whole thing began to creep up on him as the operator continued with the baseline questions.

"Are you wearing a yellow shirt?"

"No."

"Do you work for the Salem Police Department?"

"What? No. Jesus Christ."

"Just yes or no," the operator warned. "Do you work for the Salem Spooktacular?"

"Yes."

More baseline questions, testing Zachary's reactions to give them something to compare his other answers to later.

"Are you thirty-five years old?"

"No."

"Are you thirty-one years old?"

"No."

"Are you twenty-seven years old?"

"Yes."
"Are you originally from Salem?"
"No."
"Are you originally from Gloucester?"
"Yes."
"Are you the community liaison at the Salem Spooktacular?"
"No."
"Are you in information technology?"
"Yes."
"Okay. Now think about this one carefully, Zachary."
Zachary tensed. Lennox could see it along the edge of his jaw.
"Ready?"
"Yeah, sure. Fire away."
"Have you ever robbed a bank?"
"Yeah, sure," Zachary laughed. "All the fucking time, man."
"Just… say yes or no."
"No."
"Have you ever stolen anything from your current employer?"
"Nope."
"Were you born in 1988?"
"No."
"Were you born in 1991?"
"No."
"Were you born in 1992?"
"Yes."

After thirty minutes of this, Lennox thought he was probably even more nervous than Zachary. What if this didn't work? What if Zachary could beat the test?

What if they had the wrong guy?

Zachary was faced away from the operator. Lennox saw the man slide the clipboard away from him. He had repeated back all the questions that Zachary answered in writing and was now moving on to the real questions. The questions Zachary didn't know were coming.

"Have you ever hurt anyone?" the operator asked.
"What? No..." Zachary said hesitantly.
"I'm going to ask you that again. Have you ever hurt anyone?"
"No."
"Did you meet a woman on June 7?"
"Yes."
"Was her name Sarah?"
"No."
"Was her name Paula?"
"No."
"Was her name Stacey?"
"Yes."
"Did she have a tattoo?"
"Yes."
"Did you sleep with her that same night?"
"Yes."
"Are you wearing a yellow shirt?"
"What? No."
"Do you think murder is a crime?"
"Yes."
"Do you think theft is a crime?"
"Yeah."
"Did you murder Stuart Pickman?"
"Fuck, no."
"And I am going to ask you that again. Did you murder Stuart Pickman?"

If you do confess and give glory to God, I pray God clear you if you be innocent. And if you are guilty, discover you. And therefore give me an upright answer...

"This is such bullshit."
It is all false and I am clear.
"Please, just yes or no."
"No."
"Did you argue with Stuart Pickman?"
"Yes."

"Do you know who murdered Stuart Pickman?"

"No, I do not."

"Just yes or no," the operator said patiently. "Did you take anything out of the junk box in your office?"

"No."

"Do you think people who commit crimes should be punished?"

"Yes. No—wait—"

"Do you think people who commit crimes should be punished?"

"Yes."

"Do you think you will pass this test?"

"Yes."

"Did you kill Stuart Pickman?"

"No."

"Are you wearing a yellow shirt?"

"Jesus Christ. No."

"And… that completes the test. That's all the questions I have for you today."

Zachary Dykstra let out a long, ragged breath and fell back in the chair.

"Okay… so… how'd I do?"

"Let's get you unhooked and you can wait next door while we go over the results," Ouellette said. "We'll get you a water and you can chill for a couple of minutes."

"All right, whatever."

Lennox brought him into Interrogation Two and left the door open.

"Need anything?"

"Yeah, I'll take that water."

Lennox got him a cup of water, told him he'd be right back, and rejoined Ouellette in the next room, closing the door as he entered.

"So how did he do?"

"He passed," the operator said simply.

"Really?"

"Yeah. No deception indicated."

I am innocent, I know nothing of a witch, I know not what a witch is.

"And you're eighty percent sure?" Lennox asked.

"Don't blame me if your guy passed."

"Okay," Ouellette held up a hand. "Send me the results."

The operator tapped a few keys and nodded. "Sent."

He started to put away the sensors and the other equipment in a hard-shell case. He was taking his time. Stalling. Once he was packed, he turned to Ouellette and said quietly, "So, Michelle, was it?"

"Yeah," she said cautiously.

He glanced quickly over at Lennox and said, "I'm Jack. I'll be back up this way next Tuesday for another appointment. I don't know what your Tuesday looks like, but if you're free for lunch…" He held out his card.

"I'm in the middle of a homicide investigation," she said, giving him the Look.

"All right, then." Jack put his card on the table. "In case you change your mind."

"You can send the invoice to our lieutenant."

"Nice meeting you," he muttered, shouldering past Lennox and out the door.

"All right, so," Ouellette said slowly, "he passed."

Lennox looked at the summary chart the operator had given them, a spreadsheet of numbers, and thought for a moment.

"Yeah, but… he doesn't know that, does he?"

Friday
June 8th

Chapter II

SHE'S SAFE HERE, in her house in her village. Tucked away, insulated from everything else out there. She's safer here than she was downtown yesterday.

She is just back from her quick, morning dip in the ocean and sits by the open window, wrapped in a towel she bought a couple of days ago: an orange beach towel with a witch on a broom on it. And she's not sure how he feels about that towel, about the cartoony witch straddling the broom, but for now she just smiles. She sits and lets the sun and the breeze come in through the window and run their fingers over her, drying her and warming her—the water is still a little too chilly when she takes those dunking swims.

She feels safe here.

She wraps the towel tighter around her and has some breakfast: a muffin she got yesterday from the Starbucks on the edge of the university campus nearby, washing it down with an orange juice. She has laid in a little supply of bottled water and protein bars for the next couple of days. She reaches over to her jeans to check her wallet. Thirty-seven dollars left. She hasn't dared use an ATM since she left the Hawthorne. That will send up a flare, she is sure. She doesn't really know if thirty-seven dollars is enough for the remaining days. It's not much, but it will have to be enough.

She should stay here, she thinks. Just stay here until it's time. Right here in her little house—sheltered in the little house which is actually the biggest house in the village. She loves going downtown, walking the old streets, passing by the tourists and the locals who don't have any idea who she is, relishing that anonymity, slipping through the crowds, looking at dresses and eating ice cream. But she knows now that it's not safe for her.

Her father is here, and she has to stay out of sight. Out of his sight. If he finds her, he'll drag her home and this will all be ruined, all for nothing.

And her father was talking to *him*. To the man with the knife. She closes her eyes tight. She leans forward in the chair, reaches for the orange juice but the bottle is empty. She takes a deep breath and stands. The towel falls to the floor and she leaves it as she crosses to the door, taking the poppet from the beams, holding it in both hands.

Deep breath. Eyes closed. Another deep breath. Straightens her shoulders. Deep breath, calm. Deep breath, relax. Deep breath, focus.

She needs to concentrate, needs to look at what is right in front of her.

She tucks the poppet back in place over the door, and looks around the room. She has never been neat, never been organized, at least when it came to things that bored her, that didn't hold her attention. And looking around the room now—she's been here two days already and her clothes are piled on one of the chairs and there are empty bottles and wrappers on the table. It's not a mess yet, but it's going to be unless she does something.

It'll help her to claim the space, she decides, to exert some meager control. Help her get to know the place better.

She gets dressed in yesterday's jeans and a new t-shirt. She makes the bed, snapping the stale, dusty sheets until she sees motes floating around the room; they are strangely pretty as they spin around and catch the sunlight. She hadn't gotten a sleeping bag, and maybe she should have. Maybe later today. She gets the coarse broom from where it stands in the corner and begins to sweep. The floor is gritty and she can see her damp footprints on the wide floorboards as she works her way around the room. A few minutes later, she opens the creaking door and sends the dust and the grit outside, then puts the broom back in its corner.

Now she puts the big leather Bible on the shelf on the other side of the room. She doesn't have any use for it. It's not her book. She collects some of the other things—the quill pens, the chipped ceramic dishes, the little tin lantern—and puts them away on the shelves, too. More things she doesn't really think she needs. Except for the green bottle, the little, green, square bottle that was on the window sill. She leaves that where it is for now. She likes it there.

She bundles up her dirty laundry and stuffs it into the shopping bag her new t-shirts and socks came in. She doesn't need to worry about doing laundry right now, but doesn't want to leave her underwear draped over a chairback, either. That doesn't seem right.

Opening the front door again, she carefully peeks out. No sign of anyone. She still needs to be careful. She can't let herself be discovered here. No one seems to know she's here and she needs to keep it that way. She pulls the door shut quietly behind her and she steps cautiously outside.

She makes another slow, careful loop around her weird, little, forgotten village. Again, she keeps thinking it's bigger than it really is. A couple of the cottages need work; one needs some boards replaced, she thinks, and the thatch on another looks like it's getting thin in places. There is brush everywhere that should be cut back, pathways that need to be cleared. There are a few overgrown garden plots that are dry and disorganized, just tangles of weeds and rocks that probably shouldn't be there. But she smiles as she looks around, thinking that she likes this weird little village. She might even love it here. She feels safe.

She looks around and finds some flowers, purple and yellow, that she pulls up and brings into the house, for the green bottle on the window sill. She smiles and almost starts to cry, realizing she doesn't want to have to say goodbye to this place.

Chapter III

ZACHARY SAT IN INTERROGATION TWO, legs crossed, arms folded. Tight and rigid. The cup that Lennox had gotten him fifteen minutes before sat on the table, empty and crushed. His body language said angry, frustrated, and a little bit scared.

Ouellette sat down opposite him and Lennox quietly closed the door and remained standing.

"Is there some reason you would have failed the polygraph, Zachary?" Lennox asked.

"What?"

Ouellette said, "You failed."

"Bullshit."

"Why would the machine say you're lying, Zachary?" Lennox asked nonchalantly.

"Show me the printout."

"We don't have to show you anything," Ouellette said.

"So now you're both the bad cop. Look, I already told you, I didn't kill anybody. I met a girl at a bar and brought her home and that's it."

"We can't find her," Ouellette said. "And the bartender doesn't remember you."

"And you told us you were there at about the right time," Lennox added.

"I don't know what to goddamn tell you. Look, I don't have to prove myself innocent—you have to prove that I'm guilty."

"This looks very bad for you right now," Ouellette said.

"Look, Zachary, if you have anything to tell us, now is the time. Maybe you asked Stuart to meet you out there to talk, smooth things over before you went back to work the next day. You wanted to apologize. But he was in no mood. We've heard he was kind of... difficult. So maybe things got a little out of hand?"

"No."

"Maybe he wanted to remind you who was the boss, maybe he moved the deadline up even further, huh?"

"And he was nasty about it. And you had one of those carving tools in your pocket, right?" Lennox asked. "I get absent-minded and I put the weirdest shit in my pocket and forget about it and then a week later..."

"No. This is crazy. You two are crazy. You're trying to railroad me... those machines are bullshit. This is just a fucking... stunt. You're just trying to scare me."

Lennox opened the manila folder he held, silently placing the crime scene photos on the table one at a time. The parking lot. A smear of blood. Stuart Pickman's dead body.

Zachary gasped for air, pushed back from the table. The chair scraped along the floor.

"What the fuck, man?" he rasped. "What the fuck are you doing?"

Lennox inched the photos across the table.

Zachary jumped up and the chair tumbled over behind him. He backed up, staring at the photos, crossing the room and only stopping when his shoulders bumped the wall.

And Lennox saw it then. The open, honest fear in Zachary Dykstra's face. A fear that couldn't be faked.

Shit.

"The hell," Zachary said. He took a deep breath and asked, "Am I under arrest?"

"No," Lennox admitted.

"So I can... I can leave? I can get the hell out of here?"

"Any time," Lennox said.

"Then... I'm going."

He came around the corner of the table and reached for the door. It was locked. He pulled on the handle twice and then glared at Lennox.

Lennox took out his keys and opened the door.

"Fuck you people." Zachary shook his head. "Just… fuck all of you."

"That went well," Lennox said, back upstairs in the bullpen. "He's not our guy."

"No, he's not," Ouellette said. "He did look good for a while there."

She popped her cufflinks out, put them in a small ceramic bowl on her desk, and rolled up her sleeves. She opened her notebook to a blank page. Lennox wondered how she could be so calm about it. He envied the distance she could keep between herself and a case.

"So back to square one. If Zachary isn't the killer, who is?"

"We always start with the wife or girlfriend or significant other," Lennox said. "But we got sidetracked with Zachary pretty quick and haven't really looked at Jessica. She says she didn't know where he was that night, but maybe she did."

"True."

"Maybe they weren't as happy together as people say. Maybe she was sick and tired of living with Mr. Hallowe'en. Maybe she was angry that she wasn't Mrs. Hallowe'en."

"He loved Hallowe'en more than her?" Ouellette asked, not quite convinced.

"The Spooktacular is having financial trouble, maybe they were at home, too. And maybe the pumpkin-carving knife isn't a weapon of opportunity, maybe it's more of a message? Hey, pal, if you love Hallowe'en so damn much…"

"But there's a daughter at home. Can't just put her to bed and hope she doesn't wake up while you're out killing her father. She's old enough to say something about it to the wrong person."

"Right."

"But it's somewhere to start. Who else should we be thinking about?"

"Jessica has a brother. Maybe he had a problem with the victim. He didn't seem at all happy that Pickman never married his sister."

"Wouldn't make an honest woman out of her. Kind of old-school, but possible." Ouellette wrote it down. "Then we have Sonya Weaver, who wanted to get rid of him but couldn't get the board to go along."

"So she takes matters into her own hands. And he who lives by the pumpkin-carving kit, dies by the pumpkin-carving kit. Plus, she gets to pick the new director, and she already has someone in mind."

"That works. And what about David Nicholson? He says he doesn't want to be the new director, but maybe he does after all."

"No guarantee he'll get the job, though," Lennox said. "And he does not strike me as someone who leaves things to chance."

"Maybe he and Weaver have something worked out?"

"I don't think I see them playing well together, but you never know." Lennox picked up the old marlinspike on his desk and rolled it between his palms, feeling the metal warm up. He'd had it since he'd been in the Coast Guard and sometimes it helped him think. After a minute he started tapping it arrhythmically on the arm of his chair.

"Got another one," he said.

"Who?"

"Toni Basilico."

"Okay. Why her?"

"Pickman chewed out her... friend. And she seems fragile. Building is making her sick, right?"

"But why talk to us?"

"She's worried."

"About...?"

"About what we know. About Zachary going down for something she did."

"Imaginative," Ouellette nodded.

"One more," Lennox said hesitantly. "Dworaczyk's missing girl. Maybe she's not our witness. Maybe she's our suspect."

"So there's no Spooktacular connection at all?"

"Maybe not. Maybe he just crossed paths with a… troubled girl who's off her meds."

"Wrong place, wrong time."

"Maybe," he said.

Lieutenant Winters stood in the door of his office, holding an invoice.

"You two just spent five hundred and seventy-five dollars on a lie detector," he said. "Please tell me we have something to show for it."

"No," Ouellette replied. "Our suspect passed and we still went after him but he looks like a dead end."

"Fabulous. So you're back to where you started?"

"Seems like it."

"And Fred, where are you with your Missing?" Winters asked.

"I am exactly nowhere," Dworaczyk said, not looking up from the papers on his desk. "I am at the end of my rope. But I have someone coming in another hour. Expert help."

"Good. The three of you need to coordinate and get this thing figured out."

Ouellette's cell phone rang. She checked the number and turned away to take the call. All Lennox heard was "*Ce qui?*" in an annoyed tone before she dropped her voice too low to hear.

"Expert help?" He turned to Dworaczyk.

"Yeah, another hour. Enough time to eat." Dworaczyk looked into an empty coffee cup on his desk and frowned. "Going to grab something quick."

He stood up as Ouellette finished her phone call.

"I… gotta go," she said quietly.

"Everything okay?" Lennox asked. Something was obviously not okay.

"Fine," she said, fishing the cufflinks out of the bowl. "Just fine. Not sure when I'll be back. Shouldn't be long."

"Okay…"

Dworaczyk sighed as he watched her go.

"Okay, so, an hour?" Lennox asked.

"Yeah. An hour."

Chapter IV

LENNOX LOOKED UP FROM HIS CASE NOTES as a short, dark-haired woman stopped on the other side of the half-wall that formed the bullpen. She was in her fifties, professionally dressed and carrying a leather notebook. He recognized her and bit his lip, thinking he must have missed an appointment.

Linda Morrow was a Harvard-educated psychologist who worked closely with the department. Her office was in a tall, new building downtown. She helped screen recruits, offered expert testimony in court, and even did some profiling. She also did counseling, and Lennox had been her client for the past eight months, since he had been the officer in an "Officer-Involved Shooting." Seeing her out of context like this, outside the office where he met her every other week for his regular session, was jarring.

He was relieved when she looked past him and said, "Sergeant Dworaczyk?"

"Thank you for coming," Dworaczyk said. He stood up and indicated an empty chair next to his desk. "I need some help. This is a weird one."

"You said you were looking for a young woman with some psychiatric issues," she said, crossing the room to take a seat. She nodded to Lennox—a polite nod, like she was simply passing someone in the street. He knew this was some kind of professional courtesy: no one wanted to be recognized by the department shrink.

"Yes, you could say that. Apparently, she thinks she is the reincarnation of one of the witches from the old days."

"Bridget Bishop," Lennox said quietly.

"The girl must be psychotic," Dworaczyk said. "I assume. Right?"

"Well, without meeting her and assessing her, I can only speculate, at best. And I'm not sure that will be all that helpful to you, if you see what I mean."

"I am just trying to get a line on her. Like I said, I assume she is psychotic and I do not know how to… handle that."

"Okay, well, does she have hallucinations?" Morrow asked, opening the case file that Dworaczyk handed over.

"Not according to the family."

"Is she incoherent?"

"Again, not according to the family."

"And is she aware of her behavior? Is she able to navigate an ordinary day?"

"It seems like she can, yeah."

"Violent?"

"No."

"Then she's not psychotic."

"Okay, so she is… what, delusional?"

"Maybe not delusional, either, really," Morrow said. "Delusions are idiosyncratic beliefs that are maintained despite being contradicted by other evidence or argument. That's the textbook definition, anyway. Millions of people all over the world believe in reincarnation. I can walk into any number of shops downtown and buy ten books about it. And another ten about this Bridget Bishop," she nodded over to Lennox. "So I can't diagnose what's going on with her without interviewing her and making an assessment, but right now, couldn't say she's delusional. She shares a belief with many, many other people."

"But she is a witness in a homicide," Dworaczyk said. "And her father is worried. So we need to find her and we can PC her, at least."

People could be taken into Protective Custody for their own safety. It was usually used to bring drunks down to the station to sleep it off, but it could be invoked in Kelly's situation, too.

"What happened to this witch she thinks she's the reincarnation of?" Morrow asked after thinking for a moment.

Dworaczyk looked over at Lennox.

"Hanged on the morning of June 10, 1692."

"Sunday," Morrow said. "If she's here that close to the date, that's no coincidence. Reasonable to think she may visit that spot on Sunday morning."

"That's what I said," Lennox said quietly.

"Are there other spots associated with her?"

"There are stories about a few locations around town where her ghost is supposed to be seen," Lennox shrugged. "But those are just stories."

"But you should be checking out those spots, too. People like going to places they feel a connection with. Maybe you can find her before Sunday, and I think you need to."

"Why is that?"

"This witch was hanged on the tenth?"

"On Proctor's Ledge," Lennox nodded.

"All right." Morrow took a deep breath. "Now, like I said, without meeting her and assessing her situation, I am just guessing. But if that's where and when this Bridget Bishop died, this girl could be planning to hurt herself out there."

"Planning to hang herself?" Lennox asked.

"I'm only speculating, nothing definite. But it's a possibility. Worst-case scenario, yes, but you can't rule it out."

"Ouellette and I were already planning to have the area under surveillance that morning," Lennox said.

"Assume that she's smart enough to notice you," Morrow warned. "If she thinks she's one of the witches from back then, she's probably assuming everyone is out to get her, right? So she'll be paying attention."

"Great," Dworaczyk said. "What else?"

"Nothing offhand," Morrow turned a few pages in Kelly's file. "But let me look this over and get back to you. Can I have a copy?"

She left a few minutes later with a copy of the file tucked into her notebook.

"I told you most of this a couple days ago," Lennox said to Dworaczyk.

"When?"

"When I first told you about Bridget Bishop."

"Okay, fine. So where are these other locations? We should probably take a look at them."

"We?"

"I do not know where these places are, and you do," Dworaczyk said, standing up and reaching for his keys.

Friday June 8th

Chapter V

OUELLETTE DROVE TO THE MARBLEHEAD Police station, trying not to speed, trying not to grip the wheel too tight. Marblehead was a nice town, nicer than Salem in many ways. Every town had another town next door that residents liked to complain about, another town that thought it was too good. She drove past colorful old houses, the kind of old houses Lennox liked, with narrow windows and steep roofs. He'd probably start talking about the architecture if he were here. Not helping.

Joanie had sounded upset on the phone. Of course she had. Things had been getting awkward between them for the past few months, ever since Joanie had brought home Frank. The first time Ouellette had met him, she'd nodded politely to her sister's new boyfriend as she sized him up. She knew immediately—knew his type. The stubble and the faded tribal armband and the tattered jeans weren't a problem. She recognized him in the way cops could always recognize someone with a record. Recognize someone who wasn't quite finished with having a record just yet.

And she and Joanie had talked about it the next day. Joanie explained that sure, Frankie had had some problems in the past but it hadn't been his fault, not really, and people were so damn unfair sometimes. Just like she was being unfair to him right now.

"He can't be here," Ouellette had told her. "Not while I am paying most of the rent."

Michelle Ouellette had a son, Roland, seven years old now. He was why she left her service weapon at the station when she went home at the end of each shift. She wouldn't have a gun around her child and she sure as hell wouldn't have a felon hanging around the house, either.

The irony of it, of course, was that for so long, she had been the family fuckup; she'd been the one the family worried about. Joanie was the good student. Joanie had gotten the good job. Michelle, why can't you be more like your sister? Maybe applying to the police academy was overcompensating.

And then she'd gotten pregnant. Out of wedlock, to use her parents' antiquated phrase. And then they were horrified again that she was damn well going to stay out of wedlock.

Yes, Michelle had been the one who needed to get her shit together. But she wasn't the one dating a felon who evidently wasn't finished being a felon.

She pulled into the parking lot of the Marblehead PD. The station was a new building: cinder blocks and glass bricks. It looked more like a high school. She quickly crossed herself and walked into the lobby, badge in hand. Her eyes went from the duty sergeant to her sister, sitting by the window, hunched forward in her chair, legs crossed, one foot tapping manically in the air. Joanie, her little baby sister who made bad choices. Her little baby sister who was in her thirties and looking like… like someone's terrified little baby sister.

"Mish," Joanie said, jumping up. "Thank God."

"C'est que shit?"

"I didn't know who else to call," Joanie said. "They just dragged him down here."

"You know I'm in the middle of a homicide, right? Did you stop and think about that?"

"I… I didn't know what else to do," Joanie sniffled and wiped at her eyes. "Jesus, Mish."

"Is there a problem over there?" the duty sergeant asked sharply.

"Detective Sergeant Ouellette, Salem PD." She held up her badge. "This is my sister. You have a Frank Caruso here?"

"Oh, yeah. Yeah. He's in holding."

"Mish," Joanie pleaded. "You have to do something."

Friday June 8th

Chapter VI

"So what were you doing, telling the father about your little theory?" Dworaczyk demanded on the way to the restaurant.

"I was trying to help. What did you want me to say?"

"I did not want you to say anything."

"The guy's daughter is missing. I just wanted him to know that we had some idea what we're doing."

Lennox looked out the window.

"So is Michelle's kid yours or what?" Dworaczyk asked after a couple of minutes.

"Wait, what?"

"This is what some people have been saying."

"What people?" Lennox asked.

"I do not think you have the nerve, myself. And I cannot see *her* with *you*. I would not blame you, of course. I would go for it if she was my partner. Definitely." Dworaczyk had always lusted for Ouellette from across the CID bullpen, silently but obviously. She had dropped a stack of files some time ago, and Lennox thought Dworaczyk was going to have a heart attack as he watched her bend to pick them up. "And I would have her leave those riding boots on, too."

"You're married," Lennox said uncomfortably. "You have kids."

"I can dream, right? See, this is why you will never make sergeant. No initiative. No imagination. You are not a go-getter."

"Roland isn't… mine."

"I did not really think so. Like I said…" Dworaczyk shook his head.

"Oh, look—here's the restaurant."

They got out of the car, and Lennox saw Denise from Screaming Skull Tours standing across the street, wearing a tall witch hat, with a microphone clipped to her bodice. He overheard her telling a group of half-a-dozen afternoon tourists that the ghost of Bridget Bishop still haunted the building standing on the site of her old tavern. She and Billy didn't seem to notice them as they entered.

"So what is this place, again?" Dworaczyk asked.

"She used to live on this site. It's her old land."

"Great."

It was quiet in the dining room—the lull after lunch and before dinner.

Dworaczyk thrust his badge and Kelly's picture at the nearest waitress.

"Has this girl been here any time over the last few days?" he asked.

The waitress didn't look much older than Kelly herself. She squinted in the cozy dimness of the restaurant and tucked a loose strand of hair behind her ear.

"Yeah," she nodded. "That's mac-and-cheese girl. She in trouble or something?"

"No, but we need to talk to her."

"Mac-and-cheese girl?" Lennox asked.

"Yeah, she's been in two or three times, I think. Always has the mac-and-cheese."

"Just two or three times?"

"Yeah."

"So not regularly? Not every night or anything?"

"No."

"Does she come in at a particular time?" Dworaczyk asked.

"No. I waited on her once for lunch and then I think someone else had her for dinner that same night, maybe?"

"Was she with anyone?"

"Nah, she was alone. She sat in the corner, away from the windows."

"How did she seem? Upset? Or... sad, or something else?"

"Just seemed shy." She shrugged. "She gave me a little smile and a wave when she left."

"Anybody else ever try to talk to her?"

"Not that I noticed."

"Anybody creeping on her? Checking her out?"

"Not that I saw. Look, is she in trouble? Did something happen to her?"

"Did you hear about the missing girl?"

"Yeah, the one from Milwaukee or something? Think I saw it in the paper."

"Yeah. This is her," Dworaczyk nodded.

"Oh, shit."

"When was the last time she was in?"

"Day before yesterday, I think."

"Not in today?"

"No."

"All right, then," Dworaczyk said. He held out a card. "If she shows up, you call me."

"Should I, like, try to keep her talking or anything?"

"No, no. Just leave her alone. Do not bother her. Do not do anything except call me."

"Okay." The waitress slid the card into an apron pocket.

"Some place else to check out," Lennox said. "Couple of streets over from here."

"So this is where the witches are buried, huh?" Dworaczyk asked.

"What? No."

The Salem Witch Trials Memorial was a rectangular green space the size of a house lot, with granite walls along two sides and a wrought-iron railing closing off the far end. Rough ledges jutted out from the walls, each one dedicated to the memory of one of the victims of 1692, each carved with a name and a date: twenty names in all. Entering the space, Lennox stepped carefully over the threshold carved with protestations of innocence (*On My Dying Day, I Am No Witch—I Am Wholly Innocent of Such Wickedness—I Do Plead Not Guilty*), all taken down during the trials three hundred years before the memorial was built. It was one of the most popular stops for tourists to visit, and it always annoyed him to see someone sitting on one of the ledges, having lunch or checking their phone.

There were a few visitors today, slowly following the path that led past the markers, pausing to take a selfie or leave a flower.

Bridget Bishop's ledge was the first one on the left as they entered.

"Nobody's buried here," Lennox said. "When they hanged you as a witch, you weren't entitled to a Christian burial, so they left you out there swinging from a tree branch."

"Did they now?" Dworaczyk was already bored.

"We don't know where any of them are. Some of the records say they were buried near where they were hanged, but that's disputed."

Dworaczyk wasn't the only one to make that mistake. The memorial was tucked in next to the oldest cemetery in the city, and that was probably why so many people thought the accused had been buried here. Outside the memorial, just on the other side of the wall, were crooked rows of slate headstones, engraved with names and dates and winged skulls and weeping willows. *Sacred to the memory of. Departed this life.*

Visitors to the memorial often left tokens—flowers or coins or candles. Sometimes, descendants eight or nine generations down the family line left notes, held down by a rock or jammed into crevices in the granite wall—testament that they were still remembered, that the family still survived. Lennox never read them; they weren't for him, and he wasn't related to any of them, victim or judge or bystander.

There were wilted flowers on Bridget Bishop's ledge today. A few coins. And a faceless, green poppet. Weather-stained, darker than the other ones they had already found, lying on its side behind the bouquet.

"Look," he pointed.

"Same thing I found," Dworaczyk said. "At the hotel."

Lennox looked down the length of the wall. No poppets left on any of the other nineteen ledges. Nothing green anywhere at all.

"Okay, but what does this tell us?" Dworaczyk asked.

"Tells us we're on the right track."

"So she was here. Fine. But where is she now?"

Lennox hadn't been out to Gallows Hill Park since the previous October, on his first rainy day back on the job. Now the car crawled up the winding service road to the crest of the hill, tires crunching along on the old asphalt. Gallows Hill was one of the highest points in Salem, and there should have been a view for miles, but it was blocked by scrubby trees that seemed unhappy to be there. The top had all the charm of a vacant lot, Lennox thought as he got out of the car and walked a few steps into the dry, rasping grass.

He hadn't actually been to the summit since he was in uniform, breaking up the regular underage drinking parties on weekends. It was usually easier on those nights to approach slowly, creeping up the service road with the cruiser's blue lights flashing to let them know the cops were coming. Most of the kids would scatter, and that meant less paperwork, but it was also playing a long game—arresting kids for drinking only made them hate the police and that might come back to haunt everyone a few years later. Better to give them a good scare and let them get away and think they had put one over on the cops. Lennox never wanted to arrest anyone he didn't have to.

They stood in the shadow of the water tank that loomed at the summit. The tank was a sickly green, with the city's name in twenty-foot letters and the inevitable witch-on-a-broom silhouette below it. It stood behind a six-foot chain-link fence. The ground was rocky and uneven and glittering with shattered glass—brown and green beer bottles ground down to pieces the size of pebbles. And trash: some filthy clothing, moldering cardboard boxes, and even an old television with a smashed screen. There was less-identifiable junk, too, but Lennox didn't want to know what it was and didn't get too close.

"I do not want to get fucking Lyme disease up here," Dworaczyk said.

"Or tetanus," Lennox murmured. He was reminded why he never came up here anymore. It wasn't a nice spot, and while it always felt desolate and lonely, he still got the weird feeling of being watched. He was getting it again now. And the back of his throat twisted.

He quickly realized that this was more than just a two-man job. Searching the area for signs that Kelly had been there would require a dozen officers at least, fanning out over the location, step by step, for a couple of hours—like processing a crime scene. Scouring the hilltop would take the rest of the day, and they might not find any trace of Kelly anyway. But they had to check, had to follow up on every possibility.

Lennox shaded his eyes as he looked around, hoping to see a bright green poppet hidden behind a rock or tucked into the branches of a blunted tree. But there was nothing.

They made a slow circuit around the tank, looking for any sign that Kelly had been up there, that she had done her own reconnaissance on the location. But there was nothing, or at least nothing obvious now. Halfway around the tank, they startled a pair of rabbits who went bolting away through the dry brush.

"Jesus Christ," Dworaczyk murmured, hand on the butt of his holstered gun. "Those damn things almost took two."

"That's nice," Lennox replied, and kept walking.

They completed their circuit of the tank. Dworaczyk was sweating and slightly out of breath.

"There was a homeless encampment up here last year," Lennox said absently.

"Good place for one. Out of the way. Nobody would know they were up here. So this is where they used to hang the witches in the old days?"

"No. That's the next stop, unless there's anything else up here you want to take a look at."

"I am all set."

Proctor's Ledge was a lump of bedrock rising up behind the Walgreen's where Lennox used to fill his Xanax prescription. It took up an oblong of nondescript land that few people would bother paying attention to, with the store's parking lot on one side and a neighborhood on the others. The parcel itself was divided up between the homeowners, the city, and the pharmacy—a patchwork of ownership making it difficult to know just where the property lines were. A year ago, a team of researchers had confirmed what historians had long suspected: that despite what centuries of oral tradition might have said, this was the real Gallows Hill; this was the actual site of the hangings. Now it was just a piece of undeveloped land, with some rocky, wooded bluffs looking out over the Walgreen's, with a chain-link fence running along the lip to make sure no one fell off the steep edge and sued.

"I do not see the investigative value of this," Dworaczyk muttered, following Lennox up the side of the little hill. A narrow branch Lennox pushed aside whipped back to hit him on the cheek. "I think—ow, shit, watch it! —I think you are getting sidetracked."

Lennox threaded his way through the trees and didn't pay attention.

"I was wrong before when I said you have no initiative. You do, you just have the wrong kind."

"Okay," Lennox nodded.

Lennox shivered in the heat. This definitely felt like a place where people had died, where people had been killed. It felt like a three-hundred-year-old crime scene. Executed witches left swinging from a branch; at least one account described the victims being thrown into a crevice, scorned and damned, left for the elements and the animals. Lennox glanced over his shoulder, almost expecting the crevice to be right behind him. But he knew the landscape had changed considerably since the hangings. Much of the hill had been dynamited to make way for factories and mills in the nineteenth century, and the actual spot on which the hangings had taken place might no longer exist at all.

"You are not going to make sergeant, chasing after shit like this."

"Maybe you're right," Lennox said quietly.

He saw someone through the trees, fifty feet away. Then he heard a man's voice. He stopped, hand straying toward his gun. He had thought there might be a chance of finding Kelly as they checked out the various locations. It hadn't occurred to him they might find the killer instead.

A man and a woman stood in a little clearing. The woman was blonde, wearing clunky hipster glasses and a black t-shirt, standing behind a digital camera on a tripod. Not Kelly. The man was short and thick with a lumberjack beard, hiking boots and jeans, and a matching black t-shirt. They were both somewhere in their twenties.

"… at this actual location where I am standing right now," the guy was saying into the camera. He pointed to the ground manically as he spoke; his nails were painted black. He turned and scowled as Lennox drew nearer. He glanced back over at the woman with the camera and made a quick slashing motion across his throat. "Cut. Hey, we're filming something here—do you mind, dude?"

Lennox looked over to Dworaczyk, who just hooked his thumbs in his belt.

"This was your idea," Dworaczyk murmured.

"You're not really supposed to be up here, you know."

"We're filming," the woman said defensively.

"Still, you're not supposed to be up here."

"What are you gonna do, call the cops on us?" she asked.

"We are the cops."

"Well, shit, officers," the guy's shoulders slumped. "We'll be gone in another hour, two at the most. We just got started."

"Started… what, exactly?"

"Well, I don't know if you two know it or not—you're just cops—but this is the actual site where the hangings occurred back in 1692."

"Yeah," Lennox sighed. "I think I remember hearing about that somewhere."

"We're Weird Archaeology," the guy continued. He pointed to his t-shirt. The words Weird Archaeology were scribbled across the front in raised lettering over a logo: a shovel, with the blade in the shape of a skull.

"We got a YouTube channel. Over a thousand subscribers."

"Like twelve hundred, last time I checked," the woman added, one hand still on the camera.

"And this is gonna be our new upload. Right now, it's just a preliminary assessment, but we'll be back in a couple of days to really get started."

"Get started on what?"

"Excavating," the woman said.

"We're pretty sure we know where the bodies are." The guy nodded and pointed over to a couple of shovels leaning against a tree. "Now I'm not going to go into it with you—you'll have to wait for the upload like everybody else."

"No."

"Oh, we'll work fast. Always do. We'll dig fast."

"The hell you will," Lennox said, a little surprised at how angry he was.

"I don't see the problem, officers," the guy said. "If my theory is correct, this is gonna be huge."

"Hypothesis," Lennox said, rubbing his eyes. He was getting a headache. "It's a hypothesis, not a theory. And you're wrong, anyway."

"What do you mean?"

"It's the right location, but there's nothing to find up here. No bodies. Other researchers have already checked. Real researchers," he added.

Lennox had gone to the press conference when the team of historians and archaeologists announced their findings last year. The room had been packed and he stood at the back, feeling conspicuous. The team had spent nearly two painstaking years combing the little hilltop behind a Walgreen's, inch by inch, using everything from tweezers to ground-penetrating radar. They finished their work one cold December day, having concluded that there were no bodies to be found, no trace of what had happened here three centuries before.

"We took our time going over the site," the tweedy lead researcher had told the little crowd in a conference room. "We wanted to make sure that there was nothing to find, because the last thing anybody wants is for someone to show up with a shovel and start digging."

"Bullshit," the Weird Archaeologist said to Lennox now.

"How can there not be?" the woman demanded. "We did our research. We know what we're doing."

"Okay, this is city-owned land, and you're actually trespassing right now."

"If it's city-owned, then it's public property."

"Not how it works."

"We have subscribers—"

Lennox put his hands in his pockets and tilted his head back, looking calmly up at the blue sky between the leafy branches overhead.

"You are trespassing, and I am telling you to leave. Now."

"You are fucking kidding me," the guy said.

"Okay, that's it. Let's see IDs."

"You gonna arrest us?"

"Do I have to?"

"Shit. We're just trying to—"

"How about those IDs?"

The Weird Archeologists were John Sexton, 24, and April Ricci, 23, both from Worcester. Lennox took down their information, shaking his head as he did.

"How long have you been up here?"

"Couple hours."

"Seen anyone else up here during that time?" Dworaczyk asked.

"No. Like who?"

"Like a young girl, about twenty. Dark hair. Wearing a red hoodie."

"No, just us."

"I'm going to let you off with a warning," Lennox said, handing the licenses back. "But if one of those shovels even touches the ground as I watch you leave, I'll arrest you for vandalism."

"This is such bullshit."

"Look, John, I am having kind of a stupid week here, and you are really not helping. Now take your shovels and go, okay?"

Sexton shook his head. "Fine. Let's go."

April folded the tripod and angrily shoved the camera into a messenger bag. John lifted the shovels over one shoulder and together they marched past the detectives and down the hill. They stopped midway to look back. April muttered something Lennox couldn't hear and then they kept walking.

"You want to do them for trespassing, anyway?" Dworaczyk asked, watching them go.

"Kind of have enough on my plate right now as it is."

"You are way too nice to weirdoes. So this is where my Missing will be?"

"Either here or over at the park. She should be here, but she might be over there. I don't know."

"You are not being much help."

They spent another twenty minutes searching the rocky little hill for any sign that Kelly had been there. Lennox was hoping they might find a poppet hidden somewhere, but there was nothing.

"I hope I'm wrong," Lennox said. "But I think I'm probably right."

"You think she is coming out here to hurt herself?"

"I think she's coming out here to die."

Friday June 8th

Chapter VII

LENNOX WALKED HOME, his usual route: from the station on Margin, almost all the way down Washington, then right onto Church and left onto St. Peter Street, unless he took a shortcut. It took him past some of Kelly's new haunts. Rockafellas stood at the corner of Washington and Essex, on the site of the original Puritan meeting house; on the morning of her execution, Bridget Bishop had been wheeled by the meeting house in a cart on her way to be hanged. A loose board had fallen as she went by, further proof to onlookers that she was a witch. As Lennox reached the intersection, Kelly stared at him from MISSING posters on every pole, in every window, everywhere. He tried not look, knowing that her eyes were following him as he went by. She was half-smiling in the photos, but she didn't look happy; she just looked lost.

Find me, she was saying. *Find me find me find me.*

There was a you-are-here map outside Rockafellas, three feet square and mounted on posts, big red arrow in the middle. Kelly's father had taped half-a-dozen posters here, like he had been trying to paper it over entirely. Lennox saw that there was something written on one of the posters, the middle one of the group. Some heavy green scrawl that had been circled and circled. Angrily.

It looked familiar. He had seen this kind of writing before, usually chalked on the sidewalks outside witch shops, or on flyers advertising tarot readings or past-life regressions. He thought he had heard it called the witches' alphabet somewhere, but in Salem, you could never know when someone was telling you the truth, or just repeating what Wikipedia said, or making something up on the spot and trying to charge you for it. He spent a couple of minutes staring at the writing, trying to puzzle it out. Which was supposed to be the E? Was the two-letter word *me*, or *no*, or *be*, or *to*, or… *or*?

There were a couple of shops around the corner which would probably have someone behind the counter who could translate it for him. But it was better to call in official help. He took his phone from his pocket and entered a number.

"Hey. It's Lennox. I'm over by Rockafellas. Can you meet me? I kinda need your help over here. In ten? Great. Thanks."

Officer Elizabeth Harker was a trim, blonde woman who had joined the department shortly after Lennox had. In June, she was just another uniform cop, although one that might get a second glance from passing tourists who probably thought she was an actress or a model in costume rather than an actual sworn officer. But in October, as the only practicing witch on the force, she was a minor celebrity, with TV crews and bloggers all trying to snag an interview with the Witch Cop. Only Mr. Hallowe'en was a more sought-after interview that time of year.

Now she smirked when Lennox pointed to the poster.

"Wow. That takes me back."

"What is it?"

"The Theban Alphabet, supposed to be the witches' alphabet."

"Like a secret code?"

"Yeah. Kind of."

"You actually use this?" He looked skeptically at the writing.

"Yeah, when I was seventeen, in my first Book of Shadows. I think I can still write my name in it. I practiced enough." She smiled. "Plenty of people around the corner probably could have translated this, you know."

"What's it say?"

"There's probably an app."

"Okay, cool. Do you know what it says?"

"Well, those are E, those are L, those are A...."

"*Leave Me Alone*," Lennox murmured. "Right?"

"Yeah. Looks like it."

"I was worried it was going to say that."

"You think this is from your missing girl?" Harker asked.

"Until I know it's not."

"And she's your witness?"

"That's our working theory."

"And she's a witch?"

"Yeah, Wiccan. From what we know, she seems to think she's the reincarnation of Bridget Bishop. She's been visiting sites around town associated with her. Like Turner's over on Church Street, and the site of the old witch jail." He shrugged. "Probably Gallows Hill, Proctor's Ledge."

"So wait, is she a witch, or a Wiccan?" Harker arched an eyebrow.

"There's a... difference?"

"Well, yeah. Witch is general; Wiccan is specific. Like you're generally a Christian, but specifically Catholic or whatever."

"Oh. Didn't know."

"When someone calls themselves a witch, they can be kind of freestyle, picking and choosing what seems to fit. Wicca is more structured, more... initiatory, you know?"

"Okay. How did you... get started?"

He wasn't sure if this was a rude question, or at least overly personal, now that he'd asked it. Maybe it was like asking someone when they first realized they were gay.

"Well," Harker began, taking a deep breath and staring off dreamily, "when I was thirteen, I went for a walk in the woods near our house. And there was an old woman who lived out there in a hut. My parents always told me to keep away from her. But I went out there one day, and there she was. And she had this cloak, and big crazy hair, and she pointed a sword at me and said, *Thou Art a Witch!*"

"You're kidding."

"Of course I am," she laughed. "My mom was Episcopalian but not real serious; Dad wasn't really anything." She shrugged. "They kind of left me alone. I did take a lot of walks in the woods and that always felt better than being in a church. After a while, I kind of realized that outdoors *is* a church. So it kind of started from there, I guess. It's not like I had a big religious experience or anything. With most religions, they give you a book and say Do This, right? With witchcraft, eventually you find a book about it and you realize you're already doing it." She nodded toward the poster. "Is your girl in a coven?"

"Not that we know of. Does that make a difference?"

"It might give you someone to talk to in town if she was."

"Like a local chapter or something?"

"Yeah, kind of."

"The father hasn't said that she is. Are… you?" he asked.

"In a coven? Nah. I was a couple years ago, but there was just way too much fucking drama." She shook her head. "Never again. Do you know if she's reached out to anyone locally?"

"Dworaczyk says she wanted to meet Magnus."

"Okay then," Harker said.

"He's… popular, though, right?"

"Not as popular as he thinks."

"Okay, so, any other ideas?"

"I can make some calls, see if anyone knows anything, but I haven't been hearing anything about her."

"All right, that'd be good."

"You said she was visiting some of the sites associated with Bridget Bishop," Harker said. "Is this one of them? Is there some reason she did this here and not somewhere else?"

"Maybe," he said, thinking about it. It took him a moment to remember. "She was married three times—she and her second husband used to fight all the time. People kept calling the constable on them."

"Good old-fashioned domestic disturbance," she shook her head. "Nothing ever changes, right?"

Lennox had responded to dozens of domestic disturbance calls back when he was still in uniform. Harker probably had, too. Those were the calls that cops dreaded the most: walking into a violent, angry situation with no idea what was going on, no idea who was who. No idea if there was a weapon waiting somewhere. It probably wasn't any different three centuries ago.

"So she and her husband get arrested for disturbing the peace, and the punishment was either paying a fine or standing out in front of the meeting house wearing a sign for an hour. Someone pays the fine for her husband, but not for her…"

"Yeah, nice."

"The meeting house was right here." He pointed up to the Victorian Gothic brick façade of Rockafellas, with the old Daniel Low and Company sign still on the side of the building. "So she would have been standing… somewhere around here."

He looked around, almost expecting to see a woman in a red paragon bodice lurking behind him.

"Wearing a sign," Harker added.

"And not being allowed to speak."

"The good old days."

"Are you really not familiar with her?"

"Nope," Harker said.

"Thought you might be."

"Why?" she asked. "She wasn't a witch. That's kind of the whole point, right? None of them were witches." She shrugged.

"Yeah, you're right. Okay, if you can check in with… your people and let me know?"

"I will," Harker said. "Blessed be."

Saturday
June 9th

Saturday June 9th

Chapter I

STUART PICKMAN'S WAS THE FIRST civilian funeral Lennox had been to in years.

He had been to a couple of police funerals since joining the force, but they had been for officers long retired, officers he had never served with. Cop funerals were all dress blues and bagpipes and gun salutes. There were stern faces and stoic speeches about honor and duty and dedication. He didn't think he could handle gun salutes anymore—he'd probably end up reaching into a pocket for the Xanax that wasn't there. And bagpipes always made him blink away tears, even when Amazing Grace was being skirled out for an officer he'd never even met.

He'd been to his one and only Coast Guard funeral two years before, when his former CO died of a heart attack; Lennox remembered Captain Daniels having a pointed sense of humor off-duty, but being almost belligerently serious on duty. Daniels had always seen himself as Lord Admiral Nelson or something, and it was no real surprise when he'd requested that his ashes be scattered at sea. And so Lennox went to stand on the deck of a cutter for the first time in almost a decade. He still had his sea legs, and his old dress blues still fit. Gun salutes and taps and Semper P.

No dress blues for Stuart Pickman. No gun salutes nor bagpipes. Just rows and rows of mourners sitting by the grave, with more people standing behind them. Jessica had specified that the funeral was to be private, trying to keep it from turning into Hallowe'en in June. And it seemed that Mr. Hallowe'en's fans, in their horror movie t-shirts and witch hats, had stayed away. They were probably leaving their flowers and notes at the little improvised shrine in the parking lot.

And it was quiet as a crime scene.

Lennox and Ouellette stood in the back of the little graveside crowd, a few steps apart. He wore his dark blue weddings-and-funerals suit, with the knit tie that always ended up too loose or too tight. Ouellette was in a narrow black suit, with small obsidian cufflinks in a black silk shirt, her hair in a dark braid. He couldn't remember if he had ever seen her braid her hair before. He didn't think so.

Father Dutra spoke of the walking in the valley of the shadow of Death, fearing no evil, and dwelling in the house of the Lord forever, but Lennox was watching the mourners; he was good with faces, and you never knew who was going to show up, even to a private funeral. Never knew who was going to whisper something they shouldn't. But it felt cold, standing by a murder victim's grave, watching and eavesdropping and making mental notes.

The crowd grouped themselves together according to how they knew Pickman, how they fit into his life. It didn't seem to be conscious—just people naturally seeking out the familiar faces. Jessica, the new widow, stood closest to the grave, at the priest's right hand. No Emma. Lennox wondered if she was still being told that Pickman was on an unexpected trip. The next row of chairs was taken up by the Spooktacular board—he recognized most of them from the online directory he had studied the second day of the investigation. Sonya Weaver sat stiff and uncomfortable. The staffers were behind the board and, as Lennox scanned the faces, no Zachary Dykstra.

Probably just as well, Lennox thought. He wasn't sure he could face him right now.

"I believe Mayor Pyncheon has a few words," the priest said.

The mayor came to the front and stood before the tiny lectern that had been set up near the grave. He slipped his folded remarks from a jacket pocket.

"Stuart Pickman was an exceptional man, a man who truly loved Salem, and turned that love of Salem into a celebration that brought people from around the world to share it with him. His festival is the single greatest love letter to the city that anyone has ever written. Stuart and I met during my first campaign for office. He was always a strong supporter, and I was always his biggest fan. He was a generous, kind-hearted man who brightened every room he entered—a man with a Midas touch who made a roaring success out of the smallest endeavor. Mr. Hallowe'en will be missed by many thousands of visitors—visitors who never even met Stuart Pickman, the man I knew so very, very well. Today, he joins Nathaniel Hawthorne and Elias Hasket Derby on the list of Salem's favorite sons.

"And I am very pleased to say that Stuart's legacy will live on. I spoke with Sonya Weaver just this morning, and she tells me that the Salem Spooktacular's board has asked Phillip Agnew to be the new executive director. He will be joining them next week, and continuing Stuart's hard work and service to the great city of Salem."

Pyncheon looked up with his best earnest expression and held the pose for a moment, waiting for cameras to click. There were no photographers, but he was hostage to the instincts he had honed over a long political career. Lennox almost expected him to ask if there were any questions.

And Lennox saw Sonya stiffen in her seat, face flushing an angry red. Leave it to Pyncheon to make a funeral into a press announcement. Leave it to Pyncheon to make the announcement before anyone else could.

The mayor nodded to the crowd and stepped away from the lectern, flanked by a pair of bulky aides, and left.

"And let us now go in peace," Father Dutra said awkwardly.

Lennox scanned the little crowd again. Still no Zachary.

Mourners at the edges of the crowd peeled off and left in a hurry, duty done, respects paid, needing to get back to what they had been doing. Others stayed in place, murmuring what a nice service it had been, what a great loss to the community it was. A handful of others made their way over to Jessica. Going over to make sure she was *okay*, that she could *get through it all*, that she was *holding up*. And her face was a pale mask.

"Detectives?" a man quietly called to them as he approached. Lennox had seen him a few minutes before, sitting at the end of the second row, with the board of directors. He had seemed to be sitting by himself, and there was no one with him now. He was about Pickman's own age, in a dark suit over a Spooktacular t-shirt—a t-shirt with the older logo, the slightly more cartoon-looking jack-o'-lantern. The man had an angular face and straight hair pulled back in a short ponytail.

"I'm Ken Cromartie," he said, holding out a hand.

"Oh, you made it. I'm Detective Lennox, we spoke on the phone. This is Sergeant Ouellette. How did you pick us out?"

"Jessica told me." Cromartie put his hands in his pockets and looked back over the crowd as it thinned out. "Sad day. Do you know what… happened… yet?"

Civilians were never really sure how to ask the question.

"We're working on it," Lennox said. The stock cop line, as trite as *I'm sorry for your loss* at a funeral. Off-the-shelf lines used when there was nothing else to say.

Cromartie nodded and let it drop. He looked around at the uneven landscape of the cemetery.

"It's a pretty spot for him," he said quietly. "He'd like it here, I think."

Harmony Grove was one of the oldest cemeteries in town, opening in 1840 but including over a hundred graves relocated from an earlier burial ground nearby. There were thousands of burials packed into ninety-eight acres, and almost no attempt had been made to tame the landscape, to make it solemn and respectable. The steep hills and rocky bluffs and gnarled trees had been worked around, and now grieving angels and crypts and monuments shaped like cannon stood on outcroppings or were tucked into hollows or half-hidden behind boulders. Stuart Pickman's grave was not far from the Gothic chapel.

"He... didn't deserve this." Cromartie sniffed and wiped at his nose. Another glance toward the coffin. "Stu."

"We're sorry it happened," Lennox said.

"Yeah, me, too. Well, um, I should probably let you go," Cromartie said. "I am sure you have a lot to do still. Nice meeting you. Let me know if there's anything I can do." He shrugged. "I hope you catch the guy."

"Are you staying in town?" Lennox asked.

"Probably heading back tonight," he shrugged. "There's a collation back at that seafood place, used to be the Lyceum, across from the office. So I'm headed over there for a bit."

"Turner's," Lennox said awkwardly. The seafood place on Bridget Bishop's old land.

"Yeah."

"Right, well... nice meeting you."

Cromartie walked away, hands in pockets, head bowed. David Nicholson got the man's attention and Cromartie changed direction, taking his time.

"We should probably see her before we go," Lennox nodded over toward Jessica.

"Probably should."

They joined the line, right behind Kara and Antonia. Antonia was wearing a dark blue jacket that didn't match her charcoal skirt. She noticed the detectives before Kara did, and nudged her.

"Hi." Kara half-turned. "I saw you in the back. That was, um, a nice service, wasn't it?"

Lennox just nodded.

"I'm thirsty," Antonia said.

"Either of you seen Zachary?" Lennox asked.

"No," Antonia flushed. "Not since yesterday."

"Yeah, he wasn't here," Kara added.

"Know where he is?"

Kara shook her head dismissively. Antonia just turned away.

After a moment of silent waiting, Kara took a step out of line. Then another step. She glanced back at Lennox. She wanted to tell him something. Another couple of steps. Whatever it was, she wanted to say it away from the others.

"What's up?" he asked, coming over to her.

"It's been really bad over there," she whispered. "At the office."

"What do you mean?"

"Jason and Adam keep saying you're about to arrest Zachary. Like, tomorrow. Are you?"

"Can't comment."

"Jesus," she said. "You are, aren't you? Toni is really worried about him."

"I can't get into it with you. You have no idea where he is?"

"No," she sighed. She looked past him, eyes jumping from one thing over his shoulder to another. She took a deep, quick breath and blurted, "I'm quitting."

"What?"

"I gave my notice."

"Why?"

"Sinking ship," she said. "And who's Phillip Agnew? I've never even heard of him."

"Yeah, that was kind of news to me," Lennox said.

They stood together for a minute, silent and uncertain. Neither of them were sure what to say next, where the conversation went from here.

She sighed, then pointed, and he saw that the line had inched forward.

"I guess we should…"

"Yeah."

They rejoined the rest of the mourners.

When they reached Jessica a few minutes later, she looked exhausted. Pale in a black blouse, sweat on the sides of her face, scarlet hair flashing in the sun. She shook hands and nodded and said "Thank you for coming" for probably the thousandth time that day, then seemed to snap out of her little trance of decorum when she realized Lennox and Ouellette were standing in front of her.

"Oh," she said feebly. "You came."

"The least we could do," Lennox said.

"Do you—?" She bit her lip. "I mean, is there anything…?"

"Not right now," Lennox whispered. "We… should have something soon. Tomorrow, maybe."

"What?" She grabbed his arm, digging her fingers in.

"Nothing right now."

"Tell me."

"There's nothing to tell you right now. But we'll be in touch."

She let go of his arm and gave him a look, harshly disappointed.

"That could have gone better," he said once they were a few steps away.

"Could have gone worse," Ouellette said.

"Yeah, true."

The crowd was thinning as they moved back to the car. Lennox stopped and turned and looked for Zachary one last time. He still wasn't there. The familiar faces had all disappeared as the crowd dispersed.

Mr. Hallowe'en's coffin, a long box of polished wood and antiqued nickel hardware, was stark and strange there by itself as the mourners left it behind. It stood next to the fresh grave that seemed to be waiting for it. A few yards away, a couple of workmen were trying not to be noticed, shovels behind a tree, a walkie-talkie in hand, waiting to call in the backhoe. Waiting for the last person to be gone.

Ouellette stopped to thank Father Dutra for a lovely service, to assure him that he should be hearing something soon. The old priest nodded, no doubt familiar with the comforting words always offered up at such a time. Familiar and skeptical. Priests and cops saw the same things too many times, and knew that kind words and promises didn't always produce results.

They had taken about three steps when Ouellette's phone rang. She clapped it to her ear and stopped walking.

"What? Where?" She looked over at Lennox as she spoke. "Okay, we'll be right there." She put the phone back in her pocket and said, "Dworaczyk. He found something."

Saturday
June 9th

Chapter II

"**It is easy to forget** this place is even here," Dworaczyk said.

Pioneer Village was an open-air museum, a cluster of buildings meant to depict what Salem might have looked like in the very early years of the settlement, when Puritans had crossed an ocean to carve out a new world for the greater glory of God. It consisted of half a dozen or so structuress—thatched cottages, one-room cabins, an Indian wigwams, and a blacksmith shop. The largest building was a two-story house, a mansion by colonial standards, representing the kind of home the royal governor would have lived in. It had a heavy, nail-studded door and was the only building on the whole three-acre site with glass windows.

The place had opened as the nation's first living history museum in 1930, and was supposed to be staffed by costumed interpreters and reenactors offering a look at everyday seventeenth-century life. Now, nearly a century old, it qualified as a genuine historic site itself. But it had struggled to attract the ticket-buying public in recent years—it was a mile from downtown, tucked away in a public park in a quiet neighborhood. Too far away for tourists, almost ignored by locals, the cottages and cabins languished behind a chain-link fence and a palisade of wide, rough planks, and it was generally a low priority when the city voted on a new budget. The little village was now in a kind of sad, administrative limbo, neither open for the season nor officially closed, with no one to unlock the gate, no one to give tours.

On their first Hallowe'en in Salem, Lennox had let their eight-year-old daughter convince him to buy tickets to the outdoor haunt some charity was putting on at the village. Allison promised not to be scared, but shrilled as the ghouls and zombies shambled out of the houses and grabbed at her. He had been forced to carry her for some of it. It had been a fun night out with the family in their strange new city, right up until the moment he put his foot in a hole at the edge of the path and went sprawling in the mud. He was pretty sure he actually heard a bone snap as he landed. Allison bounced like any eight-year-old and was just fine. After a moment, a zombie with a rubber knife yelled, "Robert! We have an injury!"

He'd fractured his tibia and spent the next six weeks in a cast.

Now Dworaczyk was leading him and Ouellette across a little bridge and down the same path, toward the tall, two-story house. The hole was still there, and he smiled at the old memory. A fractured leg bone was still a happy memory, because they were all still together as a family, husband-wife-and-daughter, and not so... fractured, like they were now.

"I forgot about this place," Dworaczyk went on. "Only just remembered it. Figured it was worth a look. And..."

He led them past the thatched cottages, across another little bridge, and by a dry and disheveled herb garden. The door to the main building was open, and the interior probably looked pretty much as it had when the door had been locked for the end of the season last year, or the year before. There were ceramic bowls and a leatherbound Bible, and there was a dusty, broad-brimmed hat hanging from a peg over a spinning wheel. Things had been carefully arranged like a stage set; Lennox almost expected a witch-hunting Puritan to come down the stairs and accuse trespassers of consorting with the Devil.

But there was a sleeping bag unrolled on the wooden-framed rope bed. Bottles of water and a handful of protein bars were on the table. There was a plastic bag of dirty laundry under the bed, and another plastic bag of travel-size shampoo and toothpaste slung over the back of a chair, all weirdly incongruous. There was a little glass bottle of wilted flowers on the windowsill.

"We still don't know for sure it's her," Ouellette said, scanning the room. "People break in here all the time. Kids use it to party…"

"This is our girl," Dworaczyk said, pointing to the poppet over the door, wedged between the beams.

"Okay, that's weird," she said quietly.

"You have a cross over your door at home, don't you?" Lennox asked.

"So she's been here since she left the Hawthorne?" Ouellette asked. "Three nights and nobody's noticed?"

"We do not know how long she has been here, but three days and nights seems like a good guess," Dworaczyk said. "And I think she could hide out here if she was careful about it. I am not the only person who forgets about this place."

"Why here?"

"It's familiar," Lennox said. "This is the kind of place where Bridget Bishop would have lived, and, even if it's a recreation, Kelly might find it… familiar? And every time they film a new documentary on the witch trials, they film here, so she's probably already seen this place whether she realizes it or not."

Ouellette opened a bag of clothing: t-shirts and sweatshirts, still with the tags. The receipt at the bottom of the bag, dated two days ago, showed she paid cash. Another bag had underwear and socks, also new and unopened.

"She needs new clothes because everything else is back at the Hawthorne," she murmured.

"Including her meds," Dworaczyk said. "Do not forget that."

"Next steps?" Lennox asked.

"I think we should sit on this place until she comes back tonight," Dworaczyk said. "Pick her up then. Done."

"Assuming she comes back here," Ouellette said.

"She has been sleeping here, obviously. Worst-case scenario, she does not come back and I sit out here with a couple of extra guys for nothing." He shrugged. "I can always use the overtime."

"We should make sure everything is where we found it," Lennox said. "Don't want her realizing we've been here and taking off before you can talk to her."

"Obviously," Dworaczyk said.

"I can be here tonight if you like," Lennox offered. Dworaczyk nodded.

The three of them came out of the house and Dworaczyk started giving orders to the pair of uniforms standing by the nearest cottage.

And then Lennox saw her—the young woman in the red hoodie, on the far side of the little duck pond, on the opposite side of the fence. She looked at the police and then turned away sharply.

"Kelly!" he yelled. Her name echoed back.

The girl in the hoodie froze. She almost looked back and, even at this distance, Lennox could see her trying not to react, trying not to respond to someone calling her name.

"Kelly! I need to talk to you!" Dworaczyk called through his cupped hands. "Your father is very worried about you!"

And then she ran.

"*Merde*," Ouellette swore as they all sprinted for the gate.

It's too warm and it looks like it's going to rain and the park is almost empty, other than a few cars and a couple of kids on the baseball diamond. The hole in the chain link fence is around the back, and she doesn't think anyone who is in the park would be able to see her. Still, she flips the hood up and keeps her head down when she notices a police car—a blue and silver cruiser with a witch on a broom on the door.

The gate next to the ticket booth is open. It was closed when she left, closed with a padlock. But now it's open.

They've found her. All those posters downtown, the articles in the papers, she thought she was still dodging them, still slipping by everyone, but now they've found her.

And she feels the noose again.

Hands in pockets, head down, she walks casually by the cars and sneaks a look. There are two officers standing outside the house where she's been staying, where she's been hiding. And then three people come out of the house, her house. There is a rugged bald man with a moustache, and a tall woman with broad shoulders and long, dark hair. Standing with them is a skinny man, elbows sticking out, his hands in his pockets. He doesn't look like a cop. He looks more like an English teacher.

That man, the last one—he sees her and points and yells her name. And she recognizes him.

They're all cops. They have badges and guns and radios on their belts. She can see that, even this far away. But the skinny man, the tall skinny one with the sandy hair that needs a trim, he's not just another cop.

This man, the one who looks like an English teacher, he's like her. Like the people she saw at the witch trial play. She recognizes him immediately.

He was once Sheriff George Corwin, the sadistic official who had arrested her on charges of witchcraft before. Arrested her and hanged her.

And he recognizes her—she knows he does. She turns, hesitating, caught as he calls her name, her name now, and it takes her a moment to find her legs again and run. Trying to outrun him. Outrun the noose.

Tomorrow, she thinks, running. Tomorrow and it's done, it's finally over. She can't let them catch her now.

Lennox and the others got to the gate just in time to see Kelly making it over a low hill. She stopped by a tree to glance back, looking right at Lennox before taking off again, trying to put as much ground between them as possible. She was moving fast, but he might be able to catch up to her. He was a runner, too, and had chased down enough suspects and persons of interest before. But she had too much of a head start, and too much adrenaline and panic were fueling her now; he wasn't sure he could catch up.

"I need to talk to you!" Dworaczyk shouted again. His voice dropped and he shook his head. "Jesus Christ. I can have ten guys here in two minutes. Maybe we can box her in, try to corner her."

"She's a scared girl, not an animal," Ouellette said. "Is that really how you want to play this?"

"Only going to scare her," Lennox said. "Scare her more."

"No," Dworaczyk said. He shook his head, rubbed the back of his neck. "No. You are right. I will set up a watch on this place. If she comes back tonight, we will PC her and that will be that."

"She's… not coming back here."

"She didn't go back to the Hawthorne; she's not coming back here," Ouellette agreed. "Her sister said that when she gets scared, she hides, and this isn't a good place to hide now that we know."

"Well, what the hell am I supposed to do at this point? I will look pretty stupid if she does come back and no one is watching. I do not want to have to write that one up."

"At least we can tell her father that she seems to be okay," Lennox said. "She's still in Salem, nobody's got her locked in the basement, and she appears uninjured."

"But she is still listed as *Missing*," Dworaczyk said bitterly.

Find me, the posters had said. *Find me find me find me.*

Saturday
June 9th

Chapter III

"**You said you have something?**" Rick Conroy leaned forward in the chair next to Dworaczyk's desk.

"We have found where your daughter has been camping out the past few nights."

"Kelly," Rick said. "Her name is Kelly."

"Right. Where Kelly has been camping out."

"Where?"

"It's a place called Pioneer Village," Lennox said. "It's kind of an outdoor museum, replicas of old houses. It's empty most of the year now, so not a bad place to lay low for a few days. And it sounds like the kind of place that Kelly would like."

"And how do you know she was there?"

"There were indications that someone had been staying in one of the houses, and we have reason to believe it was her," Dworaczyk fell into the usual boilerplate. "And as we were searching the location, she appeared at the scene."

"You saw her?"

"Yes, we did," he smiled.

"Why… why the hell isn't she here?" her father stammered. "Why didn't you bring her in?"

"She eluded us."

"She eluded you? A twenty-year-old girl eluded the police?" He leaned back in his chair. "What are you people even doing?"

"She caught us by surprise and ran like hell," Dworaczyk said. "Your girl is fast, I can tell you that. I did not go out there expecting a foot chase."

"And she's scared enough already," Ouellette said. "Chasing after her like that would be risky."

"Risky," Rick sighed.

"The important thing is that we know she is okay, and we know she is still in town."

"You're keeping an eye on this place in case she comes back, right?"

"I do not expect her to go back, now that she knows we know she was there. But we are keeping an officer posted, just in case."

"I should probably go out there."

"No, that is a bad idea. I keep telling you, let us handle it."

"We're still pretty sure we know where she's going to be tomorrow morning," Lennox said quietly.

"Yeah. Listen, I was talking to someone downtown about that. He… had a lot to say."

"Okay. Who was it?" Dworaczyk wanted to know.

"A local." Conroy shrugged. "Someone who stopped to talk when I was handing out flyers yesterday. He asked if you were making any progress."

"So what did you tell him?"

"I told him your theory, that she'd be out at that… execution site tomorrow. Where they used to hang the witches."

"You told him that?" Dworaczyk blinked.

"Yeah. Why? What's the problem?"

"The problem is that we try to keep quiet about working theories. We do not announce them to the public." He gave Lennox a quick glare from the corner of his eye. "The fewer people who know about tomorrow, the better."

"Word gets out and you don't know who is going to show up," Ouellette said. "We can't have a crowd out there."

"Or somebody might not show up," Lennox said.

"So who was this guy?"

"I don't know. Like I said, just a local."

"You did not get his name?"

"No."

"What did he look like?"

"I... I don't know. He had a baseball hat. Sunglasses."

"Like he didn't want to be recognized?" Ouellette asked.

"I don't know."

"Would you be able to identify him again if you saw him?"

"Identify him? I... I don't know. Maybe? But... no. I don't know. I'm not good with faces. I... I feel like I've talked to a lot of people the past couple of days."

"Older or younger?" Dworaczyk asked.

"Couldn't really tell. Thirties, maybe? Could have been in his forties, I guess, but with the hat and the sunglasses..."

"Taller than you or shorter?" Lennox asked.

"Um... my height, I think? Average?"

"Fat or thin?"

"Um... average?" Rick was starting to sweat.

"And you just told this stranger everything?" Dworaczyk said.

"He was trying to help. I thought he was trying to help." He half-turned to Lennox, adding, "He had a few things to say about you, you know."

"Me?"

"Yeah." Rick's voice dropped. "He said you weren't a very good cop. He said... he said you shot someone last year."

Lennox didn't know what to say. He didn't think there was anything he could say.

"Jesus, you did, didn't you?" Conroy looked over at the other detectives. "He did, didn't he? Tell me what happened."

"Mr. Conroy—" Ouellette said.

"No, don't *Mister Conroy* me. If this guy goes around shooting people I don't want him anywhere near Kelly." He turned to glare at Lennox. "I don't want you working on this. I don't want you looking for her."

"I am the primary on your daughter's case and I choose the personnel," Dworaczyk said.

"Kelly. Her name is *Kelly*."

"And I choose who assists me in finding *Kelly* and, so far, Detective Lennox has been very helpful."

"The guy I talked to said he was… dirty."

"Dirty?" Ouellette almost laughed. "Lennox?"

"That's what he said."

"That's bullshit," she replied.

"But he did shoot someone." Rick turned back to look at Lennox again.

"I… shot a drug dealer," Lennox said quietly, looking at the floor. "He got another cop's weapon away from him and… he was about to shoot me with it. I shot first." He paused, and then whispered, "and I still have nightmares about it, in case you were wondering."

"That's… not what he told me."

"I wouldn't put a lot of faith in what he told you, Mr. Conroy," Ouellette said.

Rick Conroy leaned forward and rested his head in his hands. He sat in silence for almost a minute before speaking.

"Okay, well… I guess maybe I should go? Unless you have something else…?"

"No," Dworaczyk said.

"Okay, so… I'll just go, then." He got up and glanced over to Lennox, sitting with his hands between his knees. "I'm… sorry."

Lennox nodded, no eye contact, as the man left the bullpen.

"That went well," he murmured once Rick was gone. He took a deep breath. "Bright side… Kelly probably didn't kill Pickman."

"But whoever did, whoever the father just talked to, is probably looking for her now, too," Ouellette said.

"Looks like," Dworaczyk breathed.

The phone on Ouellette's desk rang. Two short beeps. An internal call.

"Ouellette. He's down front? Okay. Send him up." She hung up and said, "Zachary Dykstra is downstairs to report an assault."

Saturday June 9th

Chapter IV

AN OFFICER BROUGHT ZACHARY DYKSTRA up to the CID bullpen. He held his head low, and the scrapes on his face made him look paler than Lennox remembered. One eye was half-closed, not bruising just yet, but it would be soon. His lip was split and there was blood and dirt on his t-shirt. He moved slowly, flinching as he sat down in the chair next to Ouellette's desk.

"So what happened, Mr. Dykstra?" she asked.

"They went after me," he said, his voice a dry croak. "When they got back from the funeral."

"Who is they?"

"Fucking Womack and Freitas."

"All right. First, are you seriously injured? Do you need medical attention?"

"I'm… okay."

"We can have someone here in five minutes if you want," Lennox said.

"*No.*"

"Okay, so just walk us through what happened," Ouellette said.

At his desk, Lennox took off his suit jacket and loosened his tie and got out his notebook.

"I thought about going to Stu's funeral but I… skipped it." He shrugged. "I just couldn't. But then I felt bad about it, so… I went over to the what-do-you-call-it at the restaurant…"

"The collation."

"Yeah. I got there before anybody else. Nobody was upstairs. So I walked back over to the… the shrine or whatever by the office. And I was there for… I dunno, ten minutes anyway. And I heard someone say, *There he is.* And I looked up and it was Womack. Freitas was with him. And they just fucking jumped me, man. He sucker-punched me…"

"Which he was that?"

"Womack. He did this." He traced the darkening ring around his eye. "He got me twice before I… before I fell."

"Did he say anything?" Ouellette asked.

"Just crazy shit, like… like *you fucking killed him.*"

"And what do you think he meant by that?"

"Are you really asking me that?"

"It's for the report," Lennox said.

"He thinks I killed Stuart."

Lennox couldn't look up from his notes.

"So do you," Zachary added.

"What time did this happen?"

"Like, two hours ago, maybe? Little less than that."

"Were there any witnesses?"

"Yeah. David came running over, and he had Ken with him." He shook his head. "Hell of a time to see Ken again."

"Did either Nicholson or Cromartie get involved?"

"No, not really. I mean, David ran over and told them to stop, but he didn't, like, pull them off of me or anything."

"So they were still hitting you when David got there?"

"Yeah."

"They were both hitting you?"

"Mostly Adam. But Freitas… kicked me." His hand went to his side.

"What did they do when David told them to stop?"

"They stopped, but I don't think it was because of David. I think they were just… done. David told them to leave and they did." He shook his head painfully. "David asked if I was okay, if I wanted an ambulance or anything; I said no."

"What did you do then?"

"I just wanted to get the fuck out of there. So I got up. I puked. And then I walked over to Essex and sat on a bench for a while." He gave a little, unhappy snort. "Some tourist's little girl pointed at me and said, *Look Mommy, a zombie.*" He looked down at his dusty, bloody clothes, ran his hands carefully through his matted hair. "I look like shit."

"Then what?"

"I sat there for a while and I knew I had to come here and report it, but I didn't want to."

"Why not?" Ouellette asked.

He ignored the question, saying instead, "I just sat there for a while, kept putting it off, until I couldn't anymore and… here I am."

"Okay. Anything else to add? Anything else we should know?"

He shook his head.

"I'm going to need to take some pictures of your injuries," Lennox said quietly.

"Yeah, sure, why not."

"If I can have you stand over here, back to the wall." He got a camera out of his bottom drawer as Zachary rose and stood between two windows. "Just look straight ahead at me. Okay, now turn. Okay, now you said they kicked you? Can you just lift your shirt and show me where? Okay, good. Just one or two more. Thanks."

"This is all your fucking fault, you know," Zachary muttered.

"Nothing else to add?" Ouellette asked.

"No."

"Okay. I need you to sign here, and initial here," she said. "And you're sure you don't want to go to the hospital?"

"No," he said bitterly. "I'm… fine."

"We can have an officer take you home, if you like," Lennox said. "Or wherever else you need to go."

"I'm fine."

"You're sure?"

"Don't pretend you fucking give a shit about me!" Zachary Dykstra screamed. He swayed on his feet, clutched his head with both hands, steadied himself. His eyes were clamped shut, his face red. "I shouldn't have fucking come here. I shouldn't have even fucking bothered. Just… just go arrest those assholes."

"We're going to talk to them," Ouellette said.

"Are you going to arrest them?"

"Possibly, but there are procedures in place. Rules we have to follow."

"I pay your fucking salary. I want them arrested."

He signed and initialed the report with a quick, angry scribble and threw the pen down. He left without looking back.

"So what was that?" Winters called from his office door.

"Assault over at the Spooktacular," Ouellette said.

"Wasn't that your suspect?"

"Yeah."

"Does he know who assaulted him?"

"He does."

"Witnesses?"

"Yes."

"You have your work cut out for you, then," Winters said. "And tomorrow's your big day."

"Yes. We're going to have that whole area covered. We can PC her and see if she can make an ID."

"You're pinning a lot on this girl."

"Aren't we just," Lennox said.

"We have statements to get," Ouellette said. "You're driving."

Saturday
June 9th

Chapter V

THE HALL UPSTAIRS AT TURNER'S was empty, aside from a few waiters folding tablecloths and putting away chairs and snacking on untouched leftovers.

"Ended maybe half-an-hour ago," one of them shrugged. He had an African or Caribbean accent, Lennox couldn't tell which. "I think a few of them are still downstairs, though."

They found Jessica sitting at the end of the bar, flanked by her brother and David Nicholson. Three people who probably weren't sure where to go now and decided it was just easier to stay in place for a little while longer. Jessica looked up from her drink with a puzzled expression.

"Wha—?" was all she quietly managed.

"We're following up on an incident that was reported as occurring about two hours ago," Ouellette said.

"Yeah, I thought you'd be here," Nicholson muttered.

"So what happened with Zachary Dykstra?"

Jessica's expression made it clear that she had no idea what they were talking about.

"I gave Ken a ride back from the... the service and we pulled into the lot and Zachary was staring at that little shrine. I ignored him, didn't have anything to say to him. But we got out of the car, and then I saw Adam and Jason just run up to him and just start punching him."

"Both of them?" Lennox asked.

"Looked like Adam was doing the worst of it," he tilted his head. "But I think Jason kicked him once he was down. I've never seen those two like that before."

"And Ken Cromartie saw this, too?"

"Yeah, he was right there with me. He didn't know what the hell to do."

"Is he still here?" Lennox glanced around the dining room.

"No, he left kind of early."

"And you two didn't see any of this?" Ouellette asked Jessica and Trevor.

"No, I don't think we were even here yet."

"Okay. So what did you do once you got Womack and Freitas off Zachary?"

"Well, Ken and I checked to see if he was okay."

"Then what?"

"Zachary just… left, and I asked Adam and Jason what the hell they thought they were doing." He shook his head.

"So what did they have to say for themselves?"

"They said that someone had to do something."

"About Zachary?"

Nicholson nodded.

"Adam almost seemed proud," he added. "I'm going to have to fire them. Both."

"You don't seem all that… bothered by any of this," Ouellette said.

"It's been a long day and I'm just tired. And I guess I'm just not… surprised. Adam and Jason have never liked Zachary to begin with and things have been pretty… tense." "Where did you say Ken Cromartie went?" Lennox asked. "We might need to get a witness statement from him, too."

"I didn't say anything about where he went. Probably back at his hotel. Unless he told you?" he asked Jessica. She shook her head no. "He said he'd be going back home pretty soon. I guess Augusta's about a three-hour drive."

"We're going to need you to make a statement, but that can probably wait," Ouellette said. "Do you know Womack's address off the top of your head?"

Adam Womack lived on the first floor of a house near the Salem State campus. Ouellette knocked on the front door. The cop knock. The loud, clear knock that could not be ignored, the knock that let the occupant know that the police were on the doorstep. A woman opened the door and Ouellette held her badge up a few inches from her face.

"Salem PD. Looking for Adam Womack," she said. "Now."

The woman—the girlfriend, presumably, from the lack of a ring—turned and yelled, "Adam!" When he appeared a moment later with a beer in one hand, she turned and walked back down the hall, leaving him to his fate.

He took a gulp from the can and said, "What's this about?"

"We're following up on a report that you assaulted Zachary Dykstra," Ouellette said. "Need you to come down to the station."

"Maybe I… don't want to go." Another slurp, carefully insouciant. He had scabs on his knuckles.

"You can come downtown voluntarily, or I can arrest you right now." She leveled the Look at him, and waited a beat. "It's about the same amount of paperwork for me either way."

The woman's voice came from the back. *"Adam!"*

"Fine, I'll fucking go," he said, half to the detectives, half over his shoulder. He put down the beer on a little table by the door. "Let me get a jacket."

"It's warm," Lennox said. "You're fine without it."

They brought him down to the station and put him in an interrogation room and let him sit for twenty minutes before beginning. The fluorescent lights made him look pale and sullen, and brought out the black-red on his knuckles.

"Zachary Dykstra says you assaulted him," Ouellette began. Lennox silently spread out the photos he had taken on the table. Zachary Dykstra's injuries, over and over. "The assault was witnessed by David Nicholson and we have a statement from him corroborating Dykstra's allegations." She slid that across the table. "We understand that Kenneth Cromartie also witnessed the assault, and that Jason Freitas was also involved. So why don't you tell us what the hell happened."

"We came back from Stu's funeral… and fucking Zachary is right out in front of the building. He couldn't be bothered to go to the funeral, but there he was."

"Why do you think he couldn't go to the funeral?"

"You're kidding, right?"

"No. Why do you think he couldn't go?"

"If you killed someone, would you go to their funeral? Seriously?"

"That's why you assaulted him? You still think he's responsible for Stuart Pickman's death?"

"Oh, my God. Yes. He fucking killed Stuart. I know it and you know it and everyone in the office knows it. Why haven't you arrested him yet? Shit."

"You punched him. You did this, and this, and this." She pointed to the contusions and scrapes in the photos.

"This is not a big deal. Jesus. This is, like, Friday afternoon behind the gym."

"No, this is assault and battery," Ouellette said.

"This is your fault anyway," Womack said. "If you people would just do your fucking jobs and arrest him for murder this wouldn't have happened. Why am I here instead of him?"

Neither Ouellette nor Lennox answered. They waited, giving Womack a silence to fill.

"I didn't hit him that hard…"

Worked every time.

"You admit that you assaulted him in front of witnesses?"

"Yeah."

"You know assault and battery is a felony?"

"Wait, what?" He blinked stupidly. "Am I seriously under arrest?"

"Yes. Adam Womack, you are under arrest for assault and battery on the person of Zachary Dykstra at approximately eleven forty-five this morning outside Ten Federal Street, Salem, Massachusetts." Lennox handed over a Miranda sheet and a pen so Womack could initial and sign the form as he went though it. "You have the right to remain silent…"

"You know he killed Stu, right? Just admit that you know he killed Stuart!"

When they didn't answer, he bent forward until his forehead touched the tabletop.

"What happens now?" he asked eventually.

"Now we bring you down to booking and get you processed. You can call a lawyer or whoever else you want. I'll check with a clerk magistrate about bail. You're not going anywhere for a while."

"You will probably be here overnight," Lennox added.

"You are kidding me."

"No. We take felony changes pretty seriously," Ouellette said. "It's what you pay our salaries for."

*Saturday
June 9th* **Chapter VI**

Tomorrow seemed like forever away.
Lennox hadn't been able to sleep, again, and his apartment felt claustrophobic. And empty without AJ. He got his keys and walked down to the Black Museum, inhaling the warm June night through his nostrils and letting it back out. The city was quiet as he walked down the dark streets. As he walked, he tried not to think that someone had murdered Stuart Pickman, and that they still didn't really know who. He tried not to worry that Kelly Conroy, the poor, lost, afflicted girl, was out there somewhere in the dark, still missing. But if he had guessed right, she should be out at either Gallows Hill or Proctor's Ledge tomorrow—no telling which—and they could get to her before the murderer did.
Whoever the hell that is at this point, he thought.
Too much guessing, too much hoping. And not enough sleep.
He couldn't get the pale, battered image of Zachary Dykstra out of his mind.
Sometimes, he really missed the Xanax.
He unlocked the door of the museum and thumbed off the alarm. It was cool in the building, and quiet, like it always was.
He tried to distract himself with the to-do list. He wanted to try something new with the lighting on the H. H. Holmes display. He was never quite happy with it. Holmes was lit in a lurid green and he wondered now if a deep red would be more flattering or simply too clichéd. He needed to order more t-shirts; the orange ones with the seventeenth-century woodcut of a German witch

on a broom were on backorder. The maroon *I Survived The Black Museum!* t-shirts didn't seem to be selling at all; he would probably have to mark them down. He checked the register and the safe. He needed change. He would have to leave Cameron a note about that: it was past ten o'clock now, and he wasn't going to be making it to the bank himself in the morning.

He moved among the looming murderers and criminals, repositioning this mannequin a few inches, adjusting the lighting on that one, never quite satisfied. The whole museum was a sprawling work-in-progress. He could never really decide if that was okay, never knew if it was because he was always looking for perfection, or always falling short of it. Maybe he was just bored.

The last section of the museum held the witch trials triptych. He stopped by the figure of Bridget Bishop, standing on an Astroturfed Proctor's Ledge, with Sheriff George Corwin looping the noose around her neck. Corwin was a refitted department store mannequin and Lennox had always been surprised by how little work had been needed to make a jeans-and-sweatshirt display into the grim and scowling High Sheriff. Bridget had been a special commission from a local artist, her head and shoulders 3D-printed; he was still paying that off in installments. He had been unsure whether to go with the middle-aged matron of history, or the saucy younger wench of legend, so he had split the difference. Bridget Bishop had bright glass eyes, smooth cheekbones, streaks of gray in her polyester hair, and firm plastic cleavage nestled in her plunging red bodice. He had bought a poppet from Magnus years before for the display; Bridget had it clutched in her hand. That part probably wasn't historically accurate, he knew, but it seemed fitting.

But there was another one now, just peeking out from under the hem of her skirt.

The display was behind a black metal rail and up on a platform, but if someone stretched forward and was willing to risk losing their balance, the hem of Bridget Bishop's skirt was just within reach.

"You have got to be kidding me," he muttered.

Kelly had been here. Stood right where he was now. He swung a leg over the railing and retrieved the poppet. He spent a long moment wondering what exactly she might have seen when she looked at the figure.

And he jumped as someone knocked at the door.

It was past eleven. There shouldn't be anyone knocking. Unless it was the couple from the other night, back for another sneak peek. At least they had been nice.

Another knock.

Was that a cop knock?

He moved down the corridor and crossed the lobby to unlock the door and pull it open.

It was Ouellette.

"Saw the light on," she said quietly.

"Oh. Yeah, well, I couldn't sleep, so…" He shrugged.

Off-duty Ouellette looked exactly like on-duty Ouellette. A bright silk man's Oxford shirt with cufflinks. Dressy slacks and riding boots from back when she had been in Mounted. Dark hair back in a short ponytail. No makeup. The only real difference was no badge, no gun, no radio.

"Do you… want to come in?" They had worked together for seven years now, and she had never once visited the museum, as far as he knew. It really wasn't her kind of place, he thought.

She nodded hesitantly and brushed past him and he got a whiff of alcohol as she went. Was that beer? She stood in the little lobby, looking over the ticket-counter and the velvet-roped archway that led to the rest of the museum. She nodded and almost smiled.

"Never been here before," she said, sliding her hands into her pockets. "It… looks nice."

"Do you… do you want to see the rest of it?"

"What? Oh, no. No." She shook her head and then said, "I'm sorry, I am just having really shitty week."

"Oh," was all he could think to say.

He and Ouellette had been partnered for seven years now. She was very private, and they spent no time together off-duty, even after working together for so long. He really knew very little about her. He had met her sister and her son a couple of times, but the last time was over a year ago now. He had always been the weirdo, the one who didn't fit the image of a cop, and he sometimes felt she must have drawn the departmental short straw and gotten stuck with him. But now, as she stood there strangely out of place in his lobby, this tall, raw-boned woman in a man's shirt, his partner who almost never talked about herself, the resolutely single mom who never spoke about Roland's father, he realized that maybe she was a weirdo, too. Maybe they had gotten stuck with each other.

"Yeah. Sorry I had to run out on you like that the other day, but I had a… situation."

"I wondered what was going on," he said. He hadn't asked because he didn't think she would have ever told him. They might not be friends, but he still knew her.

"My sister has a new boyfriend," she began slowly. "Frank. They met at a bar a couple of months ago, and she says they really hit it off. But when I met him, he was really uncomfortable around me. New girlfriend's sister is a cop—nobody ever likes that."

Lennox knew the feeling. People became guarded and cautious around cops. They were supposed to feel safe with a cop around, but they rarely ever did.

"Just the usual, or something else?" he asked.

"He has a record," she nodded. "Possession. Did a year over in Middleton for larceny. But I told Joanie that I can't have that shit around the house. Not around Roland." She half-laughed. "We Ouellette girls, we sure can pick 'em."

Lennox wasn't sure what to say to that.

"So we had it out and things haven't been great at home the last couple of weeks."

When he had graduated the academy, the head officer, grim and straight-backed like a Puritan preacher warning his congregants to cast out the Devil, said that there was no place for lawbreakers in their lives now that they were sworn officers. No place, except on the business end. Even if this meant cutting ties with lifelong friends or even family, they could no longer associate with known criminals. They were to be shunned.

"So did something in particular happen yesterday?" he asked.

This wasn't the kind of conversation he'd ever imagined having with Ouellette. She was always so private, so buttoned-up. He never thought she would confide in him because he couldn't imagine her confiding in anyone. And besides, this kind of conversation should probably be taking place at a bar, or at a kitchen table—not next to a life-sized figure of John Billington and his blunderbuss.

"He got picked up," she said. "Hit a liquor store in Marblehead. Said he was armed but wasn't. The cashier beat the shit out of him."

"Good for the cashier," Lennox smirked.

"So he got hauled down to the Marblehead station. He called her, and she called me. Wanted me to talk to them and get him out. Wanted big sister to step in and fix things like we were in middle school again."

Lennox nodded. Everybody was uncomfortable around cops, until they wanted something. Wanted a parking ticket fixed. Or a sketchy boyfriend released. Or a weird guy in 110 checked out.

"So what did you do?"

"Went over there, talked to my sister, talked to the arresting officer," she gave an eighth-of-an-inch smile, "and I left his ass there."

"You did?" he laughed.

"What was I supposed to do?" she asked, starting to laugh now, too. He couldn't think of the last time he had heard her laugh. It was a loud, braying kind of cackle that didn't seem to suit her at all. And he could smell the alcohol again.

"You wouldn't even pull strings for your own sister. That's harsh."

"What was I supposed to do?" she asked, suddenly not laughing. At all.

"I get it. I absolutely get it. So how did your sister take it?"

"She didn't talk to me when I got home. For the rest of the night. And tonight's her night to watch Roland. I was supposed to go to yoga tonight."

"Yoga?"

"Yeah. What?"

"Nothing." He couldn't picture Ouellette in lotus position, or downward dog, taking deep, cleansing breaths. "So you skipped yoga?"

"I went for a drive. I had a beer and a shot across the street and had to tell three different guys to fuck off in just over an hour. So I saw you come in, and…"

"Well, that's good," he said clumsily. "I'm glad I was here. Is there… anything I can do?"

She shook her head.

"You think you two will be… okay?"

"Yeah," she said. "Yeah, I'm sure we will." She shifted from one foot to another, and her posture and expression shifted with it. She folded her arms. "So, tomorrow…"

"Yeah, tomorrow's the big day. And I just found something a minute ago…" He had tossed the poppet behind the counter on his way to answer the door and he picked it up again now. "She was here. I don't know when—I can check the security camera footage—but she came here and left this."

"Another one of those puppets?" Ouellette took it from him, turned it over in her hand.

"Poppets. Yeah. She was here." He shrugged. "That doesn't tell us anything, though."

"Still, good to know. I guess. So you still think between eight and twelve tomorrow?"

"Yeah. Her death warrant orders the sheriff to bring her to the place of execution between eight and twelve. So that's our window."

"And it's either the park or the hill behind Walgreen's?"

"Right. Proctor's Ledge. Legend says it's the park, history says it's behind the Walgreen's." He shrugged. "Depends on how historically accurate Kelly wants to be tomorrow."

"We're set to cover both locations starting before seven." She yawned and looked at her watch. "It's almost eleven now. *Merde.* We should both get some sleep."

"Guess so. Are you, um, okay to be driving?"

"I had a beer and a shot. And I'm Canadian. I'm fine."

"Right. Okay. I should probably pack it in, too."

She nodded and took a couple of steps toward the door. She stopped and looked down at the toes of her boots before straightening her shoulders again, turning to look him in the eye.

"Thank you," she said quietly.

"Yeah, sure," he replied. "You're welcome."

It seemed like he should probably hug her or something. But hugging Michelle Ouellette was the most awkward thing he could imagine right now.

She took a quick look around the lobby—the ticket counter with its fake jailhouse bars, the *Wanted* posters on the far wall, the scowling John Billingham—and gave another tiny grin.

"This place looks kinda cool," she said.

"You should come back on your day off. I'll give you a discount."

"See you in the morning," she said.

"Yeah. Yeah, I'll be there."

Sunday
June 10th

Sunday June 10th

Chapter I

"GOOD MORNING, EVERYONE," Ouellette said, glancing at her notes and then checking the clock on the wall of the muster room. 6:45 a.m. Two dozen uniforms crowded into the room, with Dworaczyk standing to one side and Lennox in the back. Ouellette's hair was slightly damp, but other than that, she looked like she did any other morning. No sign of her late night. Lennox sipped his coffee, and grabbed a doughnut from a box that was being passed around.

"We have a lot to go over," she said.

She clicked a button and a picture of Mr. Hallowe'en filled the projection screen behind her.

"This is our victim, Stuart Pickman. His body was found Monday night in the parking lot at Ten Federal Street, stabbed to death, pronounced at the scene."

One more click and the sullen-eyed photo of Kelly from the posters appeared behind Ouellette.

"Kelly Conroy is visiting from Milwaukee. She is missing, and was last seen yesterday," Dworaczyk said. "There is evidence placing her at the scene of Pickman's murder, and we regard her as a probable eyewitness. Lennox."

"Kelly believes she is the reincarnation of Bridget Bishop, the first person to be hanged for witchcraft, on this day in 1692. Our working theory is that Kelly is planning to visit the execution site today."

Ouellette put up a map and tossed him a laser pointer.

"Records indicate that Bridget Bishop was taken from the jail, which is where the Telephone Building is now, and put into the back of a cart that went south on Washington, then west on Essex, and then north-west onto Boston Street." He traced the route as he described it. "According to one account, she was passing the meeting house when a board broke loose and fell. The meeting house was on the corner of Essex and Washington, where Rockafellas is now, which is how we know they went south to Essex, instead of north to Bridge Street."

"Is this going to be on the test?" someone asked.

"Her death warrant orders her to be executed between the hours of eight o'clock and noon," Lennox went on. "So that's our window."

"And we have reason to believe that whoever murdered Pickman knows all this," Ouellette said. "So he will also likely be at the location, or maybe somewhere along the route, trying to get to her first. Obviously we aren't going to let that happen."

"Do we have an actual suspect?" someone asked.

"Not at this time," Ouellette said, after glancing over at her partner.

"We are positioning cars at several locations along the route she will probably be taking," Dworaczyk said, getting the laser pointer from Lennox. "One here in front of the old Telephone Building, one here at Washington and Essex, and another here at Essex and Boston. The rest of us will be down here—I am with team one, in Gallows Hill Park, and Ouellette and team two will be down here in the Walgreen's parking lot. If anybody sees Kelly anywhere along the route, pick her up immediately and PC her."

"Why are we covering two locations?" someone else asked.

Ouellette nodded over to Lennox.

"Because we don't know which of those places she's going to go to. Oral tradition says the executions took place at the top of Gallows Hill in the park, but historians say it's behind the

Walgreen's. Now Kelly's not real... grounded, and we don't know if she's going to go with oral tradition or academic research, so we're covering both."

"And we have someone covering the service road that leads up to the water tank, too," Dworaczyk said.

"You're sure she's going to follow this route?"

"It's our best guess right now."

"And she's crazy?"

"She is not well," Dworaczyk said. "And she is off her meds, as far as we know."

"One other thing," Lennox said. "Bridget Bishop was known for wearing red, and we saw Kelly yesterday in a red hoodie. So she could be wearing red."

"But there's no guarantee," Ouellette added. "Don't get lazy and just look for girls in red. Eyes on everybody."

A hand went up in the back.

"Just to be clear, what is she supposed to be doing once she gets out there?"

Ouellette and Dworaczyk both looked at Lennox.

"We're not entirely sure," he began slowly, "but our main concern is that if she is acting out Bridget Bishop's last day, then it makes sense to think that she might be going out there to hang herself. We're hoping we're wrong, but... we might not be."

We? He thought as he said it. No, make that *me*.

"And we can't let that happen, either," Ouellette said. "Finding her clears two cases. Any other questions? No? All right, everyone, let's get in position."

Twenty minutes later, Lennox and Ouellette were in the back of an unmarked van in the Walgreen's parking lot, with a uniform in the driver's seat. There were cruisers on the other two streets, hemming in Proctor's Ledge. Dworaczyk was in an unmarked car in the lot over at Gallows Hill Park, with a couple more cruisers tucked away on other streets, out of sight.

Lennox squinted out the van's tinted windows, looking up at the rocky, overgrown hill and its scraggy trees and the chain-link fence. Salem's oldest crime scene, half-forgotten back behind a drug store. He was hoping to see a flash of red, but there was nothing.

Taking a deep breath, he counted to three, and slowly blew it out. It was warm in the back of the van. Claustrophobic.

"You all right?" Ouellette asked.

"Yeah, I'm fine."

She picked up the radio. "Anybody see anything?"

"Skateboarders," Dworaczyk replied. He and his team were over in Gallows Hill Park, a short distance away—five minutes at a run, probably less—but not visible from where Ouellette and her team were positioned. "All boys, though. And a woman with a stroller, but she's too old."

The cruisers reported in: no, nothing, negative, and nope.

"What if she doesn't show?" Lennox asked.

"This was *your* theory," Ouellette said.

"What if I'm wrong?"

"It's not even nine o'clock. We still have until noon."

"If I'm right. What if I'm not right?"

"Then we'll figure something else out."

Another deep breath. Way too hot in the van. He was getting thirsty.

The radio crackled. "This is unit three, we might have something. Stand by."

Team three was closer to downtown, at the intersection of Essex and Boston—the intersection Kelly should be passing through as she retraced Bridget Bishop's last moments.

Lennox realized he was holding his breath again.

"This is team three. False alarm. We had someone in a red hoodie, but it ain't her. Disregard."

"You're sure it's not her?"

"Teenage guy with long hair. So yeah, pretty sure."

"Dude looks like a lady," Dworaczyk said over the radio.

"Everyone back to work," Ouellette ordered. "We're still here 'til noon."

Lennox looked up at the rim of Proctor's Ledge. Still nothing red.

"Should I go back up there?" he asked. He had done a quick check of the hill when they first arrived, looking for any sign of Kelly, but had found nothing

"No. We have all three approaches covered. She can't get up there without us seeing her. And we can't let her see you first."

"Yeah. True."

Kelly had seen him out at Pioneer Village. And there was no knowing what she might do if she saw him out here. She might run again. They might lose her again. She might get hit by a car trying to get away.

"All teams report in," Ouellette said into the radio. "Anybody see anything?"

Federal Street, Washington and Essex, Essex and Boston all reported negative. No sign of Kelly.

Maybe he'd been wrong about all of this.

It was way too hot in the van.

Ken Cromartie had left early. Maybe he hadn't left at all? Maybe he'd already been in Salem when the reporter from the *Advertiser* got a hold of him. In town since the night before. Maybe he'd been sitting in a coffee shop on Essex Street when Lennox called, wearing a baseball cap and a pair of mirrorshades. Maybe David Nicholson wanted Pickman finally out of the way, certain that he was the only logical choice to replace him. Maybe Trevor Meyers thought that Pickman needed to do the right thing and marry Jessica, the mother of his child.

Getting hotter in the van.

Maybe... maybe Adam Womack and/or Jason Freitas were guilty. They had just shown themselves to be violent. Maybe it was Womack, dragging Freitas along with him as an accomplice.

Maybe they had been right the first time, and Zachary Dykstra was a really good actor—good enough to beat the polygraph… which wasn't even reliable to begin with.

But maybe it was worse than that. Maybe it had been Kelly all along. The lost, delusional girl, off her meds…

Lennox pulled open the door and staggered out into the parking lot. His knees and ankles were wobbly. His heart raced and he was soaked in ice-water sweat. He doubled over and puked colorfully into a bush at the edge of the parking lot. He'd been trying to make it to the trash can, but was just a few steps short. He straightened up and wiped his mouth on his sleeve, nodding over to the officers in the cruiser parked next to the van.

He glanced over at the Walgreen's. This was where he used to fill his Xanax prescription.

He spit a couple of times, trying to clean the stinging taste of bile out of his mouth. His hands stopped shaking and he could still feel his heart, but not in the same way he had just a few seconds ago. Deep breaths. He felt better. Not good, but better.

A red car pulled up and parked a few spaces over. Something somewhere on it was loose and rattled as it drove into the lot. There was a square, magnetic decal on the side.

A shovel with a skull for a blade. Weird Archaeology.

John Sexton and April Ricci got out of the front and started taking short-handled shovels out of the trunk. John shouldered them and reached back into the trunk for the camera bag. April glanced around a little nervously. She noticed Lennox, and tugged at John's sleeve.

Lennox smiled weakly and then had to spit again.

John threw the shovels back in with a clatter and angrily slammed the trunk, swearing the whole time. He pointed April to the passenger side and got into the car. He gunned the engine and left, tires whining as he went.

"Get in the van," Ouellette called.

He climbed back into the van and slammed the door behind him.

"You okay?" Ouellette asked.

"Never better," he said.

Ten minutes later, 11:10 a.m., the call came in. A 911 call reporting a man chasing a girl in a red hoodie down South Street. A skinny man, in his twenties, wearing a knit cap. Carrying a small, orange-handled knife.

South Street was in a residential neighborhood on the other side of Gallows Hill, the opposite side from the park. It dead-ended at the foot of the hill.

"Zachary?" Lennox asked.

"We're in the wrong place. We're all in the wrong place," Ouellette said. "*Tabarnak de crisse.* Everyone, move out. Now."

"Wait," Lennox said.

Sunday June 10th

Chapter II

SHE CLIMBS THE LITTLE HILLOCK SLOWLY, carefully, eyes down, hands clasped before her. Step by step. She holds her breath as she goes and she can hear her pulse in her ears. And she can feel the noose, always the noose. It's tighter now, tighter than it's ever been.

She almost can't believe she's here. Everything has been pointing her here, bringing her here—here to Salem, here to the site of her hanging, here to this moment. This has been the longest week of her life, and she tries to step back from that now, tries to make it not matter but she can't. Because it does. Because it all matters.

She's exhausted. She barely slept last night. She couldn't go back to her little village, her little hiding place, not after the police found it. Just like she couldn't go back to the Hawthorne. She slept briefly on a bench or under a tree, nowhere else to go. Feeling desperate, cycling through fear and anger and hopelessness. Once again, Salem had become a series of places closed off to her, leaving her with no place but here.

She's filthy. The grime is in her hair and under her nails. She bought a new hoodie yesterday—a black one this time. Only fitting as she goes to the place of execution.

She tries to remember the last time, and the memory comes down to her through the centuries. She remembers Sheriff Corwin shoving her into the cart without a word, remembers rolling roughly down the narrow, dusty streets while people watched.

Not all of them stayed silent as she went by. She remembers a board breaking loose as she passed the meeting house. Some onlookers yelled that that proved her a witch, and she had just smiled grimly. Arriving here on the summer morning so long ago, Corwin grunted as he hauled her from the cart and forced her to climb a ladder leaning against a tree. The tree with a noose hanging from one bough, swaying slightly in the warm breeze. The hanging tree on the hanging hill.

She remembers the little crowd, some standing mute and others crying out to let the witch hang. Familiar faces in the crowd, friends and neighbors, staring at her and waiting to watch her die. She remembers Corwin tying her hands behind her back, tying her skirts around her ankles. Placing the bag over her head. She remembers him yanking the ladder away....

A bird squawks and flies up, startling her. And she laughs, surprised at how jumpy she is. She takes deep, slow breaths, trying to calm down.

She moves into the little clearing near the top of the hill, the little clearing that she visited a few days before. She looks up at the trees. She can't remember which one tree is *the* tree. None of them look quite right to her somehow. She folds her hands and bows her head and waits. She'll know when it is time. She kneels and waits.

Her mind is pulled back to her first night in Salem. The night she saw that man killed, the night the killer chased her before she lost him in the tangle of little streets. Terrifying. But she knew then, and she knows now, that she couldn't go to the police. The angry authorities, the grim town fathers, the hate-faced magistrates, had all betrayed her before. She can't go to them again.

She tries to banish those thoughts. That's not why she's here now. She takes a deep breath and focuses on the noose.

She has no idea how long she has been there, waiting for the right moment, the moment when she'll *know*. It'll be different this time. It'll be right. Last time was a mistake—that was never supposed to happen. But this time...

Someone's coming. Somewhere off to her left. She hears someone moving, branches crack, a shoe scrapes on the rocky ground. Someone is creeping up behind her. There shouldn't be anyone up here today. Not now. This is her time. Only she belongs here today. She shakes her black hood down; leaving it up cut her off too much, let whoever it is get too close. She turns to see who is intruding.

It's *him*.

The man she saw her second night in town. The man with the knife. The man who had been talking to her father. The killer. He's wearing the sunglasses again, like he was the other day, but she knows him. She knows that face, the same grim face she saw under harsh lights in the parking lot. That night, he looked angry. Now he just looks resigned.

He's carrying a black gym bag, ballistic nylon shimmering in the sun. She can't move as he reaches into the bag now, taking something from it and letting the bag drop.

And he's holding a noose.

She can't find her legs. They're gone.

One hand goes up to her own throat. It's the only movement she can seem to make right now. Can't get up. Can't run. Can't even turn away. Can't take her eyes from his.

Now he smiles. Slowly, with teeth clenched.

He's not supposed to be here. Not supposed to be coming closer and closer.

He raises the hand carrying the noose… and now she can move.

She scrambles in the dirt, trying to get up off her knees. She used to run track. She got away from him before and she knows she can get away from him now. She has to.

But he's too quick, bounding across the space between them in a few long strides. And then he has her by the hair. She turns and kicks, a heel to his knee.

He stumbles back a couple of painful steps.

"Fuck," he hisses.

She's on hands and knees and he lunges, catching the back of her jeans. He swings the noose, tries to loop it over her head, but she dodges, and it lands in the dirt, only a few inches away. She knows he won't miss again. She twists and kicks again—the kick doesn't connect, but he loses his grip on her.

She gets to her feet and takes a few frantic steps before her foot hooks on something, a rock or a root, and it sends her right back down to the ground. There's dirt in her eyes, in her mouth. She starts to get up but his hand is planted in the middle of her back now, pinning her to the ground, pressing her into the dirt.

She can't stop him from getting the noose around her neck. She knew he couldn't miss a second time.

He pulls sharply and she sees stars. She is able to get a couple of fingers under the rope but she knows it won't help her. He pulls and drags her as she thrashes helplessly. She gets her eyes open just long enough to see that he is dragging her toward a big tree nearby, one with a heavy bough jutting out, eight or nine feet up the black trunk. She closes her eyes, knowing that he's throwing the other end of the rope up over the branch and she can't breathe as her feet leave the ground.

Cruisers and unmarked cars shrieked down South Street and skidded to a halt. Ouellette and Dworaczyk sent the uniforms fanning out, checking up and down the street and into the playground at the foot of the hill. Just a few kids on the swings and some mommies sipping their morning coffee. Ouellette pointed to the path that ran up the side of Gallows Hill, and two officers started jogging up the rise, hands on holstered weapons.

She went over to one of the women, speaking quietly, trying not to panic anyone.

"Ma'am, have you seen a girl come through here? She might have been wearing a red hoodie?"

"What?" The young woman blinked. She was wearing a Patriots sweatshirt and baggy pajama bottoms. Her bottom lip was pierced with a small silver hoop. "No."

"Seen a skinny man in a knit cap?" She didn't want to mention the knife. Not unless she had to.

"No."

"You're sure? This would have been sometime in the last ten minutes, maybe."

"No, quiet here today."

"Any weirdoes hanging around the park?"

"Weirdoes? No. What do you mean, weirdoes?"

"Anybody hanging around watching or anything like that?"

"No." She blinked again and slurped her coffee. "You looking for someone?"

"We're just following up on something."

"Is this serious? Should I take my kid home?"

Ouellette couldn't have civilians cluttering up the area.

"It's probably nothing, but it might be a good idea for now, until we get this sorted out. You live nearby?"

"Right down there," she gestured down the street. She stood up and called to her daughter. "Caitlin! We gotta go now."

"Aw, Mom!"

"Let's go. No arguing."

The woman half-dragged Caitlin out of the park as Dworaczyk came over to Ouellette, shaking his head.

"I knocked on a couple of doors and nobody has seen anything," he said. "No guy in a knit cap, no girl in a hoodie. Nobody chasing anybody."

"And whoever called it in didn't leave a name," she said, looking around.

Ouellette's radio crackled. The two officers had reached the hilltop and there was no sign of anyone being up there so far.

"I think this is bullshit," Dworaczyk shook his head.

"False alarm. False report to get us off the real scene. *Merde*," she swore. "Good thing he's still over there." Back to her radio. "Lennox, report."

Silence.

"Lennox, report."

Nothing.

He'd insisted on staying back at Proctor's Ledge. Insisted he was right about which location Kelly would pick.

"Andrew?... *Sacrament.* Let's *move.*"

The cruisers and the unmarked cars screamed back down South Street.

Sunday
June 10th

Chapter III

LENNOX RAN THROUGH SOMEONE'S YARD. He was pretty sure it was a vegetable garden he'd just crashed through, but he couldn't stop now. There was no fence along the back of the homeowner's property, just a sudden line of unkempt brush that seemed to mark where the yard ended and Proctor's Ledge began. He jumped over a fallen log and began weaving through the skinny trees, one hand on his holstered weapon.

He could see movement ahead of him now. Two figures.

A tall, rangy man was hauling a young woman up off the ground by a rope tied around her neck.

Hand over hand, higher and higher.

Kelly kicked and twisted in the air, a few feet off the ground now, hands struggling with the rope, trying to get more fingers under it. Her body slowly turned in his direction and her eyes locked onto him as an awful grinding noise came from deep down in her throat..

The man half-turned, and Lennox saw his face.

It was just him. And the girl. And the rope.

I shouldn't even be out here right now, he thought, hauling on the rope, hand over hand. The rope burned his palms as he pulled. *This is all Stuart's fault. Stuart-goddamn-Pickman. Mr. Hallowe'en.*

This all should have ended right where it began, out in the parking lot just a few nights ago. Getting rid of Stuart was the simple, obvious solution. But Stuart was dead and buried and still causing me trouble, he thought.

He didn't want to kill this girl. He knew had to, but he didn't want to. He wouldn't have to if she hadn't blundered onto the scene, but now she was just something else to deal with. Another problem. It kept him up nights, knowing she was out there somewhere. That she'd seen his face. He was going to have to find her before the cops did.

Hand over hand. Inching higher. Just him, and the girl, and the rope. His back was starting to ache with the effort. She was struggling now, twisting and kicking and choking.

Damn it, Stuart. I shouldn't even be out here right now. This is all your fault. Just like everything else always was. Her blood is on your hands, not mine. You're the one who made this necessary.

He'd followed her out here, slowly stalking her down Essex and onto Boston, half-admiring the way she managed to slip by the police, like she knew how to be invisible, unnoticed. He couldn't just grab her off the street, with too many people around. Had to let her get out here, away from everyone, between the trees on this little hill. Then he could get this finished.

Just a little higher, he thought. A little higher and it would look like she climbed up on that branch and jumped. It would all look plausible.

The Salem PD isn't exactly the best and brightest, he'd told the father—the stupid desperate father who had no idea who he was talking to. But he was still right. All is took was one quick call from the payphone inside Walgreen's to get rid of them, to clear the way for him.

And now it was just him and the girl. And the rope. He pulled again and it slipped. She yelped as she fell a foot and he pulled again, the rope stinging his palms.

He'd been lying to that Lennox's face all week, and every time, he thought this was it, this was the last time the guy was going to believe it. This weird, awkward cop was finally going to see through him and arrest him for Stuart's murder. But no, he never did.

He smiled now. Two more minutes. If that.

Him, and the girl, and the rope.

She can't breathe.

She can't breathe and she can't see and she can't hear. She's not even sure she can feel her body anymore. She thinks she's struggling, thinks she's trying to get fingers under the noose around her neck but she really can't be sure. She can't be sure of anything right now.

Not like this, she thinks. *Not like this not like this not like this.*

She wants to scream but she can't.

Everything is slowly turning red.

"David Nicholson! Salem PD! Let her go!" Lennox shouted. *"Do it now!"*

Kelly was going to die if he didn't get her down. She wouldn't die of a broken neck like this. She'd suffocate, like the nineteen men and women hanged here before. She would stop struggling, slowly strangle, her brain would slowly die, horribly aware of everything almost right up to the end, and then her body would just sway heavily in the wind, if it moved at all.

Back at the station, there had been some talk of placing a marksman on the Walgreen's roof, but Ouellette didn't think it would be necessary. And back at the station, Lennox had agreed. But right now, it seemed like a pretty damn good idea. A civilian's life was in danger. A father's daughter. Their eyewitness. A lost tourist who had wandered into a homicide.

Nicholson all along. Nicholson had been looking for her, hunting her. Nicholson found her father, handing out flyers on Essex, trying to find out what he knew, what the police knew. So he could find her first. Nicholson must have been somewhere nearby, watching. And when he saw her, he phoned in that tip, gave them Zachary's description, sending them chasing after nothing, trying to buy himself enough time to kill Kelly and leave her out on Proctor's Ledge.

... conveyed her to the place provided for her execution and caused the said Bridget to be hanged by the neck until she was dead and buried in the place, all which was according to the time within required....

Nicholson looked at Lennox and his eyes narrowed.

"Don't," Lennox said quietly. *Don't make me.*

He took a deep breath in, and held it for just a second. Training said to pull the trigger on the exhale.

And Nicholson let go of the rope and broke into a run as Kelly hit the ground.

Lennox let out a shaky breath and blinked. There was silence on Proctor's Ledge.

Kelly or Nicholson? he thought. Chase the murderer or secure the witness?

"I've got her," Ouellette's voice rang in his ear. She was running up the hill, Dworaczyk and a bunch of uniforms right behind her, guns drawn. "Get him!"

Nicholson hadn't gotten far. Lennox could see him through the trees, pounding across the rocky soil. He seemed to be making for the chain-link fence a few yards distant. There was nothing but a rocky drop on the other side of it.

Lennox holstered his gun and went after him.

"Stop where you are!" he shouted. "On the ground! Now!"

Nicholson slammed into the fence. He whirled to face Lennox. He was out of breath, his eyes wide, his face a bright, bloody red. The fence was too high for him to get over here. He made a run for it. The fence stood on the lip of the hill, the rocky bluff rising over the Walgreen's lot. Following its length would lead him down the slope to the street a hundred yards away.

But the uniforms had fanned out and a couple of them were blocking Nicholson's escape now.

"Don't move." Lennox shook his head. "You don't have anywhere to go. You're done."

Nicholson looked at the uniforms, at Lennox, and then at the twenty-foot drop on the other side of the fence behind him. There was less than a foot of space there before the ground ended; it wasn't a cliff face, but it was still a long, rocky way down to the parking lot below.

Nicholson was the planner, the problem-solver that Pickman always needed. He was the one who came up with the solutions, found the way out. Kelly had witnessed him solving one problem, which only made her the next one. And this was his solution: kill her, and make it look like that poor, lost, afflicted girl had hanged herself, just like the police were afraid she might. And then the story would be obvious: the troubled young woman, off her meds, killed Pickman, and hanged herself behind the Walgreen's in remorse. Case closed.

But that plan was gone, now. That plan was in pieces. Now he had nothing. The only thing worse than a man who had it all planned out was a man being forced to make it all up as he went along.

Nicholson shrieked and grabbed the bar along the top of the fence, hauling himself up and over. Lennox wasn't close enough to grab him before he landed precariously on the other side. He was clinging to the fence, fingers laced in it, perched on the narrow, uneven edge. He looked down, then back at Lennox.

"What are we even doing right now?" Lennox asked.

The uniforms were a few feet away. They looked to Lennox for instructions, but he didn't know what to tell them.

"Don't do anything stupid…" was all he managed to say before Nicholson jumped.

He launched himself off the edge, twisting his body in mid-air, throwing his arms out in front of him to break his fall. He seemed to hang in the air for longer than he should have. He turned to glare at Lennox, and he vanished over the side with a cry.

"You're fucking kidding me," Lennox whispered.

Twenty feet? More? He could be okay at that distance. If he landed just right, he might be able to pick himself up and start running again. And if he landed just wrong, the fall was more than enough to break every bone. More than enough to kill him.

He heard a crunch before he reached the fence. He reluctantly looked over the side of the hill.

Below, David Nicholson was lying on the hood of a police cruiser that had just pulled into the lot. Lennox blinked and watched him roll painfully, falling off the cruiser and flopping onto the ground. Twenty or thirty feet up, Lennox heard the man groan.

"I'll be right down," he called to the uniforms getting out of the cruiser.

He turned and could see Kelly sitting up. Ouellette was crouched beside her, one arm around her shoulders.

"She okay?" he called. Ouellette nodded.

"Paramedics are on their way," Dworaczyk said, radio in one hand, phone in the other, "Three minutes. Maybe less."

"Nicholson's going to need one, too," Lennox said, slowly coming back over to join them. Kelly was sitting on the ground, knees drawn up to her chin.

"She's okay?" he asked again. It was all he could think of to say right now.

Ouellette nodded again.

Lennox sat down on the ground, slow and tired, knowing that it was all over, but there were still things he needed to do.

Sunday June 10th

Chapter IV

"Mr. Conroy," Dworaczyk said. "We have found Kelly."

Rick Conroy was sitting in an empty conference room down the hall from the CID bullpen. A uniform had brought him down to the station at eight o'clock and given him a newspaper, a cup of coffee, and a shrugging promise to let him know when she heard something. He had been sitting here for over four hours now. The cup was full, the coffee cold, and the newspaper untouched. And Rick Conroy looked exhausted, but brightened as Dworaczyk entered.

"You found her?" He stood up, almost jumping up. "Where is she?"

"She is down the hall, and she is safe," Dworaczyk smiled.

"She's okay?"

"She is fine."

"Well, let's go!"

"No, not just yet."

"I want to see her."

"In a few minutes."

"Bullshit, in a few minutes." He came around the edge of the table. "Right the hell *now*. This is my *daughter*."

"In a few minutes," Dworaczyk said firmly. "There are some things that need to get done first."

"Like what?'

"We need to get a statement from her, for one thing. Remember, she is a witness in another case."

"I should be there. She's a child."

"She is twenty-one today, right? They will be done with her in a few minutes and then I can take you to see her."

"Done with her? She's not hurt, is she?"

"She is fine."

"Right, okay." He sat back down slowly. After a moment he said, "Okay, wait—you're sure this is Kelly? You're sure it's her?'

"We are sure."

"So was that other guy right? The other detective? She was out at… that spot today?"

"Yeah, he was right. She was out there. That guy can be pretty smart sometimes."

Maybe he had been wrong about Lennox, he thought. Maybe he had the right kind of initiative after all. Maybe the weirdo would make sergeant someday.

"And the other guy?" Rick asked in a low voice, almost a whisper. "The… murderer?"

"We have him, too."

"He didn't hurt Kelly? You said she was okay?"

"He tried, but we did not let that happen. She is fine."

"What happened?"

"Nothing that you need to worry about right now. The important thing is that Kelly is safe, Mr. Conroy."

"Rick."

"Right. Rick."

"So… when can I see her?"

"They are going to let me know when they are ready."

"I'm going to be able to take her home?"

"She may need to stay for another day or two. Too early to tell yet; it depends on how quick the lawyers move. She is a witness, they need her. She is going to have to come back once the trial starts, whenever that is."

"The trial."

"There is going to be a trial. A murder trial. Gotta give that bastard his day in court."

Rick Conroy leaned forward, elbows on the table.

"She's going to be a witness in a murder trial," he said. "This is going to be… awful for her. I don't know if she's going to be able to handle something like that."

"She will be fine," Dworaczyk said. "She might surprise you. She sure as hell surprised me a couple of times this week." He checked the time. "We should be hearing that they are ready pretty soon."

"Okay," Rick Conroy said. He shook his head and gave a tired little laugh. "Okay."

Sunday
June 10th

Chapter V

KELLY CONROY LOOKED VERY SMALL and very young, sitting next to Lennox's desk in the bullpen. She leaned forward, shoulders hunched, like she was trying to fold up on herself. Trying very hard not to look up from her lap. Trying very hard not to look at anything. She had refused medical attention at the scene, and there was an angry, red rope burn against the white of her throat.

"Your girl got lucky," one of the paramedics had said to Lennox when they were still out on Proctor's Ledge. "This could have been a lot worse. Another minute...." And he had just shaken his head.

"So you're sure you're okay?" Lennox began gently now.

Kelly might have nodded; he couldn't really be sure.

"Been kind of a long week around here." He was going to say *crazy*, but that didn't seem like the right word to use with her. She still didn't look up, but he saw the corner of her mouth curl a little: a smile or a smirk, he wasn't sure which. But either one was good. "Long week for you, too, I guess."

He glanced over at Ouellette and shrugged when Kelly still didn't respond.

"Do you need a water or anything before we get started? I have some stuff I need to go over with you so we're going to be here for a little bit."

Still nothing. Maybe half a sigh.

"That burn looks pretty nasty. You're sure you're all right? I'm glad we got out there in time."

Kelly swallowed painfully, with a little cough.

"It's your birthday," he said quietly.

Her eyes strayed in his direction but she didn't look right at him.

"I didn't get you anything," he added.

Now the edge of her mouth curled upward just a little bit.

"Your father is downstairs with another detective. They'll be up in a few minutes."

She looked up. Her hair was lank and her face grimed over, but her eyes were a bright, clear blue.

"Is that going to be a problem?" he asked.

"No," she said hoarsely. "No."

"He's been really worried about you," Lennox smiled. "We've all been pretty worried around here, actually."

"Sorry," Kelly said. She paused and then gave a tiny little smile. Just the shadow of a smile.

"Okay, so…" Lennox opened his notebook to a blank page. "The man who attacked you. We need to talk about him for a minute. Is that okay?"

"Yeah, that's… sure."

"Have you ever seen him before?"

He could feel his heart in his chest. This was more tense, somehow, sitting across from Kelly, than it had been out on Proctor's Ledge, pointing a gun at David Nicholson. He tried not to let it show.

She tilted her head and took a breath. She cleared her throat and said, "He killed that man."

"I know this is hard right now, but can you just start at the beginning and walk me through what happened?"

"How far back do you want me to start?'

"Up to you."

She nodded and said, "I was in the parking lot that night. I was… just walking."

She paused, and he knew she was probably waiting for him to ask what she was doing out there, where she was coming from, where she was going. If he asked, she wouldn't tell the truth. She wouldn't be able to. And one lie only led to another lie. And then another. He had seen it too many times. If he didn't ask, she didn't have to lie. Knowing what to ask was a vital skill, but knowing what not to ask might be even more important.

"So what happened out in the parking lot?"

"I saw him… stab the tall man, the one with the beard."

"Just like that?"

"Yeah, I think. I only looked over when I heard one of them say, *What the fuck?*" She blushed as she swore. "And his voice kind of… gurgled when he said it."

She was staring blankly at the floor. And Lennox could tell that she must be watching the awful scene play out again. And the back of her throat must be twisting as she spoke. Just like his was now.

"And then he stabbed him in the neck. A couple more times."

"And was he saying anything?"

"No. It was weird. He never said anything. Just like," she took a deep breath. "Just like a little while ago."

"Okay. I know this isn't easy, thinking about all this again. But you're doing great."

She smiled and looked out the window, embarrassed.

"What happened next?"

"The big man fell, and I… I screamed."

"You did?"

"Yeah." She was embarrassed to admit it. "Not loud, but… loud enough. And the man with the knife saw me. He was, like, twenty or thirty feet away and he looked right at me. I couldn't move. I couldn't do anything. But then he looked at the man on the ground and… when he broke eye contact I could move again. I knew…" she took a deep, scared breath now, flinching as she did. "I knew if I didn't get out of there he was going to kill me, too."

"Did he say that?" Ouellette asked.

"He didn't have to," Kelly shook her head. "He started running at me and... he didn't have to say anything."

"What did you do?"

"I ran," she said with a little, dry laugh. "I ran to that little mall on the other side of the parking lot. He didn't follow me. I mean, he tried to, but I think when he realized where I was going he must've stopped. I looked back when I was inside and he was gone. I think I knocked someone down. I went out a door on the other side of the mall and... just kept running. I used to do track, so... I'm pretty fast."

"We didn't know where you were until we saw you out at Pioneer Village."

Kelly nodded, and tilted her head. She looked at Lennox seriously for a moment, and he wasn't sure what she might be thinking.

"Something wrong?" he asked.

"No. I mean... no. You reminded me of someone for a minute, when I saw you out at the village. But... just for a minute."

"Who did I remind you of?" he smiled.

"Nobody. I mean, maybe I was... wrong. It's not important." She shook her head. She'd changed her mind about something, let something go. "Can I ask you something?"

"Sure."

"Why were you out there today?"

"Just lucky, I guess," Lennox said.

Kelly nodded and smiled. A sly smile. A smile that said she knew they were both keeping secrets now, keeping each other's secrets.

"Is there anything else you want us to know?" Ouellette asked.

Kelly shook her head, exhausted.

"And just to be clear," Ouellette went on, "the man who attacked you this morning is the same man you saw stab someone in the parking lot?"

"Yes. Absolutely the same guy. I'm... never going to forget that face."

"And you're okay?" Lennox asked.

"Yeah." She leaned back in the chair, exhaling deeply and slowly. She gingerly traced the raw ring around her neck and said quietly, "Yeah, I really am."

"I'm going to have them bring your father up now, if that's all right."

"Yeah," she smiled, and a moment later wiped away a tear. "Yeah."

When Dworaczyk brought Rick Conroy upstairs a couple of minutes later, father and daughter rocketed toward one another across the bullpen, slamming into each other, embracing. Lennox and Ouellette left them where they were, sobbing and whispering and not letting go.

Chapter VI

Sunday June 10th

"How do you want to approach this?" Ouellette asked.

Lennox thought for a moment. They didn't need to question David Nicholson. They didn't even need a statement from him. They had a positive ID from an eyewitness—an eyewitness they had just stopped him from trying to kill. Now that they had him in custody, whatever he had to say for himself was irrelevant. Warrants and subpoenas and forensics would take care of the rest of it. Whatever reasons he gave for killing Stuart Pickman held no evidentiary value. They didn't need to know why.

But Lennox still wanted to.

"I think I'm just going to let him tell me," he replied, opening the door.

David Nicholson was sitting in Interrogation One—the same room where Zachary had taken, and passed, his polygraph test. That felt like it happened a month ago, and Lennox had to remind himself that it had been the day before yesterday. Nicholson had his hands on the table, palms up; they were red and raw, but Kelly's neck looked worse. He had sullenly refused medical treatment, and held one shoulder a little higher than the other, like it was bothering him.

Lennox sat down and put a file folder on the table. Ouellette shut the door and remained standing.

"I was trying to help that poor girl—" Nicholson began.

"You know, it was hard for me to believe all this was over some pumpkin-carving kits," Lennox shook his head.

"What—?"

"Well, I mean, it's obvious now that you look at it."

Lennox opened the file and started sliding photos across the table.

The first was a crime scene photo showing the old Telephone Building, standing on the site of the old Witch Gaol, looming over the parking lot. There was a dark shape on the ground.

Next was a morgue photo of Stuart Pickman: head and shoulders, with the pumpkin-carving knife still in his neck.

The last was an evidence photo: one of the carving kits arranged on a table, all eleven pieces. Carving knives and scoops and sculpting loops, with L-shaped crime scene scales at the corners. The largest knife was circled in red.

"You waited out in the parking lot that night. You knew he was out, running from one thing to another, but he had to come back for his car. All you had to do was wait for him to show up and kill him with one of these carving tools you were so upset about. It's a nice touch, really. Sends a message."

Nicholson leaned back in the chair, sliding his hands back into his lap and away from the photos.

"You actually think this was over… pumpkin-carving kits?"

"Well, you have to admit, it makes sense." Lennox glanced over at Ouellette. "It's a solid motive."

"It wasn't about that," Nicholson shook his head. "My God."

"Wait, it wasn't?"

"Jesus, no!"

"I'm… so confused right now."

"He was always in my fucking goddamn *way.*" Nicholson slammed a fist down on the table, making the metal surface ring. "Every time."

"Tell me about it," Lennox smiled.

Nicholson smiled bitterly as he realized what Lennox had just done to him.

"He was always in your fucking goddamn way?" Ouellette prompted.

"Yeah." Nicholson's shoulders slumped as he surrendered. He licked his lips. "Yeah. You have no idea what he was like. He didn't need an assistant director, he needed a legal guardian. You had to watch him every minute or he'd go off and do something stupid. Or expensive."

"Like saying an app would be ready early," Lennox said.

"Yeah. And he had no idea how to get anything done. He never had a plan. And then I'd have to run around trying to figure it out and make excuses for him. And if I couldn't, then it was my fault. Or someone else's. Never his. *Never* his."

"No way to run a business."

"Exactly. And that's what he always kept forgetting. It's not all parades and costume parties, it's a business. He just thought it was a big party he was throwing every year. Idiot."

"Be a hell of a lot different with you in charge."

"Damn right it would. No more making it up as you go along. We'd have a plan. We wouldn't be wasting time and money on stupid shit."

"You had to do something," Lennox nodded. "And you did. You came up with a plan. You figured out what needed to be done, and you did it."

"Yes."

"And with Pickman out of the way, you thought they'd put you in charge?"

"They'd have to," Nicholson said quietly.

"What do you mean?"

"Who else?" He shrugged and looked at Lennox accusingly. "Who the hell else?"

"This Phillip Agnew guy, I guess? Why not just wait it out? The board was going to ask Pickman to step down."

"No, they weren't. They were going to ask him to step down last year, and the year before that, and the year before *that*. No, they were never going to get rid of him."

"Unless someone did something."

"Right."

"What about Jessica?" Lennox asked. "What about Emma?"

"What about them?"

"He had a wife and a kid."

"They weren't married," Nicholson said. "She and the kid'll be fine."

Lennox took a deep breath. He wasn't expecting that. He wouldn't have been surprised if Nicholson had been planning to move in on Jessica, take the place of the man he himself had murdered. But realizing that Jessica and her daughter weren't part of his plan, weren't even a consideration, made the back of his throat twist once again.

"So you needed him out of the way. For the Spooktacular's own good. For your own good."

"But Kelly saw you," Ouellette said.

He took one of Kelly's missing person posters from the file and slapped it down on the table. She stared up at him reproachfully from the sad-eyed photos.

Nicholson flinched.

"She saw you and now you needed another plan, plan B," Lennox said. "You were the one who always tied up the loose ends, right? And an eyewitness is one hell of a loose end. You needed to find her and kill her. So you approached her father to see what you could find out, and he told you about our theory and now you had your plan. If you just killed her, you had a body you had to get rid of, but… if you made it look like she hanged herself out there, well, now it all just came around full circle, didn't it?"

Nicholson folded his arms and looked into the corner.

"He was always in your way," Lennox said quietly. "Things would be a lot different with you in charge. It'd be a business. You said it wasn't about the carving kits, but… it kinda was, wasn't it?"

"I want a lawyer."

"You need one."

Lennox gathered up the photos and stood. He rubbed his eyes. He was going to have this headache for the rest of the week, he could already tell.

Completely worth it, he thought, as he and Ouellette left the room.

Chapter VII

LENNOX KNOCKED ON THE DOOR of the house in the Willows. It was late afternoon now, a warm breeze coming in off Juniper Cove, fluttering the pink curtains in the second-floor window. Jessica opened the door, surprised.

"We have some good news," he told her.

She motioned the detectives into the little parlor. There was no one else there—no priest, no brother from Peabody. All quiet and empty. The funeral was over, friends and family had all departed with promises to check back in another day or two, and now the next-of-kin had run out of expected things to do, had reached the end of the list and had nothing left.

And Lennox knew the good news they brought was never really going to be good enough.

"We made an arrest this morning," he said quietly.

"You did?" She blinked.

"We've charged David Nicholson with homicide," Ouellette said.

"David? That doesn't make sense. They worked together for… years. He was at the funeral yesterday." She folded her arms and gave them a hard look. "Are you… sure? It just doesn't make sense…"

"We have a witness," Lennox said. "It's him."

"He told me you thought it was Zachary."

"We did for a while, but it's not," Lennox said. "Even the cops get it wrong."

Jessica let out a long sigh.

"Okay," she said. "Okay."

Lennox had seen this before. There was supposed to be relief, some sense that everything was fixed, that everything was going to be all right now. And he had seen it often enough to know that if it was going to be true for Jessica, it still wouldn't happen for a long time. And when it finally did, probably years from now, he wouldn't be there to see it. He would be somewhere else, trying to close another case, working to bring someone else the good news that was never going to be good enough.

"So the D.A. will probably get in touch with you in another couple of weeks," he said. "Might be sooner, might be later, I don't really know what their schedule is like."

"Okay," she said blankly. "Is there—is there anything I should be doing right now?"

"Not really, no," Lennox said. "We just wanted you to know."

"Okay. Well, um... thanks?"

Lennox smiled and put his hands in his pockets. He didn't know what to say, either.

"You're sure you want to do this?" Ouellette asked as they pulled up in front of Zachary Dykstra's building.

"Yeah, I guess."

"I'll wait here."

"Won't be long."

He hesitated, taking a deep breath before ringing the middle bell. He heard someone coming down the stairs.

Zachary opened the door and rolled his eyes. He looked tired. The bruises had darkened and changed shape, and some of the scrapes were brown and crusty.

"What do you want now?" he asked.

"I just thought I should tell you... we arrested David Nicholson this morning. For the murder."

"David?"

"Yeah. We had an eyewitness who identified him as the killer. And he confessed."

"He did?"

"Basically," Lennox said. "Kind of a long story."

"Wow. Fuck."

"Yeah, you could say that again," Lennox tried to laugh. "So I just wanted to say that I'm… sorry for everything. I was just trying to do my job."

"Just following orders, right? Think I heard that somewhere before."

"Just trying to catch a killer."

"Sure," he nodded. "This totally makes up for everything. Yeah. Totally."

He slammed the door, leaving Lennox standing on the porch, hoping that Zachary could hear him say, "I'm sorry."

"So, how did that go?" Ouellette asked as he got back into the car.

"He hates me."

"You wanted people to like you," she said, "you should've joined the fire department."

Roland came running to her as she came through the door. He jumped up and wrapped his arms around her waist with a cry of *"Maman!"* like he always did when she got home. Ouellette kissed her fingers and pressed them to the top of his head, like she always did in response. He was getting big. Pretty soon, he'd be too big to crash into her every day like this. She looked down at his smiling face; he looked more and more like his father every day and she wasn't sure how she felt about it.

Joanie was sitting on the couch, holding a big round glass of wine with both hands.

"Hi," she said, the first word she had spoken in two days.

"Hi, yourself."

Roland ran back to his room, murmuring happily to himself. Ouellette smiled as she watched him go, then put her badge and radio on the counter.

"Any of that left?" She nodded to the wineglass.

"Yeah. In the fridge." Joanie took a deep breath. "So, Frankie's gone…"

"He is?" Ouellette opened the fridge and poured herself a glass. She paused for a moment and added a little more.

"Yeah. You were right about him." She nodded toward the door of Roland's room. "And about him."

"Can't say I'm sorry to hear that he's gone."

"You shouldn't be."

Ouellette sat down on the couch next to her sister and gave her a nudge.

"Dammit, Mish," Joanie sniffled, "I just have the shittiest luck."

She leaned against her, and Ouellette reached out to stroke her sister's hair.

"Yeah, well, us Ouellette girls. We sure can pick 'em."

"Yeah, huh?"

"It'll be okay. We'll be okay."

After a few minutes of silence, Ouellette said, "Should we get a pizza?"

Roland's voice came from the next room: "Yay!"

Andrew Lennox slowly climbed the steps up to the second floor of the old jail, hoping to God that Mrs. Chevoya wasn't somewhere waiting for him. He hadn't worked a week like this since last Hallowe'en and he was exhausted. He wanted to feel great—case closed, bad guy caught. Missing girl found. Justice served. But he kept thinking of Pickman's slashed throat and Zachary's bruised face. He had the next two days off and all he wanted to do was sleep, but he wondered if he would be able to.

He unlocked the door to his apartment and smelled cinnamon hazelnut coffee.

"Hellooo…" AJ's voice lilted from the bedroom.

He found her stretched out on top of the covers, with the windows open, reading his copy of *The Devil in Massachusetts* in the late afternoon sun. All she had on were her tiny little reading glasses, balanced on the end of her nose. The nose nothing like Ellen's.

"I was wondering when you were going to get in," she said. She shifted, rolling over onto her side and he took a breath as he saw how the sunlight played along the curve of her hip. She slowly licked a finger and turned a page. "Way too warm up here, right?"

"Um… let me take a quick shower," he said.

He went back out to the living room and turned Jesse Pomeroy to face the wall, with a whispered promise to finally bring him down to the museum tomorrow. In the bathroom, as he stepped under the shower to wash every last particle of this week off of him, he heard someone knocking on the apartment door and could just make out Mrs. Chevoya's voice.

"Officer Lennox? Are ya there?"

He turned up the hot water and ignored her.

She's done what she came to do. And it worked. She stood on Proctor's Ledge on June the tenth… and survived.

She's escaped the noose, and now that it's gone, so is everything else—the dread, the doomed knowledge that everything—everything—was leading to a rocky hill on the edge of Salem, a thousand miles away from Milwaukee. But now it's over and she's not sure what happens next. And she spent so much time knowing, that now, not knowing is… amazing.

She knows she'll be back, knows she'll return to Salem. But it will be different. She'll be the key witness in the trial, and that detective, the one that looks like an English teacher, told her that it probably wouldn't be for months yet. She'll have all that time to relax, to fix things up with her father. She doesn't expect him to understand all of it, or even most of it, and thinking about it all now, there are parts of it even she doesn't understand. It's like it all happened to someone else, someone she left out on that lonely little hill.

But for now, she takes a deep breath and feels the sun on her face and she smiles for the first time in she doesn't even know how long and it feels great. She feels great.

There is no more of that fate, no more of that doom, and she wonders what will happen now, what will happen next. She doesn't know anymore, and that wondering is the most comforting thing she has ever felt in her life.

Who Was Bridget Bishop, Anyway?

As the first victim of the Salem witch trials, Bridget Bishop was guaranteed a certain notoriety the other accused witches would never achieve. Popular folklore depicts her as an outspoken woman with a plunging red bodice and a fiery temper, running a tavern where the menfolk played "shovel-board" 'til all hours—menfolk who probably could not stop themselves from admiring Bridget's womanly charms. Running that tavern would have brought her into regular contact with a variety of people—rich and poor, high and low. A woman with economic means, who spoke her mind and mixed with all kinds of people, she seems to be exactly the type that the stern, Puritan town fathers would think must be in league with the Devil. Right?

Accurate information about many of the people of 1692 can sometimes be hard to come by. Records get lost, or don't have as much detail as we'd like, or sometimes a proper record was never even taken down to begin with. But when it comes to the life of Bridget Bishop, we are a little better off than in some other cases. Enough documentation exists to probably give us a decent picture of who she was, or at least who she probably was. And we have enough information about her to show that the popular folklore is often completely wrong.

We don't have a record of her birth, but we do have a record of her marrying Samuel Wasselby on April 13, 1660, in Norfolk, England. Her maiden name was Playfer. The couple later had a son, Benjamin, but there is no further information about him to be found anywhere, and it seems likely that he died young. Bridget next appears in Boston, where she gives birth to a daughter, Mary, in 1665; Mary's birth record notes that Samuel Wasselby was now deceased. Perhaps he didn't survive the voyage to the New World, or died shortly after arrival, or died in England and never even made the journey in the first place. There is no further documentation to be found on Mary. Perhaps she died young, too.

On July 26, 1666, Bridget married Samuel Oliver, himself a widower with three children. She moved into Samuel's house in Salem, on the land now occupied by Turner's Seafood Restaurant on Church Street. Here, she gave birth to another daughter, Christian, on May 3, 1667.

Her marriage to Samuel does not seem to have been a happy one. The couple soon became famous for fighting, and not just arguing: actual fisticuffs—neighbors noticed that Bridget sometimes appeared bloodied and bruised. The authorities were called in more than once, and it seems that, in these fights, Bridget gave as good as she got, at least according to Samuel. He even went so far as to claim she was a witch, bitterly muttering that "she was a bad wife... the devil had come bodily to her... and she sat up all night with the devil."

Things got so bad that both Bridget and Samuel were sentenced to stand outside the meeting house, mute, for an hour on Lecture Day. Lecture Day was regular occurrence, when special guest preachers were brought in to speak before the congregation. Having her out there on Lecture Day assured that a large crowd would witness her humiliation. Bridget stood before the crowd that day, but Samuel seems to have escaped being made into a spectacle himself.

Strange rumors about her began circulating. On at least two occasions, she paid workmen with money that they later could not find, and somehow witchcraft seemed a more likely explanation than simple carelessness. Other men whispered that sometimes Goodwife Oliver visited them in the dead of night, occasionally accompanied by a couple of other women, only to mysteriously vanish.

Samuel Oliver died in 1679, and the court allowed Bridget to retain possession of the house they had lived in, which was a fairly unusual decision for the time. She was accused of being a witch the following year; Samuel's children might have regarded her as the evil stepmother and been trying to get the family home away from her. There was talk that she had bewitched both her husbands to death. The charges seem to have been thrown out, and Bridget retained both her freedom and the house.

In 1685, Bridget got married one more time, to an Edward Bishop. Her new husband was not the only man by that name and this has created further confusion about her and her story. There were several Edward Bishops, and one of them, along with his wife Sarah, ran a tavern in what is now Beverly. This means there are at least two (or more) women who could be referred to as "Goodwife Bishop, wife of Edward." Over time, one goodwife became confused or conflated with another, and Bridget was eventually mistakenly assumed to have been the woman running a tavern on Church Street, when that was in fact the family home, and she never owned a tavern anywhere.

The couple decided to tear down the house (perhaps thumbing her nose at her stepchildren?) and build a new one on the property. The workmen brought in to do the job would later report that, "being employed by Bridget Bishop, alias Oliver, of Salem to help take down the wall of the old house she formerly lived in, we the said deponents, on holes in the old walls belonging to the said cellar, found several poppets made up of rags and hogs' bristles, with headless pins in them with the points outward."

Walling up shoes or other items in the foundation of a house under construction is an old English superstition, a folk magic practice meant to being good luck and keep evil out of the house.

It was the kind of everyday magic that was sternly forbidden by Puritan authorities, who regarded it as at least Popish, if not actually diabolical—not that they saw much difference between the two to begin with. It should be noted that Samuel Oliver had built the house before his marriage to Bridget, and presumably that's when the poppets were put in place, so Bridget probably didn't have anything to do with them. She might not have even known they were there. But, given her reputation, some around town must have assumed they were hers. Poppets with pins were just the kind of thing a witch might secretly have.

Suspicions about Bridget and her strange doings were further aroused when she brought some items to a tailor to be dyed. The man later testified that among the articles were "sundry pieces of lace, some of which were so short that I could not judge them fit for any use." Some might have leapt to the conclusion that she had been dressing up her poppets with evil intent.

Much has been made of the "red paragon bodice" that Bridget was described as wearing. We tend to imagine the Puritans dressed in bleak colors like black and gray, but red would not have been an unusual color for clothing. For some, a woman in red brings to mind "scarlet letters" and "scarlet women," suggesting that Bridget was of questionable moral character. And for still others, the very word "bodice" naturally leads to "-ripper," creating the image of Bridget as a lusty young wench, heaving in and out of her top.

In February of 1692, when all hell broke loose in the Salem Village parsonage, it didn't take long for the infamous "circle of afflicted girls" (a phrase that appears time and again in accounts of the witch trials) to cry out on Bridget Bishop. She was an easy enough target, having been accused before. On April 18th she was arrested, along with several others, and accused of using witchcraft to magically attack and "afflict" the young girls gathered at Samuel Parris's parsonage. Being in custody didn't prevent her from allegedly sending out her ghostly Shape to harass one of her accusers that very night.

Abigail Hobbs and Mary Warren, two of the young women who had been accused and arrested along with her, quickly fingered Bridget as a witch, probably in an attempt to save their own necks. They included her on a list of attendees at a "general meeting of the witches in the field near Mr. Parris's house."

"Bridget in court was a cool one," according to Marion L. Starkey, author of *The Devil in Massachusetts*, a classic work. When she stood before the magistrates on June 2, 1692, the afflicted girls fell into their fits, but she flatly maintained her innocence. "I have no familiarity with the Devil," she said, adding, "I know nothing of it. I am innocent to a witch. I know not what a witch is."

Judge Hathorne pressed her: "How can you know you are no witch, and yet not know what a witch is?"

"I am clear," Bridget replied. We can imagine her looking him dead in the eye as she warned him. "If I were any such person you should know it."

But all the old stories and rumors came back to haunt her. The poppets. The midnight visits to various goodmen. Allegations that she scampered around town in the form of a bizarre, monkey-like homunculus. A committee performed a degrading strip-search and "discovered a preternatural excrescence of flesh between the pudendum and anus much like to teats and not usual in women." Witches were supposed to suckle their familiars from such a preternatural "witches' teat," and Bridget was said to have a snake. This only became even more sinister when they could not find it a second time.

Her guilt was a foregone conclusion. Cotton Mather, who had come up from Boston to observe the proceedings, threw up his hands and said, "There was little occasion to prove the witchcraft, it's being evident and notorious to all beholders."

The trial lasted for one day. She was found guilty and sentenced to hang. Sometime on the morning of June 10, 1692, Sheriff George Corwin took her from her cell in the jail, put her into a cart, and brought her out to what is now Proctor's Ledge, on the edge of town. Public hangings were a spectacle, and there was a crowd gathered, expecting a show.

There was no actual gallows. Bridget, and those who followed her in the coming months, would have been hanged from a sturdy tree branch. The traditional hangman's knot, which snaps the neck and kills instantly, was evidently not widely-known and the executioner probably would have used a simple slipknot. If she was lucky, she died a quick death. If she was unlucky, it could have taken her some time to die by slow strangulation. Her body would have been left hanging there for a long while, only adding to the grim scene.

After he had discharged his duty, Corwin noted at the bottom of Bridget's death warrant that he had "Caused the said Bridget to be hanged by the neck until she was dead and buried in the place…" But he then crossed out the words "buried in the place." It is unclear why. Bridget was not entitled to a Christian burial—none of the victims were given proper burials and we don't know where any of them are to this day. Some records indicate they were thrown into a ditch on Proctor's Ledge, hastily buried near to where they were hanged. But does Corwin crossing out those words mean that Bridget was spared this fate? Did someone come forward to claim her body? Who? Her daughter, Christian? (Her husband seems to have completely vanished from the records even before this point.) We will never know.

The witch trials moved on. More girls became "afflicted," more men and women were accused. Nineteen people were hanged and one man was pressed to death before it was all over in the spring of 1693.

In 1711, the legislature exonerated the victims generally. They offered compensation to the surviving family members, but evidently nobody came forward to accept on Bridget's behalf. 1957 saw the legislature passing a resolution condemning the witch trials, stating that "such proceedings, even if lawful under the Province Charter and the law of Massachusetts as it then was, were and are shocking," and clearing the name of "one Ann

Pudeator and certain other persons," not mentioning Bridget (or any of the others) by name.

In 1992, for the three-hundredth anniversary of the witch trials, the city dedicated a memorial to the victims downtown. There are twenty ledges jutting out from the granite walls, each dedicated to the memory of one of the victims. Bridget's is the first one on the left as you enter the space. Visiting the memorial, you can often find flowers and sometimes even notes left by descendants.

She finally got her legal due in 2001, when the legislature amended that 1957 resolution, specifically listing her along with other victims who were now cleared of all charges.

Bridget Bishop wasn't a witch, or a saucy tavern wench, or a Christian martyr. She was an ordinary woman, trying to make her way in a world that did not always treat her kindly. A world that ultimately betrayed her and murdered her. We can try to make it up to her now, to make some attempt at righting the wrongs she suffered. We can remember her story, and honor her memory by not making her into more, or less, than she was. It is, after all this time, the very least we can do for her.

Rory O'Brien lives in Salem with his lovely wife, their black cats, and a Treeing Walker Coonhound. His two previous titles, *Gallows Hill* and *Summerland*, are also available from the Merry Blacksmith Press. Find him online at www.roryobrienbooks.com.

Also available from
The Merry Blacksmith Press

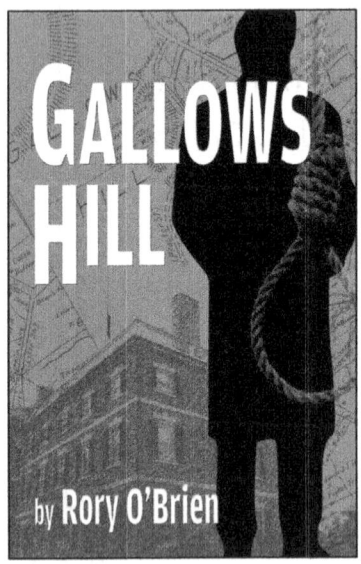

visit
merryblacksmith.com
for more details

Made in the USA
Middletown, DE
12 August 2022

70355747R00186